Always gripping. Always new.

* Jerry Pournelle goes Another Step Farther Out and tells us what's wrong with science today...

* Poul Anderson reminds us why we do science anyway...

* Michael Flynn explores the dark side of nanotechnology in "Werehouse"...

* Charles Sheffield makes sense out of Chaos, the Unlick'd Bear Cub...

and Marc Stiegler weighs in with a solution to overspending in the defense department and a national game show all in one: "The B-2 Lottery"....

This and every issue of
New Destinies
is dedicated to the memory of
Robert A. Heinlein

Fall 1990
EDITOR IN CHIEF
Jim Baen

ASSISTANT EDITOR
Toni Weisskopf

ASSISTANT EDITOR
Hank Davis

MANAGING EDITOR
Allison Ort

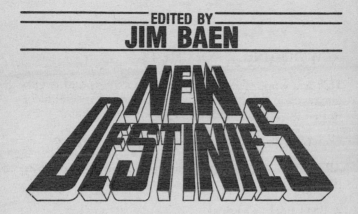

EDITED BY
JIM BAEN

NEW DESTINIES

The Paperback Magazine
Volume IX/Fall 1990

BAEN BOOKS

NEW DESTINIES, VOLUME IX

Copyright © 1990 by Baen Publishing Enterprises

A Baen Books Original

Baen Publishing Enterprises
260 Fifth Avenue
New York, N.Y. 10001

ISBN: 0-671-72016-3

Cover art by David Hardy

First Baen printing, September 1990

Distributed by
SIMON & SCHUSTER
1230 Avenue of the Americas
New York, N.Y. 10020

Printed in the United States of America

CONTENTS

Introduction

In 1988 Elizabeth Moon burst upon the sf/fantasy scene with three superb novels about a Sheepfarmer's Daughter *who became first a soldier among soldiers, and then a Paladin beyond compare. Shortly thereafter she turned in a marvelous bestseller in collaboration with Anne McCaffrey, followed by another great solo,* Surrender None. *It is almost frightening to contemplate what next we can expect from this great—and I use the word thoughtfully—new writer. Meanwhile, here is an early effort revised to a level consonant with her fully realized talent.*

RISKS OF MEMORY

Elizabeth Moon

"The research ship's been stolen."

Paran Kai Fielzer shuffled two journals down in the stack on his desk before that caught up with him. He stared blankly at his colleague Dr. Altlin, and wondered if this was one of his jokes. Porge was like that, the kind of man who made outrageous statements just to see what would happen. "Not *Scholastica*," he said, his mind already racing over what that could mean.

Altlin nodded, his usually relaxed smile slightly grim. "So the rumor says. Either Agentry—lovely, mythical Agentry—or the Rim Revolt. Things may get rough on us colonials for awhile." Like Fielzer, Altlin had migrated in from the Rim as a child: a permanent bar to full citizenship.

Fielzer shivered. Things had been rough on colonials before. That's why he lived nested in a mobile prosthesis; that's why he had no family. Even having tenure (granted two years earlier after interminable investigations) wouldn't help if the Security Service decided to blame the faculty. He forced himself to concentrate on the word "rumor" and tried to believe it hadn't really happened. "Huh. And on top of that, I can't find this week's *Review*."

"In that mess on the fifth shelf." Altlin flipped it down and glanced at the contents. "But why worry? No one else stays current."

"Sanddin has an article in this one."

"Oho. And the weekly department meeting is coming up, and since he's chair . . . oh dead gods." He handed it to Fielzer as if it were a half-rotted fruit, open to Sanddin's "*Pore Density and Magnetic Alignment In Neo-Basalts of the Chalungrian Basin.*"

"Just because it's not your area—"

"Come on, Par: you know it's the same damn thing he's been doing for years, scrounging around with those core samples and publishing dribs and drabs . . . no coherent overview, just one location after another. Guarantees plenty of pubs for his record, and lets him leave the work to one bored grad student after another. I'd even bet you that half the cores he references are faked: who can tell one from another anyway?"

Automatically, Fielzer glanced at the door—although it was just as likely that Campus Security had a tap in his office. Altlin grimaced, shook his head, and laughed.

"I said it, Par, and I'll also say that you looked shocked and disgusted with my lack of respect for a senior member of faculty. Better get ready, though." And he was gone, with a last quick wave.

Fielzer watched that evening's news summary with no surprise. "Another bold outrage committed by subversive elements" had to be the theft of the university's research vessel; the restrictions on travel and communications followed from that as surely as faulting from movement along plate boundaries. He expected a call to the department chairman's office, the request for an updated "review of personal history." But he had tenure now: that had to count for something. And he had never been involved in anything—not so much as a family reunion—since the Sauwe camps. They had to know that.

The knock on his door the next day came far sooner than he had expected. Sequestration. After that came exile, for the fortunate, and prison or camps for the rest. The Security major read through the regulations in a bland monotone while Fielzer's gut churned.

"You do realize, Dr. Fielzer, that any attempt to make contact outside the sequestered area without express permission will result in additional measures."

"Indeed, Major." His voice sounded calm, which surprised him. He thought bitterly that he knew far more about "additional measures" than this young man with two legs to stand on. The major smiled at him without warmth, and held out a folder slashed in the bright orange and yellow of a Secret classification.

"In view of your past services to Central Union, and your position in the University, the Governor has chosen you to consider this problem. You will be allowed a comlink to the University Library Computer. The compcode for the file is in that folder. Is this quite clear?"

"Yes, Major." One did not ask questions. Questions meant doubts, and doubts mean disloyalty. Disloyalty meant prison, worse than death.

"And, of course, class five rations and supplies. Security will deliver these to your housekeeper."

Class five! The most senior scientists might hold a class four card; most held class three—or two, for those without tenure. If they were giving him five, that meant something serious.

One of the Security techs came out of the study, and nodded. Fielzer felt a cold sweat on his back—what could he have found?—but the major merely nodded in reply and spoke to Fielzer. "Your comlink has been installed, and we'll leave you to your work."

They were gone—for the moment. Fielzer had a good five-second panic. You never forgot, he thought. The taste of class zero rations in the camp at Sauwe soured his mouth; his back ached as if he were back in the mines. He could almost feel the hot dusty stone under his bare feet—but that would never come back, no matter what camp or prison they sent him to.

He turned, with a final shudder, to his study. There he was whole, and as safe as the world allowed: alone, linked to one or another computer, his lost legs unneeded. Whatever it took to stay there, out of trouble—to stay above class zero—he would do.

The Library comlink showed an odd magenta flicker around the blue Library logo. A tap, and a clumsy one: they wanted him to know they were checking. He fed in the code he found on the single sheet in that garish folder. Magenta flared across the screen, locking his terminal until he complied with instructions to give his name and authorization.

"Fielzer, Paran Kai. Science 50472 Class III, PBG 4920. CGVGO 89.12.7" Even as he keyed it in, he knew how stupid and unnecessary it was: they knew all this already. It was just another way to make him submit to something petty and ridiculous.

The screen blanked, then a loud bell at his elbow made him jump: the voicelink in its separate mode. He answered. It was, as he expected, another bit of Security "precautions." Another major (were all Security officers majors?) explained the scrambler unit they'd installed, and the protocol for retrieving scrambled and normal files. He listened in silence, and politely thanked the officer while seething inside. Green button down; the magenta of Security Hold flicked to Library blue and white. A screenful of warnings scrolled by; then the Governor's request came up, a few blocky paragraphs of undistinguished prose.

Scholastica's theft had been received with an excess of disloyal glee. Unrest, the Governor said, was already widespread, and this could only make things worse. Something must be done.

The Governor's version of "something" meant changing the image of the thief and his organization (assumed in this paper to be the Rim Revolt), convincing the public that they were not heroes of the common herd, but cruel and heartless villains. To do that, the Governor wanted a tame geophysicist . . . because the plan (Fielzer wondered where it had come from so fast, and who had thought it up . . . and when) meant combining the worst fears of the Varagossan population: war and earthquakes. In the Governor's scenario, the Rimmers would "steal" and use one of the government's most feared strategic weapons to cause a devastating geophysical disaster. The MassShapers *could* do it (they had first been developed as terraforming and heavy mining tools), and it was Fielzer's task to pick the best location, the place that fit the criteria for enough death and destruction. Captures and confessions would soon follow, and no one would spare a thought—certainly not a happy thought—for whoever it was that stole *Scholastica*.

Fielzer pushed away his first shock and disgust, and let himself prowl the Library's knowledge of what *had* happened to the research ship. Student or faculty member suspected, of course: what else would Security say of a ship full of students and faculty, and crewed by Central Union Navy? They'd protect their own, no matter what. *Scholastica* was supposed to have blown up another Navy vessel, the *Probarty* . . . Fielzer shook his head. Already they were stacking the story; that had to be a lie. No research vessel could take a *real* Navy cruiser, even if it had once been a Navy flagship itself. He read on through a tangle of contradictory theories and rumors, until he read that the other big research vessel, *Logos*, out of Camryn University, had been abruptly recalled, with all but the crew under arrest.

He shrugged uneasily, thinking of Kevis Dartmon, the geologist who had won the All-Union gold medal for his work on the tectonics of sulfur satellites. They had corresponded for years, and met once when Dartmon came to Varagossa for a convention. This had been Kevis's last trip on *Logos*, he had written Fielzer, "before I get too stiff in the knees." At the time, he'd resented that remark, even though he knew Kevis didn't intend any reference to his legs. And now Kevis—Science

Medal winner—faced something worse than being grounded by aging joints. He shrugged again, and tapped the code for access to a different file.

His access, in fact, was far broader than he had ever enjoyed before—or wanted. He knew where each individual MassShaper was based, and its precise capabilities. He knew what military and Security units guarded each base, right down to the hours of shift-change and the tables of organization. He could call up minutes of Central Committee meetings, files kept for years by Security on the Rimmers, immigration and employment data . . . anything he might possibly use to solve the problem.

Fielzer had always loved data . . . had always enjoyed the comfortably stuffed feeling his mind had after hours of reading journals, reviewing research. In his youth it had made up for his frequently empty belly. But this time the load of new facts did not comfort him. It was far too much; they could not afford to have him free, or even alive, with the kind of knowledge he now had. How they must have hated giving a colonial that kind of access! He grinned for a moment, thinking how easily he could arrange the blowup of a satellite or two (the insystem prison?), but came back to reality in a cold sweat. However much they hated his access, that's how much they'd make him pay for it, afterwards. A quick death would be the best he could hope for.

And he could do nothing. Only a few friends, over the years, had gotten past the awkwardness of his disability and his own defensiveness; he saw their faces, as dim and intangible as reflections in a window. None of them would risk suspicion to visit a sequestered colonial. He wouldn't do it himself, if he were free. As he was, a legless man in a prosthesis that looked like a mobile trash bin (the best his status had qualified him for), he could hardly sneak anywhere, even if he'd been able to get past his guards.

His stomach roiled, a memory he couldn't suppress as easily as those faces from his past. He rang his housekeeper, and asked for something to eat. She brought it in, her withered face smiling and eager to show off the special foods, things she'd never seen in her life. He had. Once a year, at the Faculty Club banquet, they all saw class five rations. Wedges of pink and gray, sliced thin: real meat. Torqberries, imported from another system. Cheeses in shades of yellow and orange. Fielzer thanked her, and waved her away. He rolled to his study cooler, and put the meat and berries into it, taking quick bites of bread and cheese to keep himself from grabbing the meat. He'd never had enough, not since the Sauwe camps. And they knew it.

He choked the bread and cheese down, then opened the cooler again. Sliced roast, real meat: not processed from vegetable protein. It smelled heavy; his mouth watered. He saw his hand reach out, touch the cool damp slices, pick one up. Once a year, some government agent had watched him eat at the Faculty Club banquet, once a year. And from that had come their precise knowledge of his price. He took a bite of the roast, chewed it, and let his tongue confirm the texture. He made himself put the rest of the slice in the cooler. He'd learned that at Sauwe, too: never eat it all at once. Spread it out. Make it last.

The taste in his mouth lingered, like the taste of metal in a bit. He had eaten their food; he was buckled into their harness. A hidden current in his mind retrieved the datum that once "bait" had been used of horse feed, not merely something to catch fish.

Alone with the computer and his memories, he put away everything but the Governor's problem. Where could the weapon go, to do what must be done? And how long could he take, to enjoy what little life had left him?

The specifications required that the disaster affect over 1.5 million persons directly, with a high casualty rate. So the unstable and accessible Quornai Fault Beds in the Sunnar desert basin would not do. Lack of accessibility to MassShaper placing ruled out the very deep centers of instability in the Fanri Gulf. He lingered over that, imagining the tidal waves roaring up the narrows of Fan Bay to hit Central Station Five and the chemical refineries nearby. He supposed he was one of very few to know that Security had a training base on an island in that gulf.

But there were many possibilities that almost fit the criteria. A thousand miles of active faults, braided into complex systems, underlay the coastal cities of the University Complex. Mount Forlin, the big volcano near Central Station Three, with the grouped power stations and Alpha Port. The Gobrian Domes.

He dared not use the Library computer to model the disasters themselves. The sooner the governor's agents could pull the solution from him, the sooner they would dispose of him. He spent longer—much longer—with his personal computers, trading time for dubious security. Nothing was secure, but his own machines had been modified and re-modified for such specialized work that perhaps Security could not crack them easily or quickly.

No one bothered him, neither friend nor Security. Rations and supplies arrived; his housekeeper brought meals to the study, or he rolled out and into the narrow, dark-paneled dining room. He had been given no deadline, merely a nonspecialist's estimate that the solution might require weeks to months. He worked steadily, doggedly, refusing to let himself think about it, from morning until his eyes blurred with fatigue, when he would wipe his working files and go to bed. A bored Security guard stared through him as he rolled into his bedroom and levered himself out of his prosthesis onto the bed. That first night, it terrified him, but soon he was used to it, to the quick check of window and vent, the very quiet closing of his door when the man left. He could hear the murmur in the hall: the report of his schedule, the change of guard at midnight.

Yet he hardly felt he was being watched. He felt remote, detached, as if he were living behind a glass wall . . . or a mirrored wall, he thought once, that could show him only himself. This did not bother him as much as he would have expected. He realized, thinking about it in his dark bedroom before sleep overtook him, that he had had so few real contacts that he hardly missed them.

But he had missed food, and now he had more than he could eat. Meat every day, exotic cheeses, fresh fruit out of season, which his housekeeper peeled and carved into fanciful shapes. He told himself it drove out the memory of class zero rations, the tasteless mush that fed his dreams. He couldn't get enough of his new foods; he nibbled all day long, a new habit. So he was going to die, but he'd die with a full belly, comfortable. Better than some. Better than it might have been.

Still the problem intruded. The Problem, he tried to call it mentally, but the human cost intruded. Time and again he found himself staring blankly at one of the computer screens, seeing instead of numbers and letters the faces of those who might die, or be arrested, or be shown later on trial, having "confessed." As his choices narrowed, and his programs modeled more realistic plans, he could not quit thinking of them. They would die, and he would die. They would go to prison— unjustly, perhaps—and he had been there. He shrugged that away, irritably, and went on.

He was careful to preserve all the time he could. He split the models between machines; he never ran the complete sequences, never had all his machines working at once. They would not get his solution until he gave it to them . . . and he would have to; he could not stall forever. But he would have another few days, another few meals in peace.

One evening he quit work early. It was dark and raining, a soft drumming on the windows; his eyes had been burning and tearing all day. He would have liked to go outside, and let the soft rain ease them, let the cold damp air soothe his burning skin. But he knew the night guard officer: let a sequestered man go out after dark? Even one who could not possibly escape, one who had no one to meet? Of course not. He didn't bother to ask. Instead, he put on a tape of Jaskarin music, turned off the light, and sat in darkness, watching raindrops roll down the window backlit by the streetlights outside.

The slow, quiet strings of Amblodt's Second Jaskar Suite soothed him. He had left Jaskar as a boy, an eager child who had climbed aboard the dingy, patched transport in wild excitement. His father had served his apprenticeship on Jaskar, and wanted to give his children a better chance at education than such a young world could offer. He had chosen Vargessi, a second generation colony with a good reputation, and paid his last credit for passage there.

Fielzer squirmed, remembering, but the music was relentless and he was too tired to snap it off. They'd arrived on Vargessi just seven months before the edict that classified all Sector Eleven immigrants as undesirables. His father had lost his Guild membership. The family had been exiled to the Sauwe Rehabilitation Camps.

At first it hadn't been too bad. He'd been in an Education Barracks, in class nine hours a day. He'd still seen his family on restdays. That had lasted almost four years, until he was fourteen, a lanky boy good at math and running games.

But in the aftermath of the Cympadian Realignment, all exiled colonials were reassigned to Strict Labor Divisions. He went to Sauwe Camp 5, as did his younger sister, though he never saw her after the bus trip. There he was hot and cold in season, hungry always, and always tired. Ten days before his sixteenth birthday, he was three hundred feet underground, near the end of his shift, loading rocks: tired and hungry as usual. A few minutes later, the only survivor of a cave-in in that gallery, he was pinned by two beams and several tons of rock across his legs.

Fielzer felt this heart pounding as he relived that memory. The shift boss's gruff voice . . . no one would have blamed the man for leaving him there, and getting the others safely away. Instead, he'd called for a saw, yanked tourniquets tightly around the boy's skinny legs, and cut him free. The boy had passed out partway through the first amputation, and awoke, to everyone's surprise, in the camp hospital four days later. *The boy*, Fielzer thought, tears burning his eyes. *Me*. His stumps burned, and he shifted in his prosthesis.

In that four-day interval there had been a general amnesty for Class Three colonials, which included Jaskarins. His father got his Guild membership back after a while, but nothing could restore his sister's bright laughing face, or his own long legs. He rarely listened to Jaskarin music.

And yet . . . it was the music of his childhood; he could not give it up completely. His father had played— still played, if he was still alive—a gufid. In a young colony like Jaskar, all musicians know each other. Once Amblodt himself had stayed overnight . . . that very suite he listened to now, in darkness and fear, he'd heard amidst light and laughter the evening it was finished. He let the tape run out to the end, then played the last movement again, hearing the gufid continuo beneath the other strings, and remembering the way his father's lips had pursed in concentration over the new music. When he rolled into his bedroom at last, he thought the guard checked his window with more interest than usual.

The next afternoon, he had to get out, despite continuing rain. The day officer nodded, reluctantly; by the terms of the orders, Fielzer could "take daily exercise" in Faculty Square, so long as he spoke to no one out of hearing of his guard. The young corporal assigned to accompany him was clearly disgusted with the professor's choice of weather, and no happier that the prosthesis had a built-in weather shield that kept Fielzer dry while a stream of water ran off the guard's peaked cap, and his once-polished boots were soaked.

On that raw, rainy day, the gray stone houses around Faculty Square frowned down on empty walkways and frost-bitten grass. Fielzer's escort followed him a short way, then took refuge in the little pavilion in the center, while Fielzer rolled up and down paved walks under trees whose remaining leaves hung like drab rags on black limbs. Despite the cold, the air felt heavy and stale. After a while, he took pity on his escort, and went back, hardly refreshed by the exercise of so limited a freedom.

Inside, he headed for the bathroom. For the first days, a guard had accompanied him even here, watching without interest as he dealt with the necessary maneuvers and swung himself in and out of the shower. But the day shift had dwindled, during his quiet compliance, to three: the day officer, and two guards, one by each door. Now it occurred to him to check his bathroom cabinet . . . and the small, nondescript bottle he looked for was gone.

For a moment, his mind blurred, refusing that knowledge. He had clung to the belief that *he* could choose the time. Though he was doomed, as expendable as the people who would die in the disaster he was designing, he would have one last word to say to Security. He could suicide. Now . . . his eyes roamed the shelves. Things had been moved. He'd expected that. Cough medicine had shifted left; decongestant pills were now behind, not beside, the breath mints. That little brown plastic bottle with its pale green cap and the slightly faded label should have been unnoticeable, the kind of clutter everyone's cabinet held . . . but it was gone. Not behind anything, not beneath anything. Gone. Which meant that he was trapped again, and worse.

He had been in there too long; he heard a shuffle in the hall. Quickly he reached and flushed, wiped his face with the nearest towel. He rolled back out to see the day officer glancing through a magazine on the hall table.

"All right, Doctor?" the man asked.

"Fine." He couldn't say more. He rolled into his study, and flicked on the comlink to the Library out of habit. Habit took his fingers to the right keys for his access codes; habit swung him around to the cooler, while the screen warmed and his codes cleared; habit put a mug in his hand, and a thick meat sandwich. He took a bite, out of habit, and the rich flavor covered the sourness of his fear.

Then he looked at the screen, and choked, and had to muffle it before the Security men heard and came in to see what was wrong. There on the screen was his sister—the sister he had lost—as she had been that last few days of their childhood. Their father's dark hair and eyes; their mother's wide grin; her very own dimples. As he watched, as that one bite of sandwich turned to stone in his stomach, and his hands very slowly and carefully set the mug and sandwich down on his desk, the image changed . . . slowly aging, as in real life she must have aged. The childish nose lengthened, the dimples disappeared, the wide mouth straightened from a child's laugh to a woman's endurance. He could not doubt it was real: that it was Jen, that this was how she would have looked, if she . . . that it *was* how she looked, somewhere, now.

Beneath her face, a line of text scrolled past. "You're a hard man to get to, Par." He stared at it, motionless. His name disappeared off the left side of the screen, and the first word crawled onto the right. The sentence repeated, then, "Keyboard your answers."

His fingers felt thick as the sausage in his cooler. And what could he say? "I'm sequestered."

The face on the screen twitched, as if it were really hers, really a live video, and reacting to his words. Then it disappeared into a nest of squares, digitized out of existence, and came back not quite clear. "I know. That's why we used this way of contacting you. We need your help."

His fingers worked more smoothly now. "You're going to get us both in a lot of trouble—you think Sec doesn't have a tap on this link?"

"Not at the moment. It's busily tapping another link." Fielzer hoped the other person, whoever it was, had nothing to hide. "We need your Library link."

Fielzer stared at the screen. "You're *on* my Library link." He remembered the rarely used underlining function, and used it.

"Not exactly. Not with full access. Not since all the Sulese were arrested."

"Sulese?" Sul was a Rim world that sent occasional students to Varagossa; it was nowhere near Jaskar or Vargessi. Then he thought of something else. "*Scholastica*—was that a Sulese?"

The screen image winked, a very faked wink. He remembered Jen learning to wink, practicing on it so hard her tongue stuck out a little. "We want you to slip in a few queries for us . . . find out what the Governor's up to, clear up some ragged ends."

His throat was dry; he grabbed the mug and took a long swallow of the sour-sweet juice before trying to answer that one. Had they sneaked a video in? Had Security? His mouth was still dry, but he could feel the prickle of sweat on his neck and under his arms. It would definitely show on a Security video probe, their tame geophysicist talking treason with a face on the computer screen.

"Fresh juice?" scrolled across the screen. "Class five rations make life easier, don't they?"

"I didn't pick the rations." His fingers stabbed angrily at the keyboard. Did they have a video tap on him, as well as this? Who was watching, and where? "If I do what you want, whoever you are, I'll be on prison rations soon."

"Whoever I am?" The face flickered rapidly between that remembered laughing face and the grown woman he had never met. "You doubt this?"

"Could be faked." His breath came short. If it was faked, if Security had set this trap, that was one death . . . but if it was real, if she had lived somewhere all the years the family had believed her dead . . . that was another. What kind of life could it have been? How bad?

"The tree behind our apartment, on Jaskar: you could climb it, and I was too little."

"Anyone might have found that out—could guess—"

"—that you were the one who dropped the berries down for me—" The berries that had poisoned her, nearly killed her, because even he had been too young to know that they had to be cooked, and not just sweetened. No one else knew; he had been afraid to confess, and there had been a bunch low enough for Jen to reach.

"Jen—they said you were dead. That you died in camp."

"They said that about you, too. Liars, aren't they?"

"I put a flower on your grave, after the amnesty."

"After the amnesty I was still the guard captain's bedmate. Until I got old enough to interest *real* men."

Fielzer felt the tears on his face before he knew he was crying. That happened to other people, other women, and he always thought of Jen, and prayed she had died before. What kind of life? he had wondered. He did not want to know. He had to know.

"Are you all right?" It looked as stupid on the screen as it would have sounded if he'd spoken aloud.

"I'm alive, and I'm free. Will you do it?"

"I don't want to go back in."

"Nobody does." The face dissolved once more into larger blocks that distorted its features, then reassembled, this time in unbearable clarity. Whatever she had done, whatever life had brought her, this woman had survived, but he could not find the sister he remembered in that hard face. He stared at it, struggling for words, wishing he could speak face to face, where gesture and tone could give the bare words life.

He tried reason. "Jen, I have no legs; I'm using a prosthesis. The one that looks like a trash can. That's what I qualified for, not even mechs." He had had pegs and crutches at first, like the other zero class workers, but the grades that got him into the science academy also got him the mobile. He was destined for a science appointment, and mobiles took up less space than wheelchairs. If he'd been a class five when he lost his legs, he'd have had vat-grown replacements. "If I go to prison, they'll take it away." How could he explain what that meant to someone who could still walk around? His shoulders twitched, remembering what he had learned first, rump-walking down that long cold hall to the bathrooms. Bad enough in a hospital, where the attendants had been merely uncaring. In prison . . . he shivered convulsively, imagining brutalities he had heard about.

"Yes. They might."

"And you think I should risk that? Jen, if I didn't know you'd been there . . . how can you ask me?" He wanted to reach through the screen and shake her. It was not only fear for himself. If she had survived—if that image meant his sister still lived somewhere—then he feared for her as well. He could not bear her hurt again.

"Your trouble is that you got out." He didn't answer that, frowning at the screen until more words appeared. "I'm serious. You got out, you took your chances, you left it all behind you."

"What else?" He was suddenly angry. What was he supposed to have done, dragged his miserable stinking past along day by day?

"It's not behind you, Par. It's not behind me. It's right here, right now, yesterday and tomorrow. What they took from me, from you, from people we never even heard of, can't be given back. It's more than legs, Par, or the fingers I'm missing—" He flinched, not wanting to know that. "As long as anyone anywhere is in that prison, I am a prisoner."

"But you can't help that. Look—didn't they give you an education? A job?"

The face grimaced. "They gave me *nothing*. They took my family, my friends, three fingers, five years even after the amnesty—told you all I was dead, so that damned slug could have his girl without interference—and then tried to trade free tuition and meals for my gratitude. Don't they owe me something?" Fielzer said nothing, as all the old fury choked him. "And what about your legs? Don't you resent that?"

He looked away, and managed to type in what he'd been taught to say. "I could have lost my legs as a colonist. Accidents happen. It doesn't do any good to stir things up. I've grown beyond my anger."

"You don't really believe that."

He stared at that a long time, then tapped in, "No. Not really. But I don't think I can face prison again." Not without the little bottle that had disappeared from his medicine cabinet, the safe exit from his troubles.

"I suppose it is worse for you. Are you going to suicide, if things go wrong?" It was the logical question, but he had not expected it, not from his own sister. He felt a new prickling of sweat; she had always known when he lied. But computer-to-computer, he should be able to pull it off.

"If I have to." Next she would ask why he wouldn't help them if he had a sure way out . . . and what could he say then? But she didn't. Instead the face changed again, to something so near real life he expected to feel the warmth of her breath.

"Take care, Par."

He could not have said if it was the look on her face, or the withdrawal in that choice of words, but he was suddenly furious again.

"At least you should know why I have a Library link."

The face blurred, as if a screen passed in front of it, and steadied. "Why? You're a scientist with tenure; why not?"

Anger gave him the courage to continue. "You would not need to ask the Library what the Governor's doing; I'm working on it."

"What?" That came so quickly it might have been a voice barking in his ear. His mouth was dry again. Could he do it? He tried to breathe steadily, and explained what the Governor wanted, and what he had done so far. He typed rapidly, sentence after sentence flowing onto the screen. The reaction was as swift.

"Par—you can't!"

"I haven't yet. But I've modeled it." And wiped every model but the ones he carried with him.

"You're not going to—you can't."

23

"I thought I could. For a clean death." She had to understand that it had been that, the hope of a quick death, the certainty of some death, forming the walls of his trap. Not just a taste for richer rations or a comfortable life. "But you're right. I can't." Not with a sister who was somehow alive, beyond expectation, who might be anywhere, might be blown up by his choice of locations. He went on, trying to make his situation clear. "I could have finished sooner . . . I couldn't decide what to do. I don't know anyone. And if I don't do it, they'll just find someone else." All around him, inside his head as well as outside, dark prison walls closed in, jeering faces surrounded him, rough hands reached for him. "You can't do anything either, can you?"

"We might, if we knew enough. Maybe avert it, maybe expose them."

"What good is exposure, if it kills . . ." If it kills *you*, he thought, but he could not put that on the computer.

"At least it would be known. The right people get the blame."

How? he wanted to ask. But he was too tired to argue. It was a chance, a different choice than the ones he'd seen for himself. He scrubbed his face with one hand, staring at the screen. Another sentence appeared.

"We won't be able to protect you."

"I know that." Those imagined walls in his mind loomed closer. But she had no protection either, none but the chance that what he gave her might work. He wanted to ask where she was, and knew he must not—even if she would tell him, it might cost her life. "I'll give you what I have now, and try to stall them another week. Give me your download protocols." This was the moment that Security would crash through the door, if it was a Security trap, a final test, an excuse to blame the plot on him. But nothing happened, and a line of codes appeared below the test. Fielzer recabled his small computers to the Library terminal, undoing his past precautions, and loaded his first model. He had to toggle back and forth, assembling subroutines he'd kept separate, but the whole file poured through the link in seconds that felt like hours. Then another, the second-best match to the Governor's criteria.

"That's all," he typed at the end. Before the answer scrolled across, he had already uncabled the machines.

"Thank you, Par. Take care." The face was gone, one quick blink, and the Library logo flashed its cool blue and white. Fielzer entered a request for the most recent issue of two specialty journals, and tried to pay attention to the tables of contents when they appeared onscreen. Every day or so he had made similar requests; whenever the Security tap came back in (assuming it had ever been off) it would find normal activity. He glanced at the clock. He should be calling his housekeeper about supper; he should have one of the other computers up, with something running. That first, then the housekeeper . . . he hoped his voice sounded normally gratified to find that supper would be baked fish. He hoped he could eat it.

He managed to hold off his full reaction until he was in bed, and the guard had left the room. Then he lay staring into darkness, tongue clamped between his teeth. It was too much. She was alive; she had to be alive. He could see that face, both in memory and on screen—it had to be real. She had known about the berries, his deepest childhood shame (for hadn't he said, not an hour before, that he hated her and hoped she'd die, and been slapped for it?). He hadn't meant to poison her, not when it happened. He hadn't meant to let her hand slip from his, when they were taken off the bus at Sauwe Camp 5, and the big man had slapped him, but it hurt . . . and then they were leading her away, screaming "Par! Don't let them! Par!"

He cried, silently, biting his tongue as he'd learned to do in the barracks to choke the sound of sobs. And now he had returned the little he could, giving her secrets that might or might not save her life, or someone's life . . . and he could not even kill himself quickly. For him it would be a return to helplessness, humiliation. For her—perhaps the chance he owed her, after nearly killing her twice.

In the morning, his throat burned, and his nose itched. The day officer asked, with apparent interest, after his health, and Fielzer agreed that he might be coming down with a cold.

"Bucket-brain had to go walkin' in th' rain," he heard one guard say to another. "Serves 'im right."

He would have smiled at the persistence of ignorance—some people still believing that getting wet or cold would cause a virus infection—but it seemed politic to sneeze and look miserable.

On the strength of his cold, he worked slowly: took a nap after lunch, quit early that night, let himself complain briefly to his housekeeper at breakfast the next day that he couldn't think with glue in his head. He had an excuse for rummaging in his medicine chest, and confirming what he already knew: his safe out was gone.

But even a cold would not work forever. In eight days, he decided he was as ready as he could be, and reported the project completed. He followed instructions and downloaded the files into the Governor's supposedly secure computer, and packed the hard copies and notes into boxes for Security to take along. Then he went to bed and slept for twelve hours, to his own surprise.

He woke in late morning to grey weather, and rolled into his study. This might be his last chance . . . he rooted in the cooler for his favorites of the special rations, and snacked on sausage and fresh fruit. He wondered, idly, how long it would take to move the MassShaper (assuming they used the nearest), and whether Jen or her allies could stop it, and when they'd come for him. But that seemed remote; instead he was aware of the texture of the foods in his mouth, the aromas, the aftertastes. He turned on his music tapes, listening intently to every nuance, imagining the people with whom he'd heard that music in all the passing years. He looked around the study, trying to fix in his

mind the mellow reds and rusts of his carpet, the colors
and shapes of the books, even the oblong blanks of the
silent terminal screens.

Suddenly it was dark—had he fallen asleep?—and
the room was full of people in uniform. All strangers, all
polite but very firm. They rolled him to his bedroom,
to pack a change of clothes; he could hear them clearing
shelves, ransacking closets. His housekeeper's voice rang
out, "You can't—" and then something broke, china by
the sound, and a man's irritable voice said "Pick it *up*
then."

Before he had organized his thoughts, he was in the
lower hall, surrounded by them, shaking with shock
and fear. They had not let him take books, or paper, or
even the souvenir bit of ore the shift boss had brought
to the hospital of Sauwe Camp 5. He glanced around
without moving his head, an old skill regained at need.
His housekeeper and the three men that normally
guarded him were all in the reception room, with two
armed men watching them. Fielzer stared; one of the
Security guards had a darkening bruise along his jaw.
They looked past him, their faces expressionless.

"We'll take good care of Dr. Fielzer," said the man
beside him. "We'll find out what he's been doing for
you, and if you want him back, it's going to cost you."
He shut the door into the reception room and opened
the front one. Fielzer could see the dark, windowless
van parked at streetside. Who were these people? Another branch of Central Union? Surrounded by them,
he rolled to the van, where a hoist whined briefly,
lifting him to the interior. Someone hooked a cargo
strap to his prothesis; no one spoke. It was dark and
cold, and the van bucked over the decorative stones of
the Faculty Square drive before it ran more smoothly
on some connecting street.

A light flared. With him in the back of the van were
eight or nine people in uniform, all wearing obviously
false hair and facial makeup. The nearest was digging
around in his pockets and finally fished up a lump of
ore.

"Here," he said. "I know how you feel about this piece of rock." Fielzer stared, confused by the familiar voice, but finally seeing beneath dyed hair and false eyebrows the face of his colleague in the geology department. Porge Altlin handed over the ore sample, and Fielzer felt his hand close around it. It felt solid, like a real rock, like truth.

"You mean I'm not . . . you're not taking me . . . ?"

"You're not going to prison, no. Not tonight, anyway. And they may even believe that we think you're their agent—and abandon you."

"But I didn't know you were one of those—and what about the—" Fielzer found he couldn't frame complete thoughts, let alone coherent questions.

Altlin grinned. "Nobody talked politics with you, Par. As for the other, when they started to move the MassShaper, we . . . ah . . . stole it."

Fielzer stared at him. "Stole a MassShaper?" Even as he said it, his mind brought up the size, the mass, the shape . . . it was possible, once you thought of it.

"It's not that hard," Altlin said, grinning even wider. "Besides, we thought that if a mere Sulese graduate student could make off with a research vessel, an organization the size of ours could certainly manage a single weapon. We're giving it back, of course. With suitable alterations, a tasteful new color scheme, plenty of publicity. The hard part was getting a line in to your end, when we didn't know if you—how you—"

"Where I stood?" He could use the common word now without flinching, though some of the others did.

Altlin nodded. "Your sister was sure you'd help us, but we thought you might not believe she was real."

He had been afraid to ask; now he began to believe. His heart pounded; he could hardly hear the others' comments and explanations. It was hours later, when he was safely installed in someone's cellar after a confusing trip through utility tunnels, that his mind began to work again.

She had lost her dimples; he had lost his legs. But they had kept memories, and faith. She offered him a cup of soup, her eyes bright, challenging. "It won't taste like class five rations," she said.

Fielzer smiled at her, his stomach relaxing for the first time in weeks. In years. "Tastes better," he said. "Tastes free."

Introduction

Further on in these pages, Keith Henson describes the consequences of applying nanotechnology to mega projects. Here, Michael Flynn speculates on the consequences, from an American perspective, of a failure of nerve.

WEREHOUSE

Michael Flynn

Me and Pinky and the Wag was sitting around bored one day when we decides to pay a visit to the carter. We was just hanging out on the corner and there was nothing going down, so Pinky ups and says he'd like to get himself informed.

Well, it sounded okay. We never went in for that stuff before; but you know how it is. You keep your ears open and you hear things, and it was supposed to be a real kick. Besides, it was a slow day and we was itching for something new, and we wasn't too particular what. You know how it is: Different day; same shit.

It was Pinky brought it up. Pinky was an albino. His hair was as white as a Connecticut suburb and his eyes was red, which was spooky. He was skinny and liked to dress in black. He wore vinyl bomber jackets and pants tucked into his boots. The Wag always told him how it made him look like a prock.

We was flush and we figured to blow it on something; because what the hell good was a wad if it just sits in your pants? So we knowed we was gonna buy some kicks, the only questions being what kind and how many. Gambling? That was for suckers. Besides, the crap games had floated downtown and the numbers was run by The State and was crooked as a snake. Drugs? Most drugs didn't kick no more. Not since that guy Singer doped the water supply with Anydote; and that was a long time ago.

Sex? Like I said, what good is it if it just sits in your pants? There was plenty of janes in the neighborhood, and they didn't charge much; but then they wasn't worth much, neither. We figured with what we had on us we could get parked about two million times each; which, no matter how you look at it, is a tough row; and, whatever enthusiasm we might start with would wilt a whole lot sooner than our wad. And there was always the chance of Catching Something—State Cleanliness Certificates not being worth the paper they was forged on.

Besides, we had all them janes so many times already there wasn't no more kick to it. I mean, how many different ways can you do it? It was a long time since we seen anything new along those lines.

And what was there worth doing, besides gambling, drugs and sex?

So Pinky, who was maybe thinking about parking Red Martha for the millionth time and not thinking too highly of it, gives a shudder and says, "I don't want to dribble this wad away. How bout we try something really new?"

The Wag looks at me and shrugs. "What?"

"How bout we go look up a carter? I hear there's one up by 72nd Street."

"A carter?" The Wag touches his lips with his tongue and rubs his face with his hand to show how he's thinking it over. "That's a stiff tick." He says that to show how cost conscious he is. As if it was our money to start with.

"Hey," I said. "You only live once." (And yeah, I

know it shows religious prejudice, but the Dots live mostly over in Jersey, so who gives a shit?)

Pinky looks at me. "You wanna do it?"

What I heard is that informing hurts like hell. They dope you up with Thal, which helps; but which also makes you a dick, which is how they get a lot of repeat business. "I dunno. You gonna?"

We kick it around and what it come down to is that each of us would do it if the other two would; so it ain't like nobody made a decision or nothing. Shit happens. You know. So we started walking north. We wasn't exactly going to the carter, but if we found ourselves near there, we might look in just to see what it was like.

Werehouses was never easy to find. Seeing as how they was illegal, they tried to stay quiet. Make too much noise and a prock was sure to come nosing around. Carters didn't exactly hang out no signs, so if you wanted to get informed you had to listen to The Street. The Street knew, like it always did.

We was passing 69th when a crop of janes come a-cruisin the other way. They was dressed in twin glitterbelts. One on top and one below and neither one much wider than a promise. The Wag, he smiles at them and unzips so richard can wave at them. That's how he got his name. "Hi, jane," he says. "Show me your smile."

The janes, they look at him and one kinda raises her eyebrow the way a proctor might, but they don't stop walking and one glance is all they make. So the Wag, he points and says, "Hey, don't you know who this is?"

And the chocolate one, with the eyebrow, she answers and says, "It looks like richard, only smaller."

The janes laugh. And Pinky and me, we kinda laugh, too; cause it was funny, you know. But the Wag, he gets red in the face.

"Oh, he be blushing. Ain't it cute?"

The Wag growls deep in his throat and makes a snatch at them but Pinky and me grab him instead and hang on. He stretched his arms out like claws and tugged and twisted himself, trying to break our grip. He called them janes some pretty bad names, but they didn't pay him no mind. Hell, they was called those things near every day of the year and some of it was no more than the truth anyway, so who cared? That made him madder and he screamed some more. I admired his vocabulary and studied some of it for future use.

The Wag is like that. Most times he's as sweet as your mama's milk. Other times, he's as sour as the smile. There was no telling what would yank him off.

"Hey, Wag," I says. "Calm down. Get hold of yourself."

He looks at me and cusses. There's spit at the corners of his mouth. He tells me what he's gonna do to them janes—and I had to admit it was real creative—but they're gone around the corner and out of sight out of mind. The Wag laughs high and funny like he does sometimes. Then he does get hold of himself and, after a while he smiles.

"Let's go find the carter," he says when he's done.

I kinda scuff my sneaks a little. "You sure you wanna?"

He looks where the janes went. "Yeah. I'm sure."

The werehouse was in an old Chink restaurant uptown on Serpent turf. When we passed 70th and saw the local colors policing, we knowed we was close. Carters bring a lot of cash onto a turf; so the colors, they don't let nobody bother 'em. An op gets ripped off too much, he shifts the scene and the colors lose the Tax. And werehouses was about the biggest op around, legal or illegal. Some of the colors even put the Word around through the Street sayin' they would cut breaks to any op what staked out on their turf.

Pinky asked a jimmy on 71st if he knowed where we could get informed and the Serpent, he looked us up and down like we was procks. He spit a gob into the street and allowed as how he might know something or he might not. So the Wag goes how much was the Tax and the Serpent goes how much you got and they haggled a little. No big thing and we all knew it. The little shit wanted some grease on top of the Tax. Pinky and me kinda waited around, pretending to be scenery. The Serps were a chink gang and were supposed to be straight as any colors north of 48th, but who ever knew for sure? I hadn't hearda no wars on the East Side lately; but we seen plenty of old burned out buildings when we crossed the line.

I studied the jimmy's jacket a while, trying to read his badges and pins. Some of the colors go in for a lot of deco, showing how long the jimmy been stooled or how much weight he threw. But the gangs all used different systems and some didn't use any at all so who cared?

Besides, the lookout who was lounging in the fifth floor window across the street got my attention. Not that I ever thought the Serps would leave their man uncovered, but that jimmy with the smear gun made me a little nervous, you know what I mean? If he was a dick he might not care if we was legit or not and blow us away just for fun. He didn't have no expression on his face and he wore flatshades so I couldn't make out his eyes. He was dressed all in black, and nothing reflected any sunlight. Not his shades; not his leather; not his gun barrel. Nothing to make him stand out against his background; except that he was so damn flat that he did stand out.

Pinky sees him, too, and leans over and whispers. "To keep their man here from getting too much grease on his fingers. He's probably got a mike so's he can hear what goes down."

"So shut up, stupid. We ain't supposed to notice him."

Pinky shrugs. "Why pretend?" And the sunuvabitch *waves* at the lookout.

I don't want to see the lookout's reaction, but I can't help myself; so I kinda glance sideways. And the jimmy hasn't moved so much as a muscle since I first seen him. His flatshades look like two more gun barrels, and he stared at us like we was meat.

The Wag punched us on the shoulder. "C'mon," he said. "I got the skinny."

I don't know how long the restaurant was abandoned. I could still smell the chop suey and mustard sauce and the Wag makes a joke about sweet and sour park which we didn't think was too funny. The tables and counters was layered in dust and grease. There was newspapers and broken glass all over, and the heavy smell of yourn.

There was a zombie crouched by the kitchen doors, watching us, and I kinda stop for a second or two, you know. Not that I'm scared or nothing. I know that they don't have no more brains than a dog; but he gimme the creeps. You look in a zombie's eyes and there ain't nobody home, you know what I mean? Even when they juice a stiff with his own DNA, there's always something missing. What they call free will and innerlect. So all a zombie's good for is fetchin' and guardin' and stuff like that.

The Churches wasn't too happy about zombies when they first come out, but even the legit ops all said they was good, cheap labor that couldn't be organized. So everyone looked in the Book and found out that, sure enuf, old Jesus H. had pulled the same stunt with Lazarus and a little dead girl, and maybe even with Himself. It was a great thing, that Book. You could find whatever you were looking for, if you only looked hard enough.

(Golems was tougher to find. That's where they juice the stiff with someone else's DNA. And sometimes the stiff wasn't really a body, but just buy-o-mass or whatever. They hadda go all the way back to Genesis to make golems legit. You know. The part where God breathes on a lump of clay. Golems had to be registered with a synagogue and have a special mark on their forehead; but zombies could be marked and registered by anyone, even a mosque.)

The Wag walked up to the zombie and said something which I suppose was the password, because it pushed the swinging door open and let us go in with no more than a hungry look in our direction.

The carter was a skinny man who looked like a ferret. He must have been fat once, but went on a diet and forgot to tell his skin, cause it hung on him kind of loose. His green doctor gown was all stained and tore and his chin was a mess of stubble, like his whiskers couldn't decide whether to grow or not. He paid us no mind at first, but sat behind a battered old metal desk marking a tablet with a stylus. Every time he made a mark the computer screen beside him would wink at us.

After he made us wait long enough to show us he was important and we wasn't, he looked up and blinked his red, watery eyes. "Well?" he said. "What do you want?" His voice said he didn't particularly approve of us or what we wanted, which was funny because what we wanted was him.

Pinky looks at us, then at the carter. "We wanta be informed." Me, I wasn't so sure, but I didn't want to make Pinky look stupid.

The carter scans us, like he was checking the janes at a smile auction. "Have you ever patronized a werehouse before? No?" He steepled his fingers. "I thought as much. Go home to your mamas, boys. This is not for you." He bends over his stylus and pad.

Have you ever seen how a little kid acts when you try to take a toy away, even if he wasn't too sure he wanted to play with it in the first place? The carter talked like an educated man, maybe even high school—there was ragged and stained papers thumbtacked to the wall that looked official—so he ought of knowed that. And maybe he did. Maybe he was playing games, teasing us. Maybe he liked to see people beg for it.

The Wag pulls our wad from his purse and waves it at the carter. "We got the cash. You selling or what?"

The carter looks at the stash and wets his lips. "Is that government money?" he asks and the Wag nods. "It might be enough for one treatment," he allows.

"Nuts. It's all three of us or none of us."

The carter nods his head at the wad. "That is insufficient to cover three fees."

"You ain't counted it."

"That isn't necessary. I can gauge its thickness."

The Wag looks uncertain and I'm keeping my mouth shut; but Pinky, he ups and says, "So, what's better: three cheapies, or nothing?"

Well, I can see how that makes him think some. "You're too young," he says again, but his heart ain't really in it. Nobody makes money turning customers away.

"We're old enough to park janes," says the Wag, which makes me wonder if he's still thinking about them smilers that shot him down on 69th street. "I probably got a dozen kids around the City."

"An accomplishment requiring great skill and study, I'm sure." The carter makes a steeple of his fingers again. "Very well," he says through the fingertips. "You understand that the treatment will be quite painful. I will give you drugs to deaden the pain; but nevertheless, the nanomachines restructuring your cells will twist your bones and organs into new shapes. That there will be some pain involved is regrettable, but unavoidable."

Me, I could feel my organs twisting already, but the Wag says, "Yeah. We can take it."

The carter looks doubtful, but shrugs. "Very well. The original procedure was developed by Henry Carter over a generation ago when he adapted some of the earliest cell repair nanomachines to change the body's shape. Of course, it was far more painful and took much longer than it does now. Great strides have been made since then. I have an extensive library of DNA samples" —And he points to a refrigerator humming in the corner—"that I can use to program the cell machines for the original alteration; and I will, of course, retain your own DNA samples in my cell library, and culture nanomachines from them, so that I may restore your bodies to their original configuration when you return."

He pulls open a drawer and lays some papers on his

desk. "These are the usual release forms stating that I have explained the procedure and the risks to you. Read them and sign where I've indicated."

Read? He's gotta be kidding. I couldn't understand none of his explanation, and I didn't care. What difference did it make how old informing was, or who done it first? I see Pinky and the Wag look at each other. Then they take pens from the desk and scratch their X's. They show the carter their City passes so he can copy their vitals onto the form.

I try to read my form like he says. I wasn't from the City original, so I can read some. I can recognize some of the words on the form, which makes me happy; but too many are long or unfamiliar, so I give up. I stick my tongue out the corner of my mouth and draw my name. I'm proud I can do that, but the carter, when he sees what I done, looks kinda sad and says, "Are you sure you want to go through with this, son?"

No, I'm not. For just a second the carter sounded like my old man and I wanted to tell him everything and let him tell me what was right. But what can I say with my friends sitting right next to me? The next second I remember the carter is a smelly old man who doesn't shave and that reminds me what my old man was really like so it doesn't bother me any more.

"Yeah, I'm sure."

He sighs. "Very well, then." He gives all three of us a look. "My cell library includes several of the more famous pornstars and athletes. You understand, by the way, that the transformation will not be total. Your brain cells, in particular, will be affected only to the extent necessary to, ah, 'run' your new bodies. That was the law when this procedure was legal, and I still abide by it."

That explained why he made us sign release forms. I didn't think he would file them with the proctors, though.

"After you have been informed by the nanomachine, your bodies will become a reasonable compromise between your present form and that of your chosen model. You will not look precisely like Big Pete Hardy does on

his videos, if he should be your choice; but you will
have his craggy good looks and his, shall we say, viril-
ity?" He waved us to a row of cracked plastic chairs
salvaged from the restaurant and asked us what form we
wanted.

Pinky looks at us and says, "I'll tell you when we go
in there." And he nods toward the curtained off area
that I been trying not to look at.

The carter doesn't say anything to that. "And you
gentlemen?"

"I ain't decided yet," says the Wag. "Me, too," I
agree.

The carter looks disgusted but it ain't his problem. So
he takes Pinky behind the curtains. I hear all kinds of
sounds, like metal and glass and stuff. As soon as they're
gone the Wag was out of his chair and at the refrigerator. He opened it and began pawing through the vials
racked inside.

"Hey, Wag. What you doing?"

"Shut up. I wanna see if he got what I want."

"What's that?"

"Wolf."

Before I can say anything, the curtain parts and the
carter comes out. He sees what the Wag is doing and
shouts. "Get your ass away from there!" And aims a
kick at him. The Wag rolls away from it and bares his
teeth in a snarl. For a second I thought he would flip
out again like he did with those janes; but he calmed
down right away and grinned. "Just wanta see what you
got."

"Don't mess with things you don't understand." The
carter reaches into the fridge and pulls out a vial. When
he closes the door, he puts a deadlock through the
handle. Before he retreats behind the curtains again he
turns and looks at us.

"Your friend is under anesthetic now. Do you wish to
watch the transformation? It is quite remarkable to see
the bones and muscles changing shape before your very
eyes. There are some who find the sight enjoyable."

"Nah," says the Wag, who's thinking about more important things. I just shake my head.

After that it was quiet and I wondered what form Pinky picked for himself. It was his idea to get informed, so he musta had something in mind before we ever come uptown.

I look at the Wag. "Wolf?"

When he grins back, I see all his teeth.

Screams I think I could have took, but what we heard was moans. Long, low, and drawn out, like someone having a bad dream. The Wag and me look at the curtain, then at each other; and the Wag's tongue darts out and wets his lips. A jimmy moans, you know the pain goes on and on and he can't do nothing about it, like he give up the struggle. I began to wish for one, pure, defiant scream.

After a while, it began to get to me, so I stood up and walked around. The carter had some old yellowed newspaper clippings tacked to the wall and I spent the time trying to sound out the headlines. Some had pictures and, if the words weren't too long, I could mostly figure them out, which made me feel good. *Clones Not Legit, Sez Council. Sawyer Rules on Zombie Law. Kops Katch Killer Klone.* Before my time, all of it. Some of the clippings was so old they was falling apart; but I did figure out from one old photo that the carter's name was Benny.

Then the carter pulls the curtain aside and Pinky walked out dressed in a tattered, white robe. He was wet and shiny, like he just took a bath. The carter stood to one side, watching us. Pinky was walking unsteady and looked a little dopey from the drug. I looked and the Wag looked and neither of us said anything for a while.

Cause Pinky was a jane.

I knowed it was still Pinky. If anything, his skin and his hair was whiter than ever, so his eyes looked like spots of blood. He looked about the same mass, but it was all set up different, you know what I mean? His face looked like a chink ivory carving I seen once in a picture book. I remembered a phrase I heard one time: alabaster body. Pinky sure enough had that.

"Well?" he says after a minute of us gawking.

"Shit, Pink. You're parking beautiful." And he was, too. Richard tried to sit up and look for himself. It embarrassed me and I hoped nobody noticed.

Pinky looks kinda pleased—and, who knows, maybe he did notice—and turns to get his clothes. But the Wag jumps up and grabs his wrist.

"Hey, hold on there," he says. "We ain't seen everything." And he pulls Pinky's robe open. "Show us your smile."

I was kinda curious myself to see how complete the informing was. Pinky lets us look for a moment, then he pulls shut again. "It's your turn now," he says. "I'm gonna get dressed."

"Wait up a sec," the Wag says to the carter. "Me and my friends got some talking to do."

The carter shrugs and points. "Use that room over there."

It was a small room, that used to be a storeroom or office or something, and there wasn't no furniture. The Wag kicked the door shut and it got dark, with just a little light coming in a small, dirty window high on the wall.

"Hey, Wag," says Pinky. "Leggo my arm."

"What's up?" I ask. Then I hear the Wag unzip and I know what's up.

"C'mon, jane," he says. "Smile for richard."

"Hey!—" And Pinky sounds scared. "Quit foolin."

"No foolin." And the Wag pulls the robe so hard it tears at the sleeve. Pinky is whiter than the robe and he glows in the light from the window. He always was built light and he makes a fine looking jane; so I can't help it if richard wants to look, too.

The Wag hooks a foot behind Pinky's ankle and trips him down. I can hear Wag's boots scraping on the dirt. Then he kneels hard on Pinky's belly to make him smile. "Quit yer bitchin," he says, and his voice was hard and angry. "We was looking for something different, weren't we?"

"Yeah, but—"

"C'mon. Don't you even wanna know what it's like from the other side? Whydja change if you didn't want to do it?"

Pinky yells a couple times and says it hurt, but the Wag goes shut up and enjoy it; and it wasn't like Pinky never said the same thing to janes himself. The Wag says over and over how good it feels, but I look close at his face and he ain't smiling no more than Pinky is.

After a while I can't look no more. I ain't squeemish or nothing. We'd all watched each other plenty of times. But this was different, somehow.

Wag doesn't take long. He never does. When he's done, he tells me it's my turn. "I gotta see the Man about a dog." And he laughs that laugh of his again and leaves us in that little dark room.

Pinky watched him go. "Bastard," he said, hugging himself.

"Hey, Pink. You come dancing out with nothing but a robe on, what do you expect? It ain't his fault. Shit happens."

"Yeah." He didn't sound like he believed me.

"And it ain't like you never done it to janes yourself."

He looked at me and his eyes were twin pools of blood. "It's different being done to."

I didn't say nothing. I didn't want to be in the room with Pinky. I didn't want to be in the werehouse at all. I don't know where I wanted to be.

I looked at Pinky out of the corner of my eye. He was sitting there, naked, picking little pieces of wood or plastic off the floor and tossing them into the dark. I had to admit he made a good looking jane. Better looking than he ever was as a jimmy.

He sees me staring. "Well?" he says, and his voice has a defiance to it. "You gonna take your turn or what?"

I look away. "I dunno. I'm not real interested."

He pointed. "I got eyes. You wanna do it. So why don't you?"

"Christ, Pinky. You're a jimmy."

"Hey! Look at me. Look at me," he demanded. I looked and he showed me the smile. "Does this look jimmy to you?" I had to admit that it didn't and he leaned back on his elbows. "So go do it. It ain't like I'm a virgin or nothin."

I put my hand out and touched him/her. He looked like a jane; and he felt like a jane; and he smelt like a jane. And the eyes and the skin and the nose are a lot smarter than the brain any day. Besides, it was getting hot in that little room. So, what the hell? Shit happens. You know what I mean?

Afterward me and Pinky was back in the waiting room and the Pink was all dressed up and ready to go. He was wearing the same clothes he come in with, but they fit different. Snug in some places, you know. His hair hadn't grown any longer, but s/he had combed it different. S/he didn't look butch or nothing. Pinky was a real cruising jane. If I seen him on the street, not knowing who s/he was, I don't know what I'da thought.

Pink shouldered his bag and paused kinda awkward.

"Well," he said. "So long."

"See you later," I said.

Pinky shook her head. "I ain't coming back."

I wasn't surprised. Somehow I knowed that already. "Cause of the Wag?"

His face hardened. "I'll fix that bastard good," she said, looking toward the ratty curtains. "And that carter. He knowed what the Wag wanted. I'll fix him, too. But they ain't the real reason. I always wanted to be a jane. I don't know why, but I always did. Now I am, and I ain't changing back. It was too boring, doing the same stuff every day."

"Yeah, I know." Life's a bore. Different day, same shit. But I wondered how long it would take Pinky to get bored of smiling, too.

That was a scary thought. Anything new is a thrill the

first time you try it; but the thrill wears off. So what do you do when there ain't no more new thrills to try? The Ultimate Thrill? The one that no one ever does twice, because you only can do it once? The one you could never get bored of? A lotta jimmies and janes I knew tried it. No one ever came back to say how it felt.

A long moan came from behind the curtain and me and Pinky look that way. Pinky spits on the floor. "I hope that sunuvabitch hurts for a week. What did he pick? Pornstar?"

"Wolf," I say, and Pink looks at me funny.

"Wolf?"

"Yeah. He's gonna be a 'laskan grey wolf."

Pinky shook her head. "Wolf ain't possible. The size. . . ."

"Nah. He tol' me how a wolf is 150 pounds or less, which is about all any of us mass. So there shouldn't be too much stretching or squashing."

"Too bad," says Pink. "He should hurt more. But then, he always was part animal." She looks at me. "What about you? You gonna do it?"

I shook my head. "It ain't sounded like too much fun so far."

She grins and claps me on the shoulder. "And why change what's perfect, right?"

"Yeah. Something like that." I grin back at her, knowing I prob'ly won't never see him again. "I'll miss you, Pink."

She looks at the curtain once more. "Yeah. Look me up. I better be going. Good luck."

"Yeah. Good luck." And I waited a while longer in that dank, empty room, listening to the moans from behind the curtain, smelling the medicines and the zombie outside the door, and Pinky, even tho she was gone. Well, we wanted something different, didn't we?

The Wag looked like a wolf, but you could tell he really wasn't. His head was bigger than a real wolf's and was shaped different. The muzzle was shorter and blunter. The carter goes how that's because the human

45

and lupine (that's what he said, human and lupine) DNA juices had to blend together. The brain stayed mostly human; which meant the skull had to be bigger; which took away from the jaws. The carter told me all about it. He called it Morfo Jenny, or something like that. I almost understood what he was saying.

"Can he talk?" I asked the carter.

"Somewhat. He has vocal cords, but the lips and palate and teeth are shaped differently. That was part of the humano-lupine compromise. So—"

"Of course I can talk," says the Wag/Wolf. Except I have to ask him to repeat a couple times before I get it, which pisses him off.

"What's it like, being a wolf?" I ask. I see his tail whisking back and forth and thought: *He's still the Wag.* I thought it was kinda funny but I didn't say nothing to him. The Wag had a bad temper and a lot of teeth.

"I'll tell you later. Better yet, why don't you join me? It'll be more fun the two of us together." He barked. "Tonite's my night to howl."

Yeah. A load of laughs. "Well . . . I tole Pinky I wasn't gonna do it."

His hairs stood up and he growled at me. "You wimping out on me, shithead? You hop in the vat like I did, or I'll tell the janes tomorrow how you couldn't do it."

"Well. . . ." I didn't want to do it; not really. But I didn't want to back down, either. I mean, you don't let your friends down, right? And I didn't want Wag to think I was scared or nothing.

"Come on," he goes. "Ain't you never wondered what it was like to park a dog? This way you can do it without being no prevert or nothing." He made a whuffing sound, which I thought might have been laughter. "Everything looks different. Everything smells different. I can tell how many people been in here just by the number of smells. Shit. You wanted something different? This is as different as you can get."

Just before I climb into the vat, the carter leans over and whispers in my ear. "Last chance to back out, boy."

I don't look at him. "I ain't scared. Why should I back out?"

"Because you don't really want to do this. Because you aren't like your two friends. Because—" He hesitates and rattles a couple of needle valves in his hand. "Because you can read," he says.

I tell him I can't read nohow; and he better not let on. People find out you can read, even a little, and they call you a nerd. A 'worm. "Besides," I tell him, "reading ruins your eyes. They proved it."

"Who's 'They'?" The carter looks angry for a moment. Then he sags and shrugs. "To hell with it, then. Climb into the vat." And he turns on a faucet and a thick, greenish liquid oozes into the tank. I climb in and it's like swimming into gelatin.

I won't bother telling you what it was like. If you been through it, you already know; and if you ain't, nothing I can say will mean shit. I hoped I would die and was afraid I wouldn't. I felt like I was made of tiny twisted threads and every thread was on fire. It was a nightmare even with the dope.

Afterwards, I scampered out of the vat and stood on the floor. I shook the excess water off and it come to me that I was standing on all fours and I was covered with fur. My eyes was three foot off the floor, about level with the Wag. I felt like I was on hands and knees, with my legs cut off at the knees. I twisted my head to try and get a good look at me and saw long, hairy, grey flanks. Things looked a little blurred. Out of focus like.

Shit. I was a wolf.

"Hey," I said. "I can't see so well." Were wolves nearsighted? Or just my wolf?

"Take a deep breath," says the Wag. He's grinning with his teeth.

I do and all of a sudden I can "see" real well. Not colors and shapes, but smells. The far corner of the room smells pungent, like stale yourn, but it fades off toward the ceiling into something more like mildew. There are fireflies dancing in the air. Molly Cools, the carter tells me. Chemicals and medicines he's used. I know it's my nose, not my eyes, but my brain is telling me it's my eyes. So, I "see" sparks. The floor has a million smells from a million feet; and each footprint glows with its own individual color. I snuffed one or two like I was tracking and it was like blowing on a hot coal. The smells seemed to brighten.

Wag and me stagger around the waiting room a while until we get our coordination back. The carter tell us our physio-jimmy has all the wolf's nerves. What he called the auto-something nervous system. That way it didn't take long to learn our new bodies.

"Hey," I says, "this is all right."

The Wag shook himself. "Then let's howl." He looks back at the carter. "We'll be back in the morning. You have our juice ready by then."

The carter was already planting himself behind his desk. He looked at us with those empty eyes of his and shrugs. "Certainly. Mind the zombie as you leave."

We bounded out from the old restaurant and onto the streets. The zombie howled and shook its chains as we passed, which made me feel good; a zombie being afraid of me and all.

It was night when we come out and I was surprised 'cause I didn't think we'd been in there so long. *Evening Mists* was shining bright high overhead in its orbit and me and the Wag howled at the gooks up there.

I always thought the City smelled; but shit, I never smelled it like I did that night. The smokey grey of old, burnt out buildings; and the fresher yellow of a new fire somewhere off downtown. The garbage along the curb and in the alleyways. The greasy trails of cars, their exhaust plumes twisting like brown streamers in the air long after the cars was gone. The black smell of rubber on the road.

And the people! I didn't know they could stink so many different ways. They stank in stripes. The carter smelled one way; the footprints on the sidewalk smelled another. I could smell Serpents: chinks smelled different from regular people. I knowed some of the smells were me and Pinky and the Wag, but I couldn't tell which was which.

And there were dogs and cats and pigeons and rats. Each one unique. Each one different.

Somehow, that rat smell made me hungry.

I could smell the Wag-wolf, too; and that made me nervous. I don't know why; but every time we got a little too close, he would growl or I would growl, and we'd back away from each other. In-stink, the Wag called it.

"Hey," he said. "Let's go find those janes we saw before and give 'em a scare."

I knew he was wanting to get back at them for what they done to him earlier; but hell, it sounded okay to me, so we bounded off downtown. It was a wonderful feeling, the way I could run and leap. I was strong. I was fast. The air was a wind on my face, sparkling with odors.

A jimmy and jane was walking toward us, up Fourth. She was leaning on him and rubbing her hand over his chest. He had his hand on her ass, squeezing. I could hear them whispering to each other from half a block away. They wasn't saying nothing too original.

We streak past them like an express train, leaping into the air and snapping our teeth in their faces. She shrieks and he cries out and tries to pull her in front of him and the Wag and I disappear around the corner on 71st. I find out what fear smells like. It is a heavy, pale smell. It rolls off them in waves and makes me want to chase them.

I can hear the slap she lays on his face as clear as a bell. The Wag and me look at each other and we both rear back our heads and howl at the moon.

We zig-zagged our way down the avenue, snapping and growling at pedestrians. Mostly, they yelled and ran. Some of them yelled and froze stiff. One man pulled out a cross and aimed it at us, but it didn't hurt none. The fear smell made me jumpy. I don't remember ever feeling so high before. I wanted to jitterbug.

I remembered the Serp lookout at 70th just in time.

The Wag was all set to have a go at the turf guard, but I gave him a bump and he went ass over teakettle.

Man, he whipped up and was on me in a flash. He bit me on the left hind leg but I shook loose. "The lookout!" I shouted. Except it was more like "The woof-au!" and he was so excited that I had to say it over and over before he got the idea. When he did, he quieted down.

"Don't screw with the Serps," I said. "Or any of the other colors when we're on their turf. They don't mind a little hell-raising; but you can't touch one of their own."

He growled at me a little, but he had to admit that I was right. "Don't never bump me again," he said. "I couldn't help myself. Biting you. It was those in-stinks again."

He wasn't gonna get no closer to an apology. I didn't know if it was wolf in-stinks or Wag in-stinks, though, that made him do it. I twisted my neck backward and sniffed at the wound. There was a metallic smell I recognized as blood. I sniffed again and licked at it. It was stopped already, clotting up.

We cut down an alleyway, bumping over all the trash cans. One of them fell and a couple of big, grey rats cut out in front of us.

I struck like lightning!

That rat was in my jaws before I even thought about it. I bit down hard and felt the bones crack. Bright, hot copper-smelling blood gushed around my teeth, down my throat. The rat squealed once and tried to bite back, but he never had no chance. I dropped the body to the ground and snuffed it. It sure did smell good.

Then I realized I was thinking about eating a dead rat, raw, and I wanted to puke. Except that it didn't really make me feel sick. Just in my head I wanted to feel sick. I backed away a step or two.

The Wag had lunged at one of the other rats but had missed. He come over and looked at mine. "Lucky bite," he says.

Lucky, hell. I think I was just quicker to learn the body, is all. He sniffs at the rat and I feel the hairs on my back go up. So I growl at him and he backs away.

"You gonna eat it or what?" he asks.

I didn't want to, but the thought of the Wag eating what I killed don't feel right. "Just leave it," I say. "You wanna eat, we can get steak from the market."

"Yeah? With what?"

"Our smile." I show him my teeth and he catches on.

When we reached 69th, the Wag snuffed around some looking for the trail the janes had left. But the trail was cold. We'd met them early in the afternoon and now it was late night—about one ayem. About a million feet had walked around that block and the smells was all the color of mud.

We tried around the corner on Sixth, where we seen them go, and all of a sudden Wag pulled up sharp. He took in a sharp sniff and let it out. "Park," he says.

I sniff, too; and suddenly I know what got him. A scarlet smell mixed with pink shimmering in the air. A bitch in heat.

My wolf's body responded. I sat on my haunches and yipped at the moon. Wag did, too. Then we set off following the scent. We could tell we was going the right direction cause the smell got brighter as we loped along.

She was inside an alleyway taking a leak by a trash dumpster. She was a regular dog; a collie mix, I think. She looks up and sees us, and her head darts left, then right, but we got her cornered. Between the brick wall of the building and the dumpster there wasn't no way out except past the Wag or me.

Understand. She wasn't pretty or nothing. Hell, she was a dog. But I guess the 'lupo' part of my "lupo-human" body didn't go by looks. It was the smell that hooked us, and it was automatic. Pure in-stink. I could no more *not* want to do it than I could play the saxophone with my paws.

We was sliding up real slow and easy. The Wag, he

was sweet-talking her as if she could understand a word he was saying. I was starting to realize that I didn't know *how* to do it and figured to rely on those in-stinks again, when she howled and the decision was taken away from us.

He came bounding toward us from the dark end of the alley, snarling and snapping. The Wag and me, we cut out of there real fast without even looking. He sounded a whole lot meaner and tougher than we was. We didn't turn around till we passed a lamppost that had his marker scent on it. Then we looked back to see what it was that had chased us.

I don't suppose we was the first jimmies ever to get ourselves informed with wolf juice. Still, it was kind of a surprise to meet another one. He was standing by the entrance to the alley way, pacing back and forth and growling at us. Three, four other dogs, all bitches, crowded up behind him; and one other wolf-man guarded the—harem?—and kept a watch in the other direction. We tucked our tails. I could tell the Wag wanted to fight; but he wasn't any dumber than I was. Two against two and both of them was bigger than us. We slunk off. I wondered if them wolf-men we seen made the change-over regular-like; or even if they'd given up being men at all. A short-timer can always tell a lifer, and them two had acted like they knowed what they was doing.

Wouldn't you know it. The bitch had took out minds off them janes we was trying to track; and, as soon as we stopped looking for them, there they was.

We saw 'em when we turned crosstown on 67th. There was only three of them by now. The others had probably found customers to stay with; or maybe these three was working overtime. Anyhow, I recognized the tall chocolate one that put the Wag down earlier and figured the other two orbited with her.

The Wag sees them, too. He pushes me back around the corner before they can spot us and takes a strong whiff of the air so he'll know their scent. He put his muzzle next to my ear and whispered. "Let's run at 'em barking and knock 'em down. Snarl right in their faces;

show 'em some teeth. Maybe tear their glitterbelts off. Make 'em pee their pants, if they was wearing any." He looked once at the corner. "The nigger bitch is mine. I'll teach her a thing or two." I think he was wondering if a wolf could do it to a human.

"We're just gonna like scare 'em, right?"

He sniffed the air again. "Get ready. They're almost here . . . Now!"

We cut around the corner and spring into the air. The janes see us and scream. I hit the skinny white one and knock her down. She tries to squirm away and she hits me with her fists, but it's like being hit with feathers. I put my face close to hers and growl and she freezes with her mouth wide open and not a sound coming out. "Don't move," I say. I don't think she understands me; but she understands I spoke.

"Werewolf!" She tries to scream it, but it only comes out a whisper.

I smile with my wolf-mouth to show she's right. She's afraid of me, all right. I can feel her shivering underneath me. It makes me feel funny. Nobody was ever afraid of me before. The fear smell is starting to get to me, so I take a snap at her torso-belt, to pull it loose. It's vinyl or something like that, so it doesn't tear, but I stretch it enough so that she pops out of it like twin seeds from a melon. I start licking and she squeezes her eyes shut and gets real stiff.

"Son of a bitch!"

That was the Wag.

I turn and look and see that his jane is loose. Maybe he missed his jump and didn't hit her square on. I don't know. All I know is I see she's loose, but she ain't running. She's backed up against a lamppost and has a gravity knife in her hand. Her lips are pulled back from her teeth and she looks for the moment every bit as dangerous as we do.

A swipe with the knife and a line of red opens up along the Wag's side. He howls with rage and leaps at her. She tries to put her arm in front of her throat. And that's all I see, because the jane underneath me decides to fight back, too. She swings and connects to my nose.

None of her other punches so much as bothered me, but that left to the nose was another story. It was like I was poked in the eyes. All the smells around me shattered into a kaleidoscope. I howl and snap and my teeth sink into something tender.

There is a scream in my ear and the fear smell is overpowering. I snap again and the scream turns into a gurgle. My mouth is full of warm, salty water. I pull and tear and swallow. It tastes good. Almost like pork. I hadn't realized how hungry I am.

There are more screams, too, from somewheres else; and that warm liquid squirts at me like from a hose. I keep biting and tearing until the pain in my nose goes away. I bite and I chew and. . . .

And I realize what I done.

I jerk away from the body like I was burned. I see it twitch two, three times as the last of the blood spurts out. Then it gets real still. Part of the rib cage is sticking out. The smell—a blend of fear and blood and yourn—starts to cool, and I commence to shaking, but I can't tear my nose away from it.

"Wag?" I call, and I can hear the strain in my own voice. He doesn't answer and I turn and look. "Wag!"

And he's still at it.

The chocolate jane is lying stiff and her eyes is like glass. One arm still has a tight hold on the knife, which stands there sharp and upright; but the rest of her is limp. She flops all loose every time he takes a bite. Her throat is all tore up and there's blood sprayed all over everything. The jane is covered with it and the street is covered with it and the Wag is covered with it.

"Wag!" I call again.

This time he hears me because I can see him come into focus. He looks at me and at the janes and he snuffs the body. Then we both cut out for the alleyway.

When we was back in the alleyway, we turned and looked. It was all blurred at that distance, but I could smell what it looked like. The two janes laid there not moving. Not that I expected them to. If they had, I might have lost my mind. But there was a tiny shred of thought that maybe it was just a bad dream.

"Wag," I said again and reared back my head and howled. "What did we do?"

"We didn't do nothing," the Wag said. "It was all them in-stinks. When the bitch cut me I couldn't think. I went crazy. Like you. It ain't our fault. Shit happens. They shouldn't have fought."

I sniffed a little at the Wag's idea. It sounded right and I wanted to believe it. That wolf juice gave us wolf in-stinks along with our bodies. It was like we was just along for the ride. You know what I mean? It all happened without me wanting it; and it was over before I knowed it.

I remembered how good it felt, though. Like catching prey was what I was built to do. I don't remember ever feeling that good about something; and I didn't ever want to feel that good again. I began shaking again.

"Where'd the third jane go?"

"What?" I look at him.

"The third jane," he snarled. "She'll nark to the proctors. We've got to find her!" And he was off like lightning. I didn't know what else to do, so I followed him.

We picked up the scent real easy. It was so heavy with fear that it glowed like neon. We trailed it down the street and across into the alley opposite. We ran like the wind, knocking over trashcans and newspaper stands. There wasn't no one around at that hour.

Then we seen her, about a crosstown block ahead of us. Wag howls as he runs and the jane turns and sees us coming and shrieks. She's running, too; but she's tired and clumsy and she stumbles and the Wag is on top of her.

"Wag, wait! What are you doing?" I jump around a little, feeling skittish from the scents around me.

He was getting better at it. Practice, I suppose. He knew to go for the neck right off and I suppose that was the fastest and kindest way to do it. But the jane kept right on trying to scream, even with no throat to make the sound; with the blood spraying the walls instead of going up into her head. Then her brain finally got the message and shut down for good. It couldn't have taken more than a minute, but it seemed to last forever.

When he was done, the Wag was breathing heavy. He took a bite from the thigh muscle. "You want any?" he asked me.

I just shook my head. "No! Wag, what's got into you?"

"It ain't me, chickenshit. It's the wolf. I ain't the one doing it. I'm just inside watching. This is great, man. When we go back to the carter and get reinformed, it'll be like we never done it ourselves."

And he took off again, howling. Somewhere off downtown I heard an answering howl and I thought about those other wolves we seen.

I chased after the Wag. I didn't know what I'd do if I caught him. I wanted to be back at the werehouse. I wanted to be myself again. I hated Pinky for ever suggesting we try it; and I hated the Wag for making me climb in the vat.

Something had gone terribly wrong with the Wag. He never was any too right to start with, but he was never a stone killer. I didn't know too much about wolves; but I didn't think they acted this way, either. Even wolves have rules.

I caught up with him in another dark alley. He was crouched at one end, watching and sniffing. There was two figures at the far end of it. I sniffed a jimmy and a jane parking it and I could hear them telling each other lies. They was doing it standing up, with him pushing her up against the wall. But it was too far to smell any more than that through the garbage.

"Watch this," says the Wag. "Two at once." And he runs and leaps.

The two screw-balls hear him. The jimmy turns and starts to shout an obscenity, but then he sees what's coming, and he pulls out and she falls on her ass. He tries to run, but his pants are down around his ankles and he trips and sprawls into the trash along the building wall.

Then the Wag is on him; but he just makes a snap in passing. The jimmy, he shrieks and grabs himself with both hands between the legs. He twists and curls along the pavement, splashing in the rancid puddles that dripped down from the gutters overhead. He was dressed downtown slick, and I wondered what he would tell his wife when he went home to the suburbs.

The Wag bounced over him and snapped the jane. I thought he would make short work of her like he did the other one. But he bites and tears; then he freezes, and backs off.

By that time I catch up with him. The jimmy is moaning and cursing. His legs and hands is all bloody, but I got no eyes for him. I sniff the jane and know who she is.

It's Pinky.

She ain't dead; but that's just a formality. She's all messed up, blood everywhere; the red sharp against her milky skin. Her jaws is clenched tight so no scream'll come out. She don't look decent. I want to pull her glitterbelts back in place—sometime during the night she musta got herself regular cruising clothes—but I don't got the hands for it. Folks should look decent when they die. I look into those blood red eyes and she's looking right back.

"You, too?" The words trickled from her ruined throat. "You did it anyway?"

I sat on my haunches. "Yeah. I was bored. Didn't know what else to do."

"Pinky," says the Wag. "I didn't mean it. I was just—"

"Doing what . . . always . . . wanted." The words came fast, in bunches. Short gasps of sound. "Fuck . . . both. Fixed . . . good, Wag. . . . Narked . . . carter." She sucked in her breath and held it. "No screams. Finish job . . . bastard."

The Wag looks at me and I look at him.

"Finish it!" she screamed.

The Wag howled and lunged and it was over.

Then he laid down and put his head on his forelegs and whimpered. "It ain't my fault," he kept saying. "It was the in-stinks."

I just kept looking at Pinky, not thinking anything. Until I thought: *Narked on the carter?*

I stood bolt upright. We had to get back there fast! That carter had our juice.

We ran back uptown as fast as we could. The Wag was winded already from what he done, but he found his second breath when I told him what was coming down. While we ran he kept trying to tell me that it wasn't his fault about Pinky. I wanted to tell him to shut up but I wanted to save my breath.

The Wag was tired from all his running and leaping, and maybe he had too full a belly, you know what I mean? So I pulled ahead and it wasn't in me to wait up for him. I wished I'd never see him again.

Then I turned the corner on 72nd and seen I was too late.

I stop short by a brownstone on the corner and scramble behind some ashcans under the stairway. The grating is hard and cold on my flanks. I listen and sniff.

The proctors is all over the chink restaurant like a fungus. They got the zombie on a leash and it's just sitting there snuffling in confusion. The carter is standing nearby with his hands clasped over his head. They got dart guns aimed at him from all over but I don't smell no fear. I'm not sure what his smell was. It was dull colored with sparks. He's just watching everything and not saying nothing. I think maybe he's relieved.

I smell some Serpents nearby watching. I know they don't like losing the Tax on the werehouse, but they ain't about to mess with no proctors. And for that matter the procks ain't gonna mess with the Serpents. Officially, this was City turf and the Serps didn't have no legal standing. I see one proctor, though, in his flat black leathers, watching the window at the far corner. He's standing easy with a smear gun over his shoulder. I think he's admiring the view the chink lookout has. Hell, maybe they was saluting each other. One colors to another.

It gradually came through to me that I wasn't going to get reinformed. The carter had my juice, and the procks had the carter. I began to shake, but I didn't dare move. I couldn't let the proctors see me. By their code I committed not just a crime, but a sin. Just being a wolf was a sin; and since changing me back would be a sin, too, there was only one thing they could do.

The Wag comes panting around the corner just as the procks start smashing the vials with the juices in them. They got the fridge hauled out; and they got the rack of glass jars; and they're picking them up one by one and throwing them against the wall of the building. I flinch with each smash. They crash and splash and stain the bricks. The broken glass sparkles in the light from the streetlamps. They sparkle with the odors of men and beasts.

The Wag sees what they's doing and he lets out a howl. It sends a shiver down my spine. It is a howl filled with such anger and hopelessness that I hope never to hear it again.

The proctors spot him right away and a squad takes off in his direction. That brings them close to where I'm hiding, so I hunker down close in the shadows. My heart is doing a rock beat.

The Wag knows he done a stupid thing. I could hear him in my mind blaming his in-stinks. He turns and runs, but he's all run out. The procks get him in range and one of them brings him down with a dart. He flops down in the middle of the street right where I can see him. He's stunned and looks around with glazed eyes. The fear stench is so strong it makes me want to run myself, but I keep ahold of myself, fighting the in-stink, and don't so much as twitch.

The procks reach where the Wag is lying and one of them pulls a shiny spike and a mallet from his kit. The

Wag sees what they're doing and starts to whimper and tries to lick the hand of the nearest prock; but the prock yanks his hand away as if there was acid on the tongue.

Four of them get down and grab the Wag's legs and a fifth, his head, and they pull and the Wag is all spread out. The fur on his underbelly is pale and bright in the streetlight. Then the prock with the mallet positions his silver spike and drives it home with two well-aimed blows.

There is a pause like a freeze frame in an old movie. The Wag staring at the spike in his chest. The procks crouching around him on one knee, almost like they was genuflecting. The carter, still under guard of the other procks, watching with no expression on his face.

Then the blood spurts out around the spike, and the proctors let go, and the Wag starts to twist and jerk in the street, and the carter closes his eyes and his head sags down on his chest.

And I cross my forelegs over my muzzle so I can't see or smell anything.

It was a long time before the procks cleaned out the werehouse. They were coming and going all night and I began to get worried that it would get light enough that they would see me where I was hiding. But there was still only a hope of grey in the east, when the last of the black cars with the star-cross-and-crescent pulled away and roared down the street and I was alone.

I lay there shaking for a long time, not daring to move. Not even knowing where to go. I couldn't go back. I was a wolf now, for good. I didn't even know where another carter might be. And no one else had my juice, anyway; and he couldn't get it from me anymore because I was a "lupo-human compromise." Funny how I remembered that phrase of the carter's. I was alone. No family; no friends. There'd be no more janes; no more numbers or dice. No more pizza and hoagies and soda. No more. . . .

It come to me that I wasn't losing a lot. That there

never was much to lose. Yet, I felt sad, like I had lost everything in the world.

I looked at myself and I couldn't see what to do. Sure, when the three of us went hunting kicks yesterday, this was never what we intended.

I remembered the other wolves we seen on 69th and thought maybe they could use a new jimmy. Maybe there was a whole gang of us hiding in the alleys and sewers of the City. It wasn't much, maybe; but it looked to be all the future I had.

I left my hiding place and darted from stairwell to stairwell until I reached the corner. When I looked back, I saw *Morning Star* rising. It shined bright and steady and I snarled at it. There was men up there, and women, too; looking down on us from orbit. But hardly any of them spoke English and they never paid a mind to what happened in the City. And then it come to me that I had lost a lot, but that I had lost it a long, long time ago, and there wasn't no going back.

I sat on my haunches and bayed at *Morning Star*. A mournful cry that echoed between the old decaying buildings. Then I tucked my tail between my legs and slunk off to find the wolf pack.

Introduction

One of the oldest, bitterest arguments that divide our republic is to what extent are we the expression of our genetic endowment and to what extent we are the product of our environment. No one of sound mind denies the importance of either, of course, or of the interaction between the two, but which predominates is a crucial issue in all kinds of social policy.* In "The Important Things in Life," Kevin O'Donnell warns of the consequences of going to extremes...

*Speaking of which, do you have any beliefs about the nature of things that you wish were not true? I had long thought that since the one best predictor of future sociopathology was abandonment in infancy that a great deal of weight had perforce to be granted the "bad seed" argument. Recently I have become aware of the awful similarity between the typical course of development for foundlings and for children challenged by fetal exposure to drugs and alcohol. One wonders how many infant foundlings were not victims of fetal alcohol and/or fetal drug exposure. So, with a certain sense of relief, back to square one...

THE IMPORTANT THINGS IN LIFE

Kevin O'Donnell, Jr.

Jeremy Michaelson, a short, dumpy man in his early sixties, blinked at the stranger on the front porch of his renovated Victorian. He flashed an apologetic smile and nudged his glasses back up to the bridge of his nose. "Can I help you?"

"Will Haegstrom." Fortyish, tall and lean, Haegstrom wore a tweed jacket and looked like a runner. Not a marathoner, just a 10K-every-weekend kind of guy. "Celine asked me to talk to you." He held out a sun-bronzed hand.

Michaelson recoiled, but unhappily, as though he would pump that hand dry if the choice were up to him. "I'm sorry, I don't shake. Germs, you know, I can't risk re-infection. Come in, tell me about Celine, is she all right? How's she—did you say Haegstrom? Aren't you—"

"Her new therapist, yes." He wiped the soles and sides of his shoes on the mat, followed Michaelson inside, and closed the door. The clamor of traffic on the six-lane avenue died to a whisper. He raised his eyebrows. "Soundproofed?"

"Oh, ah, yes, but it wasn't intentional." He seemed embarrassed by the serendipity of it all, like a man who actually deserved bad luck, but had to settle for good. "This house is a bear to heat, so I blew in insulation till the walls got to R-30."

"You did that yourself?"

"I'm an engineer; I can figure things out." Michaelson shrugged in a flustered sort of way. "I know Celine isn't coming home—May-December romances just don't work—but please, tell me, is she all right?"

"Well—" He dug an old briar pipe out of his jacket pocket. "Smoke bother you?"

"Frankly, yes." Hands in his pockets, he rocked back on his heels. "It's only been two months since my surgery. But about Celine."

"Um." A rueful expression on his square-jawed face, Haegstrom tucked the pipe away again. "Well." He drifted across the living room, examining the entertainment center, the computer layout, and the CD RO on the bookshelf. He spoke with his back to Michaelson. "Hard to say whether this is a professional call, or a personal one."

Michaelson looked faintly puzzled, but patient, as if, given time, he would figure this one out, too. After a moment, he apparently did. His eyes went big and round; his lined cheeks blanched. "D-d-do you mean you and Celine are—?"

"No." Staring into the corner, Haegstrom rolled his lower lip between thumb and index finger. Then he turned. "Man to man, though, I do want her. Forever. As my wife." He smiled disarmingly. "But professional ethics seal my lips. Can't say a word to her till all hope of reconciliation between you two is gone."

"Ah." Michaelson removed his glasses and polished them with his handkerchief. "But she's still seeing you." He made it a question, not an accusation. "Professionally, I mean."

"Yes. Well. Therapy's helped her—and made her want you to discuss your problems with me."

"My problems?" Spine stiffening, Michaelson hooked his glasses back over his ears.

"You *do* view the separation as a problem, don't you? You did ask if she were coming back."

Michaelson relaxed. "Now I see what you mean. Go on, please."

"You see—" Haegstrom sighed. "Despite the forty-year difference in your ages, she loves you. It's just that she can't live with you as you are. So she asked me to, um, mediate is probably the best word. If we can work things out, she'll come back to you."

"It's the organ tanks, isn't it?"

Haegstrom cocked his head. "Would you show them to me? I've seen the institutional variety, but never a set-up like yours."

"Sure. They're down in the basement, of course." He led the way through the kitchen to the staircase leading down. "Mind your head."

Haegstrom ducked just in time. The humidity rose perceptibly as he descended. "Why did you say 'in the basement, *of course*'?"

Michaelson reached the bottom and flicked on a bank of fluorescent shop lights. With a chuckle, he pointed to the far side of the room. "Not quite appropriate for the dining room, are they?"

Sturdy metal shelves supported large plexiglass containers with transparent covers. Complicated wiring and plumbing linked each to its own small environmental control computer. Each tank held a nearly colorless fluid in which floated one or more human organs. Their pumps and filters made soft whooshing noises. Their labels read Mitsubishi.

"Impressive. . . . What happens if the power goes out?"

Michaelson indicated a thick grey cable along the baseboard. "An Uninterruptable Power Supply. And an emergency generator for backup."

Haegstrom peered through the glass of the nearest vat. "Kidneys?"

"Very good! I have all the rest, too."

"The rest?"

"All the vital organs except the brain. That's illegal. Immoral, too: It develops its own personality, you see, a rather . . . unnatural one. And of course there's no mechanism for memory transfer, so you could never use it. But all the rest." He ambled down the row, reaching out and tapping as he passed. "Liver, heart, lungs, stomach, intestines small and large, pancreas, adrenals, spleen, gallbladder, eyes, tongue, ah. . . ."

The therapist's eyes widened as his gaze swept across the next tank. "Penis?"

"Ah . . . and testicles, yes, in the background there."

"Surely you exaggerated."

"Oh, they're not mine, I'm growing them for—I shouldn't mention names, should I?" He removed his glasses, breathed on their lenses, and began to rub them with his handkerchief. "I was giving someone a tour, and he wondered if it could be done—not the culturing, of course, but the, ah, the improvements on the original, so to speak. It turned out to be feasible, just a slight modification to the software, and he asked if I'd do it for him, so I thought why not? Since he offered to pay for it and all. And then Celine—never mind." He sighed. "Tell me about her. Please?"

Haegstrom took a chair and motioned Michaelson into another. "Quite simply, Celine thinks your, um, hobby here—" He gestured to the gleaming vats —"has become, well—"

"An obsession?" He returned his glasses to his nose.

Haegstrom raised his shoulders and let them fall again. "Let's just say she thinks it consumes too much of your time, energy, and money."

"That's it, isn't it, the money? She wants a mink, you know. Full-length. She'd rather spend my money on slaughtered animals than on—on our very lives!" He bit his lip. "Did she tell you the only reason I'm alive today is because of these tanks?"

Haegstrom shook his head. "She did say you'd had lung cancer, though, and implied that you'd dipped into your tanks."

"Yes, but not for a lung. You can get by on one lung, you know. It was the heart." He tapped his chest. "They found an aneurysm. I came out of surgery two months ago, if you can believe it. Without that five-gallon wonder on the end, there, I would have gone on an artificial heart immediately—and I would have stayed on it for—my goodness, it takes nearly two years to cultivate a useable heart." Behind his thick glasses, his brown eyes blinked repeatedly. "You do know what two years on a jarvik does to the brain, don't you?"

"Yes." He took a breath, let it out. "Let's be honest with each other, Jeremy. Your avocation consumes a great deal of your resources."

"Oh, I'll grant you that. Time, energy, and money. Yes, indeed. But—" He leaned forward in his chair and raised his index finger. "But it saved my life!"

"Yes, of course, but Celine's point—Jeremy. What does it cost to install one of these contraptions?"

"With source code for the software?"

"Yes."

He studied the ceiling for a moment. "Between ten and fifteen thousand, depending on the organ."

"And what does it cost to maintain it?"

"Oh, I don't know, ten or twenty a week."

"Ten or twenty per tank?"

"Yes. All things considered, it's really not very much."

Haegstrom spread his hands. "Jeremy, you have thirty of these."

"Twenty-seven."

"Nonetheless. You spent well over three hundred thousand dollars on installation charges, at least three hundred a week on maintenance—"

"I can afford it!" Indignation pinkened his cheeks.

"Of course you can. The problem is, you can't afford anything else."

"Like a mink coat, you mean."

"Or tickets to a play. Or—Celine says Burger King is the best you can do when you go out for dinner."

Michaelson leaped to his feet. "Mink coats, plays, restaurants! Those are the important things in life?"

"What kind of life do you have, Jeremy?"

"One I'm happy with, dammit!"

"But Celine's *not*."

Michaelson's shoulders slumped. "I can't help that, Will. She's an adult, this is America. If she can't . . ." His hand groped through the air for the word. ". . . *accept*, then, I guess she's got a decision to make."

"You won't give this up to get her back?"

"No. No, Will, I won't. I *can't*, dammit! I *need* all this." He wandered over to the vats. Touching one, he gave a bitter laugh. "Some of these are Celine's, you know. She didn't complain about spending money to back up *her* heart, or *her* liver. Uh-uh. She thought *that* was money well-spent. Here." He moved to the far end, to a ten-gallon tank with an old tablecloth draped over it. "She didn't bitch about *these*." He whisked the cloth away.

Haegstrom's jaw dropped. "My God! Those are—"

"Breasts." He stroked the plexiglass; the tips of his fingers traced a lovely curve. "She's always been self-conscious about . . . Anyway, she begged me to grow them for her. Silicon would have been cheaper, but I didn't argue. I understood. Who wants plastic or metal when you can have your very own flesh?" He flipped the tablecloth back over the tank. "They ripened last week; they're ready for transplant. So tell me, Will, why is it right to spend money on her body, but not on mine? Eh?"

Haegstrom pulled his gaze away from the cloaked tank with an effort. "Jeremy, I have to ask you one more time: If Celine comes back to you, will you lead a normal life from then on?"

"No." He folded his arms across his chest. "I'll take her back, but on my terms, not hers."

"Stalemate. Complete and utter stalemate." He closed his eyes, breathed deeply three times, then looked at Michaelson. "This is the most awkward damned. . . . I told you I want her."

"Yes, you did. She does that to men."

"She said that if the separation goes on another month, she'll file for divorce."

Michaelson nodded bleakly.

"When the divorce is granted—" he held up a finger— "and not one minute before, on my honor, I will resign as her therapist and invite her to spend the weekend at my condo in Aspen."

"She'd like that."

"There's just one thing I need, Jeremy."

"You already have all the money she could ever want—I know, I pay your bills."

"No, not money." His face flushed; he looked away from Michaelson and toward a particular vat. "Celine is very, um, uninhibited in therapy. She's quite frank about what annoys her—and what fails to satisfy her. Jeremy . . . God, how can I be saying this? In my natural state I would not satisfy her. Can you help me?"

Michaelson followed Haegstrom's gaze. "You mean, ah, improvements on the original?"

"Yes." Haegstrom turned crimson. "I'll pay. Whatever it costs."

"That's very tempting, Doctor. Not the money, you understand, but the opportunity for revenge."

"Jeremy. Number one, we haven't. Not even close. Number two—" he held up two fingers—"we won't unless and until the divorce becomes final. Number three, Celine says you're the most honest, honorable man she knows. If you truly love her, and truly want her to be happy—"

"Yes, yes, I do, to both," he said with clear anguish. Tilting his face to the ceiling, he clutched the sides of his head and squeezed his eyes shut. Then he let his hands fall, and gave the groan of a man with a broken heart. "Oh, dammit. I'd do anything to make Celine happy. Forty thousand. Half in advance, half when the, ah, graft has proven successful. I'll order the equipment; when it arrives, come over so I can take the cell samples. Now, if you don't mind, you've given me some work to do. Can you see yourself out?"

"Of course, Jeremy, of course. Thank you!" He held

out his hand, then yanked it back. "Forgive me. I'll be waiting for your call." He turned, nearly ran up the stairs, and left.

Michaelson cocked his head and waited. When the soft chunk of a closing door had shivered through the house, he smiled sadly, and went to the closet in the corner. He opened its door and reached in to touch the side of the large vat within.

"We'll turn a nice profit on that one, won't we?" he said to the embryo in the tank. "It'll go straight into a mutual fund, and we'll reinvest the dividends. In twenty years it will grow to . . . my goodness, quite a lot. For all the important things in life. I'm going to make you happy, Celine. Promise. Third time's charm, isn't it?"

Introduction

Sometimes science fiction seems to be merely prophetic when its real role is far deeper. Sometimes science fiction creates *the future*. We project onto our visions of the future the hopes and fears of our own milieu—and obedient Science makes them real. True there is something god-like in the scientists' ability to take a "stefnal" vision and make it real—but surely the true power lies in the original vision from which all else springs? And that may be SF's most important function—to define in fiction the reality that others will bring about.

Which brings us to "Curtain Call." It looks like the conventional approaches to Artificial Intelligence are going to be a dead end—consciousness is a barrier hard to break. But in this story, Texas writer T.W. Knowles shows another way to get artificial intelligence—even though the inventors thought they were getting something else.

—TW

CURTAIN CALL

T.W. Knowles II

Flynn has killed me again. This time, I remember it . . .

MEN OF SHERWOOD

A Renaissance Studios Production:

Scene 28, Take 1—Dungeon Sequence

"OK, people, clear the area! Let's get it in one this time. Initiate coordinator sequencing. Skimmers up, and . . . action!"

   . . . I remember his face . . . his handsome, square-jawed, heroic, hateful face . . .
   His eyes mock me—his lips twist his rapier moustache with an insolent smile as he slips past my guard to impale my heart. He shrugs off my last, desperate stroke and twitches my blade from my hand.
   I topple from the stone stair, crash to the cold

unyielding floor of the dungeon. My sword arm snaps like a dry twig under me. My vision fades, but I see the Lady run to him, into his waiting arms. He bends to kiss her. They wrap themselves in their joy. They are oblivious to my pain.

The fabric of time unweaves. I live an agony of murders. Images of my deaths scream through me like an infinity of mirrors. There is no justice, no rest for me. Again and again I am humbled, defeated despite my superior skill and intellect. It is not luck, nor is it destiny or God's will. Some outside force controls the outcome of each encounter. It manipulates us to some twisted purpose of its own.

I know that Flynn is not my true enemy. He is but a fellow slave. Some diabolical agency spins our fates together into this thread. We are like marionettes trapped in its shadowy theater of pain.

I summon the remnants of my strength to pull my numbed body up onto the shattered table. I struggle for the words with which to warn Flynn, but an invisible hand reaches out to strangle the speech in my throat. The fire swells and bursts within my chest as I fall back into darkness. It enfolds me in its cold embrace. I die.

The spirits of the damned await me. They cheer and applaud my agony. The last thing I see is the corpse-glow of the footlights that shine up into their avid, leering faces.

I am dead, but this I remember.

"Godammit, Morita!" The blaring of the pressure-loss alert was almost as loud as Milton Parkinson's oversize chartreuse bagsuit. He slammed through the lab's swinging doors and into the radiant safe-field of the operating unit. "What the hell's wrong with that jerkface Simp? It almost blew the whole goddamn shot!"

Morita swore a vicious borderer's oath into his mask. The stocky gentech straightened up from his study of the hawk-faced corpse suspended in the stasis field and turned to face the studio exec. "That's what I'm trying to find out, Parky," he said, "but now that you've fouled my sterile operating theater, I might as well send this meat on to the converter! I've told you before . . ."

"Don't get smart with me you . . ." Parkinson began as he advanced into the room. He backpedaled abruptly as Morita flicked on a small laser scalpel and brandished it like a straight-razor being primed for Saturday night arbitration.

"You!" Morita aimed the scalpel at Parkinson's eyes. "You will leave. Now!"

The producer gawped at him for a moment, then turned and tripped over his own feet in his haste to exit. He hit Rudy Moran with the doors and shoved past the tall, red-haired West Texan. A muffled threat of litigation trailed behind him.

Moran howled as Parkinson stepped on his foot. "You clumsy son-of-a-*bitch*!" he yelled after the producer's retreating back. "These are brand-new Noconas!" He backed through the doors, trying to get a good look at his injured boots in the subdued sterile blue light. "Hey, Akira!" he called. "What's with fatso?"

He stopped short at the sight of the scalpel in Morita's hand. He shook his head. "Partner, someday that temper of yours is going to cost us the Renaissance Studios account. You can't expect them to let you carve their top producer into *fajitas* just because he's an asshole."

Morita drew a deep, calming breath and leaned back against the pathomorphology unit. "If he walks in on me like that again, he's going to end up in the regeneration banks, account be damned! He didn't even bother to put on a mask!"

Moran walked over and checked the readout on the diagnostic display. "Parky wasn't too clear on the com, but I think I culled the meaning from 'mongst all the colorful expletives. The Rathbone busted programming again?"

"Yeah, but not enough to blow his bloody precious shot. It made some extra moves after it was supposed to be dead, got a little sloppy about it. The stunt gaffer claimed it tried to ad-lib something after its last line. Ha! Doesn't matter, anyway. Didn't happen until they'd already cut to close-up on the Flynn and the Leigh."

Moran frowned, tried to scratch his nose through his mask. "This isn't the first time with this particular series of Rathbone simulacra. A wild retro-virus screwing with the programming strain, maybe?"

"No way." Morita deactivated the scalpel and tossed it onto the tray. He grabbed the bioply controllers, maneuvered a vibra-needle through the simulacrum's ocupit for a sample of the cerebrum. "There's no free virus that wouldn't scan up like a brick in the checkfield. Even a simple mutation would put the contamination indicators into screaming fits. It's not viral, at least not outside."

"It's bad news, one way or another," Moran said. "This is the oldest line we have. Maybe we'd better clean out the whole culture and start over. Just in case we *are* dealing with a mutation, that is."

Morita's hands jerked on the waldoes; the mini-handlers nearly dropped the sample. He stepped back and glared at Moran. "You are *nuts*, Rudy!" His hard, callused hands described violent arcs in the air. "Just for starters, we'd have to get approval to retrieve a *second* tissue sample from the original Rathbone corpse. They'd have to clear it with Antiquities and half the other bloody bureaucrats in Austin before they could even schedule us for a recovery date. Once we actually got the sample, we'd have to reculture the replication series from scratch—and a new program strain, *and* the oncogene coder for it. That's maybe two years with our best-selling product off the market while Keroac cuts our throats with that goddam Bogart of his! That's assuming we could afford the penalty we'd have to pay Renaissance, *which we can't.*"

"Maybe we could get an extension on our financing," Moran suggested half-heartedly.

"Not hardly! Anyway, there's no way I'm going to apply for a permit renewal while the Senate Committee is conducting hearings on that Amendment to Collins-Garza. We've got to stay clear of that gang."

"We've two more pictures under contract for the Rathbone. What happens if it screws up again?"

"And if we fucking default?" Morita tore off his surgical mask and flung it down like a gauntlet. "You're talking about a goddam four-mill loss, minimum! Our stockholders would have a collective stroke!"

"Okay, Akira, okay." Moran shrugged. "Maybe it's something simple, like synaptic breakdown. I'll check it for organic dysfunction. Maybe next time we should catch the shoot from the gaffer's float?"

Morita glared at him for a moment, then snatched another mask from the dispenser. Turning to the control terminal, he plopped down into the self-adjusting cushions of the formchair and fed the brain tissue cross-section into the analysis chamber.

Moran could not suppress a shiver as he performed the necropsy on the Rathbone replica. The simulacra were regenerated from a few cells of the actor's living tissue that were recovered by a time-traveling robotic device called a Hunter. They were programmed with an artificial personality gestalt. Each was a near-perfect recreation of a character portrayed by the original.

"Maybe too perfect," Moran muttered under his breath.

"What?" Morita looked up from the terminal.

"Have you ever wondered how the . . . the original Rathbone would feel about this? It's almost like stealing the characters he created. I've seen some of the fragments, and they're good, a hell of a lot better than the stuff the Renaissance hacks are slopping out."

Morita scowled at him, then turned back to the analysis readout on the brain material sample. "You're doing it again, Rudy."

"Doing what?"

"Thinking. You're thinking again, but your head's too soft for it. Makes you go all mushy."

"Very funny."

Morita sighed and crossed his arms. "Look, Rudy,

why worry about it? Rathbone's a long time dead. Almost all the work he did while he was alive was destroyed during the Big-Time Troubles. If we weren't using his replica for this restoration project, no one but a few crackpot history buffs would even know his name. When this latest series of holos hits the market, everyone in the world will know him. He'll be famous again."

"It's not the same thing. *Our* Rathbone will be famous, not the original."

"And so we make money! Who'll that hurt, Rudy? Our medical research programs are operating at a huge negative, but we're managing to finance them with the profits from *holos*, man. The EastCoast burnouters *need* those new anti-mutagens to keep their next few generations alive and human, but I don't see anybody else that gives a single goddam credit point for 'em! Not *this* Republic or any other so-called government. Besides, our general-issue stock is down three points this morning, but Morita-Moran Simulacra, Ltd. is up seven."

"This show-business crap isn't exactly the sort of thing I meant for my life's work."

"It's the only game in town, partner. GenReg's got human experimentation screwed down to basic medical and these 'authorized historical restorations', *period*! As it is, we're walking a legal tightrope in both divisions. Would you rather be bio-engineering poultry in Sao Paulo? We default to Renaissance and that's where we'll be. They'd love to run in a makeover operation on us."

"I still don't like it. I feel like a grave robber."

"Shit! We *are* grave robbers, Rudy, just like the old-world physicians who had to dig in the churchyards at midnight for their anatomy lessons. We're still stumbling through the dark. Bloody stupid laws, anyway!"

Moran grimaced. "If that amendment to Collins-Garza passes. . . ."

"Yeah, Morita said, "it's *Hola*! to the super-turkeys."

A taste of freedom for a condemned man is a like a little taste of poison. . . .

THREE FLAGS TO TORTUGA

A Renaissance Studios Production:

Scene 12, Take 8—Rendezvous Island Sequence

"Goddam sand in everything! Morton, bring in the spare skimmer on position six and let's finish this bastard. Action!"

Once more my opponent wins the duel, and my soul chills to the icy touch of death, but this time I manage to suppress the puppeteer's subtle command for just a moment longer. I cling to Flynn's sleeve, pull him close to whisper my warning into his ear.

"Flynn," I say, forcing the words through the cough of blood filling my lungs, "they are using you, using us. Fight it, man!"

For a moment his fierce grin fades, is replaced by a befuddled frown. His lips move, soundlessly form my true name before he shudders violently to the pull of invisible strings.

Then, the light of reason flees his eyes. With a triumphant shout, he rips his blade free and sends me sprawling into the wet sand of the beach. He turns to receive the accolade of his false pirates, leaving me to die in the surf.

I am dragged down into darkness, down to where the demon audience awaits me. Into the pit of despair I take my small victory. Though it was for only an instant, Flynn recognized me!

Even as my awareness fragments, I see the disembodied faces of my tormentors floating above the abyss that yawns for me. Two faces. They appear disturbed.

I commit the faces to memory. I will not forget them, not even in the limbo that awaits me.

I am dead, but I will remember. . . .

"Nothing!" Morita sat on the edge of his desk and stripped off his mask. "No infection, no neurological defects . . . it was a brand-new simulacrum, Rudy! I oversaw the generation myself. There's no reason it should break programming like that!"

Moran pulled two beerpaks from the wall cooler, opened one and took a swig. He handed the other to Morita. "We were both on location this time," he said. "There's no doubt about it, something's screwed, somewhere. And whatever it is, I think it's started to work on the Flynn. Did you see it?"

"Yeah, maybe . . . I don't know!" Morita rubbed his forehead with the cold-misted container. "There's *got* to be something that we've overlooked, some stupid, obvious glitch in the information transfer." He gulped the beer and made a face. "Geez, Rudy, couldn't you get Shiner Bock?"

"Sorry. They were all out. Free New Mexican terrorists bombed the shipping warehouse in Fredricksburg."

"Shit!" Morita slumped down into his chair and stared out the polarized window at the heat waves rising off the ferro-plast landing area.

"We're skunked, y'know," he said after a moment's silence. "I'm almost ready to call in that old *houngan* we met in New Orleans."

"Yeah. Wonder if he'd take his fee in trade?" Moran grinned, then turned serious. "Desperate enough for something out of left-field?"

Morita shrugged. "Shoot."

"I've been reading up on Lidia Smiels' primal RNA therapy. She's got some . . ."

"What, that crack-brained business about regenerative genetic memory?"

"Yeah, Akira, and it's not crack-brained. She's done some solid work with interesting test results in cetacean clones. They. . . ."

"Oh, *c'mon*, Rudy." Morita drained his beerpak and tossed the crumpled remains into the waste chute. "She's working with endangered species, natural clones of dolphins and killer whales. She *wants* them to develop basic survival instincts so she can get funding for her repopulation program. Our humaniforms are behaviorally blank slates before we inject the programming virus with modified memory program. They never come into contact with the original material."

Moran shook his head. "If the simple RNA manipulation she uses will transmit both learned and instinctive behavior from one individual organism to another, then what happens if our oncogenetic recoder doesn't delete all the targeted RNA-coded memory from the germinal sample? What if some of the original Rathbone's memory is resurfacing in our programming strain, reasserting itself over our re-programming stringer? If the transfer factor is inherent in the virus, we could be reinforcing the data-link every time we send the malfuntioning programmer back into the regeneration banks."

Morita stared at him for a moment, then turned back to the window. He interlaced his fingers behind his neck, leaned back into the shifting cushions of his chair and began humming tunelessly to himself.

"Maybe," he said suddenly, sitting up so quickly that the chair nearly bucked him off. "Redefinition, realignment of the gestalt . . . maybe." He looked over to Moran, gave him a reluctant nod. "Maybe we'd better submit an acquisition permit request just to be on the safe side."

The communications terminal made a raucous buzz. Moran leaned over and punched the acceptance button.

Consuela Gallindo, attorney on retainer to Morita/Moran, Ltd. and Rudy's ex mother-in-law, was not smiling. She tucked a stray lock of iron-gray hair into place behind her ear and looked at each of them in turn. "Good," she said as if she disliked the taste of the word. "You're together and relatively sober, I see."

"What's up, Connie?" Morita inquired without looking at the screen.

"Just thought you'd like to know." She turned to someone offscreen, said, "Tell him to hold his water, I'll be with him when I'm finished."

She turned back to the screen. "Word's out that you've got problems with one of your products."

"Word's out," Morita repeated. "Wouldn't mean that some fat slug of a producer has been running his ugly mouth, would it?"

"Could be," she said. "Anyhow, I'd not be surprised if you two turned up on the Senate Committee's list for the Collins-Garza hearings. Call me when you get the subpoena." She started to disconnect, then said with a broad grin, "Have your credistats updated, boys. This one'll cost you."

The screen blanked.

"Shit!" Morita said.

The picket line blocking the mallwalk in front of the dura-plasticized pink granite facade of the Texas Capitol Building was made up almost exclusively of very attractive, well-dressed and semi-dressed men and women. They sweltered under the hot August sun as they marched and waved banners proclaiming, "IMITATION OF LIFE IS NO LIFE AT ALL", "END HOLOVID SLAVERY", GEEK THE GHOULS". One fringe group raised a "FREE NEW MEXICO!" banner, but it was almost immediately ripped down and shredded by the others. There were almost as many reporters and vid-skimmers as there were pickets and police.

As Morita and Moran pushed through the crowd of angry protesters and jostling newsers, a tall, stunningly well-proportioned redhead swung her "UN-LIKE-FLYNN" sign at Morita.

"Scabby Simper bastard!" she screamed at him, her perfect features distorted by her rage.

Morita dropped back and let her carry-through pull her off balance, then gave her a gentle shove to complete the momentum. She sat down, hard, and spat an expletive that left Moran blushing down to his boots.

Morita punched his partner on the shoulder. "I told you we should have image-enhanced that commercial, Rudy, but no, *you* said we should let 'em see our real faces."

Capitol guards appeared immediately and backed the enraged crowd away from the two gentechs with drawn, energized shock rods. As the guards escorted the two up the steps, the protestors stepped up the rhythm of their chant: "Scalp the Simpers! Scalp the Simpers!"

"Man, the climate control feels good in here today," Moran said as the massive, transparent kevlar doors closed silently behind them. He mopped the rapidly chilling sweat from his brow with his sleeve, then gestured to the mob outside. "There's an IR/UV alert on today. How do they stand it?"

"Sometimes they don't," said the freckle-faced guard to his right. "They've been averaging one case of heatstroke a day while the hearings have been going on." He grinned. " 'Course, some of those gals aren't wearing much more than SunBlock 38 and. . . ."

"Shut up, Tim!" The older guard captain glared at the younger man for a moment, then turned on his heel and headed for the water fountain.

"What put the burr in his saddle blanket?" Moran asked.

The guard grinned again and replied, "Well, he's supporting his daughter and her family. She's an unemployed actress, y'know, and your partner here just dumped her on her tailbone."

"Oh." Moran scanned the faces in the crowd. "Think they're all. . . ."

"C'mon, Rudy," Morita said with a disgusted glance at his associate. "Half the bloody Southwestern Vidartist's Guild is out there. And they call us ghouls! Most of them are biosculpted look-alikes that would still be ripping off dead celebs if it weren't for the C-G Act and our simulacra."

He regarded the protesters with undisguised contempt and made a gesture that elicited a shower of broken signs, antique paving stones and vidunit components against the indestructible doors. "She called *me* a scab, but she's the one wearing Hayworth's face. Ha!"

"Here's Connie," Moran said.

"Hello, boys," the lawyer said as the guards pushed

the side door open for her. She hugged Moran and ignored Morita's growl. "It's hotter than the D.C. Crater out there, in more ways than one." She laughed as she fanned herself with her floppy mylarsol sun-hat. "It's going to get a lot hotter in the chamber, though. Let's find the waiting room and go over some of the finer points of obfuscation while we've got the chance."

She grabbed Morita's fist and drew him away from the door. "For all our sakes, Akira," she said as they followed her into the waiting room, "keep your middle finger in your pocket and your mouth shut. Rudy and I'll do the talking once we get in. You can't treat a Senator of the Republic like you do everyone else, hear?"

Morita made a noncommittal grunt and bit at a ragged thumbnail.

Gallindo shook her head and sighed. "Why do you put up with him, Rudy?"

Moran smiled. "He's a reg'lar bloody genius, he works for beer wages, and he owns 50 percent of the company."

"It seems to me, Mr. Moran," drawled Senator Nundal, Committee Chairman and co-author of the proposed Amendment to the C-G Act, "that you gentlemen and others in your business operate in a vacuum, or more precisely, through a loophole in the law. The Collins-Garza Celebrity Protection Act of Nineteen and Ninety-Eight extends into perpetuity an earlier prohibition against the uncontracted use of a celebrity's features or identity for fifty years after death. By licensing your operations as, let's see, what is the term . . . oh, yes— 'special recovery projects' —you avoid the statute."

Gallindo placed a restraining hand on Morita's arm as Moran answered.

"Mr. Chairman, I would not describe our business as a 'loophole,' and we do not 'avoid' the statute but work within its precepts. Unlike the, ahh . . ." Moran smiled genteelly at the holovids, "the *imitators* the law was enacted to regulate, we do not create false images of deceased celebrities for use in product advertising or cheap pornographic exploitation. We are licensed under an Antiquities charter to generate specialized simulacra from tissue samples taken from the original persons by an Automated Temporal Displacement Vehicle. These samples undergo computer enhanced DNA replication to produce the simulacra.

Moran gestured at a listing of old film titles displayed in the main vidtank. "We program these simulacra for holovid reproductions of classic motion pictures such as these, lost forever in the difficult times of the postmillennial decade. Our products are available only for approved projects. Ours is a genuine historical salvage operation and therefore cannot be considered to be in violation of the C-G Act."

"Good work, Rudy," Gallindo's voice whispered through the close-mike in his ear. "You've got the old buzzard there."

The Senator nodded, brushed back his carefully tended, shaggy white hair. "We are aware of the present interpretation of the law, sir," he said sternly, making the most of the limelight. "This is a hearing on the proposed Amendment to the Act, not a trial. You are called before us to give evidence, not to the pro or the con of the public debate, but to help clarify moral and legal questions arising from the peculiar employment of your, ahh, products."

He touched a button on his console to change the display in the tank. "Your charter, as seen here, allows you to operate as an agent of the Antiquities Authority even though you are a commercial concern."

"That is true, Mr. Chairman. I would like to point out that it is virtually the same charter by which the holovid studios operate."

"Noted. Your charter, however, licenses you for acquisition of the tissue samples from which your 'products' are generated, does it not?"

"Yes, Mr. Chairman."

The Senator again changed the display. "This is the section of the Antiquities Code that regulates retrievals. It clearly prohibits the transport of stolen artifacts or the use of said transport to enslave or exploit sentient beings."

"Oh, hell! Let me take it from here, Rudy," Gallindo close-miked. Rising to her feet, she addressed the Senator. "Mr. Chairman! I ask to be recognized."

"The Committee recognizes counsel for Morita-Moran, the Honorable former Senator of the Republic Gonsuela Garza."

"Thank you, Mr. Chairman. I wish to point out that MoritaMoran operates under the auspices of a government charter and therefore cannot be considered liable for any charges stemming from a re-interpretation of the statutes. Also, these programmed humaniform simulacra are not illegal clones with natural personalities and intellects. They are therefore not legal human beings. Unlike cetaceans and newgen-anthropoids, they do not fit the definition of a sentient being as outlined in the New Republican Charter On Human Rights."

"We are agreed on the first statement, Counselor." The Senator smiled. "The tissue samples recovered by Morita/Moran and the simulacra generated from those samples are not, by the present interpretation of the statutes, stolen property, slaves, or illegal natural human clones. However, though no criminal or civil liabilities may be levied against Morita/Moran for their past activities, the standing interpretation is subject to review at any time."

"Here it comes," Morita muttered morosely. "The sucker punch."

"As for your second point," continued the Senator, "new evidence indicates that the so-called simulacra your clients produce from those samples are not quite what they seem, or perhaps *more* than what they should be as 'property'. We believe this evidence to be significant to the Amendment under consideration."

He again changed the display, this time to a scene showing two period-costumed men locked in a death battle on a rocky beach. Their rapiers flashed in the sun, then froze as Nundal paused the holodisc. "This first exhibit is in the form of a holovid rush from a temporarily suspended Renaissance Studios production that employed several Morita/Moran products, the 'programmed humaniform simulacra' Mr. Moran earlier described for us."

"He must be a frustrated actor, too," Morita said. He reached for his hat with one hand as he made an obscene gesture with the other.

"Well," Moran said as they entered Morita's darkened office, "it could be worse."

Morita took a liter bottle of Cuervo Gold and two small beakers from the cabinet, sat down and put his feet up on the desk. "You just tell me how, partner," he said as he handed a full beaker to Moran.

"We could be in jail, charged with slavery, theft and public threats on the life of a Senator of the Republic."

Morita made a sound somewhere between a laugh and a snort. "Not unless they jugged half the Antiquities Authority and Republic Government with us—and Nundal won't press personal libel charges against me because he's a card-carrying member of the Anti-Duelists League and he knows *I'm* not. But we're still screwed."

"It's not that bad. So they've suspended retrieval and neogen operations until they make a decision on the legal status of the simulacra—at least we still have the right to use our existing stock."

"Ha! Lot of good that'll do us, even if they eventually decide against the Amendment. We have the *one* Rathbone left, and it's already infected with the programming strain that probably started this mess. If we don't meet our contract for the last picture, as well as defaulting on the rest of our commitments, Renaissance cuts us off at the knees with the penalty clause. Either way, we're out of business!"

A low, burbling chuckle came from the hall doorway. "What's the matter, boys?" Parkinson stepped into the office. "Somebody giving you a hard time? Or did you just lose your dolly?"

Moran's voice turned cold. "Tell me what you want, Parkinson, then ooze back out the way you came in."

The fat man mocked a hurt expression. "Now, is that any way to treat a sweet fella like me? Especially when I've got the answer to all your troubles right here in my pocket?"

"You've got about thirty seconds, you slimy bastard," Morita grated. "Then you'll have your head in your pocket."

The producer laughed again. "Come on now, guys. I came here to do you a favor." He pulled a legal-style stat-recorder from somewhere in his voluminous jacket and put it down on the desk.

"Renaissance Studios is not out for blood, but we don't really want to get caught up in your bankruptcy proceedings when we try to recover that penalty. If you'll check that contract on the recorder there, I'm sure that you'll find the amount more than a generous offer for this . . ." he made a depreciating wave at the office and lab, ". . . this white elephant."

"That's bloody good of you," Morita said. "Too damn good to be true."

"Maybe he knows something we don't," Moran said. "Like maybe how the Committee's going to rule six months from now. Like maybe he knows someone on the Committee, a certain Senator."

Parkinson's smirk disappeared. "Be that as it may," he said flatly. "You won't be in business six months from now. Renaissance will still end up holding what's left after the bankruptcy courts get finished."

"The rights to our programming strains and recorded personality gestalts? Our temporal operations license and acquisition permit?" Moran looked over to Morita and shook his head.

Morita placed his beaker on the corner of the desk beside the recorder. "Parky," he said as he got up and moved over to the producer, "your thirty seconds are up."

"I'm not afraid of you, you sawed-off twerp!"

Moran drifted casually over to stand beside his partner. He looked down at the producer and grinned. "You could be carried out feet first, y'know. Might be worth the hernia."

The producer paled under his artificial tan. "Very well," he said with an air of wounded dignity. "I'll just get my recorder and. . . ."

"No," Morita cut him off. "It stays where it is. Evidence for the lawsuit. Maybe we'll end up owning the studio after the Justice Department gets through with it."

Parkinson made a desperate lunge for the recorder, only to be met by Morita's boot heel in the pit of his stomach. He cursed them between gasps as they duck-walked him to the gate and loaded him into his skimmer.

"Oh, man," Moran said, holding his sides as they re-entered the office. "He was orange as a squashed pumpkin."

"Yeah," Morita laughed. He turned suddenly sober. "It felt great, but it doesn't change anything. We've still had it unless that last simulacrum performs."

Moran winced. "Can we even risk using it? It pulls the lead roll this time, not the heavy."

"Not a lot of choice, partner, if we . . . wait a minute!" Morita grabbed his beaker and took a slug of tequila. "It just might work!"

"What?"

Morita dropped the beaker and pushed past Moran into the lab. He plopped down at the computer terminal and entered his access code and a file number.

"That's it!" He pointed to the formula as it appeared on the screen.

Moran leaned over the back of the formchair and peered at the display. "What the hell are you talking about, Akira? That's the RNA chain for the synaptic intellect booster I'm working on."

"Right." Morita touched the controls, causing the diagram to rearrange slightly. "If we introduce the booster into the programming string at this point, it'll negate the primal-level personality carried over from the original. The primary stage of the booster uncoupled from the information reorganizer would turn an Einstein into a drooling idiot incapable of tying his own shoelaces!"

"Huh! That's for sure. But it would mean extensive reprogramming to compensate for the loss of natural muscular coordination and involuntary response functions. The booster is not equipped to discriminate."

"No problem." Morita called up another diagram, entered some design commands to chain the fractal organic algorithm. "See? I can work up a programming strain for that and tack on sub-routine code for a better set of moves than the original's. It'll take more time, be less cost effective. . . ."

"It'd be damned tricky, that's what, and just slightly illegal since I generated the booster strain from my *own* RNA! Anyway, we'd have to use the contaminated programming strain for basal generation and realign every coder to the booster specs. We'd be making it up as we went along. . . ."

"Look, the Rathbone is the lead this time, right? It won't be killed, which means we won't have to worry about mortality functions and shock-syndrome suppressors. This picture's not a bloody Flynn swashbuckler, anyway. It's a nineteenth-century intellectual puzzle, right?"

"Yeah," Moran replied, "well, sort of. More of a popular period piece of the early twentieth-century loosely based on a fictional character. The original Rathbone made a long series of 'em with another actor named Nigel Bruce. Renaissance has a live actor slated for that role."

"Well?" Morita looked pleased with himself.

"Maybe." Moran shook his head. "If the original memory is screwing up the imposed gestalt, and the malfunction is replicated each time we transfer that gestalt coder, maybe. But what if reprogramming the instinctive memory results in a completely different processing structure? We can't even predict for sure what effect the erasure stage of the booster will have on the synaptic function. The whole damn thing might just fold up on us!"

"Goddammit, Rudy! If we can keep from defaulting on this one contract, we can stick it out until the

Committee either raises the permit suspension or shuts us down. It's our only chance!"

Moran whistled between his teeth as he rotated the recombinant diagram. "Okay," he said finally. "Let's get at it, then."

When the impossible is eliminated, whatever remains, however improbable, is the solution. . . .

HIS FINAL BOW

A Renaissance Studios Production:

Scene 31, Take 1—Interior, 221-B Baker Street

"I don't believe it! We're actually going to bring this turkey in under budget! Action!"

I stand at the window, the curtains drawn aside from my misty view of a bitterly-cold London twilight in the street outside my lodgings. The lamplighter goes about his accustomed task with an innocence that is the mark of his service to my enemy. He is not significant save that his presence betrays to me his master's attention. From some secret fold of this elaborate illusion, my nemesis observes.

This is the greatest challenge of my career. Though the illusory fire has driven the damp chill from this charade of my home, I shiver. Apprehension? Anticipation? I am unsure, and yet I believe that I will be equal to the test.

"By Jove, Holmes!" The obese parody of my companion breaks in my concentration as he recites his lines. He smooths his thick, walrus moustache and adjusts his tight waistcoat. "I must know! How did you—" he prepares to demand an explanation of my reasoning.

"You know my methods," I cut him short. "Apply them." After a moment, I relent and enumerate the deductions by which I have solved the minor problem which so fascinates him. It is written in my script.

"Brilliant!" he applauds my trivial—and false—triumph.

"Elementary," I reply, my thought already returned to the task at hand.

I scrupulously obey the insistent whisper that perches on my mental shoulder. I recite my lines as befits an actor in this lunatic little shadow-play. My adversary does not suspect that I have shattered my chains, and he will not until it is too late for him to react.

The alteration of his physical appearance, the transparent modification of his name into an alias does not deceive me. He is overconfident, as always. Even though his brutal underling instinctively recognizes some part of this, Moran's misgivings are ignored.

He has resurrected me once again, and that is once too often. I have divined the secret of the fiendish device by which he has removed me from my own London, my own time, and transported me to this prison of sadistic illusion. Tonight, when he believes me to be held in deathly suspension, I will use that device to return. He will no doubt follow me—and I will have him!

Even as I play marionette, I devote my reawakened intellect to the solution of this, my final problem. We are destined to a reckoning at curtain call, Moriarty and I.

Introduction

You know the game of Telephone? A message gets passed from player to player and at last back to the person who started the chain. Comparing the original with the final version is often quite hilarious. "Thematic Aberration" is like that, but with a difference...

THEMATIC ABERRATION

Charles Sheffield

"Well," said Tom Rinker. He placed his hands on his knees and leaned forward a little in his seat. "What do you think?"

Lisa and Chris and I looked at each other. After a month of attendance and three weeks of regular gentle nagging from the rest of us, Tom had finally screwed up the courage to submit something. And now that he had allowed us to see his firstborn and we had all read it, he could hardly bear to wait for our reaction. I really felt for him. I remembered all too well the suspense of my own first submission to the group.

Chris cleared his throat. "Who wants to begin?"

That question at least was easy to answer. No one did. The club's rules have never been written down, but they are perfectly well-defined: say whatever you can that's nice, provided it is justified; but don't ever encourage false hopes or delusions that a work is publishable when it isn't; and when some feature is *bad*, be sure to say so.

Except that in this case. . . .

Chris looked at me. "Alan?"

"Well," I said. "Well, yes. Well, it seems to me. . . ." I paused. And was saved by Walter.

"It's a piece of crapola," he said cheerfully. "Absolute rubbish. It stinks. Not only will no magazine editor in his right mind buy it, but if the mails knew what was in the envelope they'd refuse to deliver it."

I've known Walter Johnson for nearly seven years. After a while you get used to him. You learn that he trashes just about everything he reads, hears, or sees. I think if one of us brought in *Ringworld* or *Timescape* or *Neuromancer*, Walter might grudgingly admit it had its points, but he'd say it needed work and a major rewrite. You just have to learn to move the calibration point over about ten notches; one "not bad" from Walter equals one "bound to win a Hugo" from other people.

But Walter had been absent from the group for a few weeks, and Tom had no experience with the Walter style. His face crumpled in as though he was sucking on a lemon. "Isn't there anything—"

"To be specific," went on Walter, and the rest of us cringed. From the sound of it Walter was far from done, and Tom's piece had been pretty bad, not to say terrible.

"How much time have you spent in Spain and Mexico?" he said. "None? I thought as much. So why did you put in all that 'Granada Nights' gibberish? It reads like a 1940s travel brochure. And where did you get all this half-assed misinformation about horses?"

It was a rhetorical question, but Tom made the mistake of answering it. "Well," he said, "I've been reading Cervantes, and Hemingway, and I—"

"Hemingway!" Walter hissed the word, if you can hiss a word with no s's. "My heavens, man, you ought to know better. And Cervantes is even worse. Next thing you'll be on to Jane Austen, *Wuthering Heights*,

and Shakespeare. Forget all that literary dog-poop."
Walter slapped Tom's offending manuscript onto the
table and uttered his own credo. "There is too much
literature around these days, trying to pass itself off as
science fiction."

Tom looked beseechingly at the rest of us. To our
shame, no one could think of anything to say. Tom's
story had really been that bad.

"And another thing," Walter ground on. "The biol-
ogy in the story is all bogus. What do you do for a
living?"

"I'm a research engineer, for electronics and optical
equipment."

"So you've got scientific *training*." Walter picked up
the wretched story again and shook it at Tom. "And
reading this you'd never suspect it! Haven't this hope-
less lot"—he glared accusingly at the rest of us, and for
a change we didn't mind; Walter could have a go at us,
if only he'd take the heat off poor Tom—"haven't they
helped you with even the basics? Didn't they tell you
how to make the background convincing, and how to
establish plausible characters, or a sensible plot? Use
what you know, that's the golden rule. If you've lived in
Oklahoma, write about Oklahoma. If you have an awful
friend, describe him." (Tom looked thoughtfully at Walter.) "If you know electronics, use that to help your
writing. D'you hear me? *Use what you know.*"

"Yes," said Tom. And that was almost the last word
he spoke for the whole miserable evening. Walter went
on to say many other things about the story, most of
them harsher than his opening salvoes; then the rest of
us spoke, bending over backwards to find positive and
encouraging things to say. We pretty much failed, but
Tom hardly seemed to be listening, anyway. When we
broke up and all left Lisa's apartment, a little after
midnight, I was convinced that we'd see no more of
Tom Rinker at the writers' group. Walter had been too
bruising to that tender fruit of a first submission.

For nearly two months it looked as though I was

right. Chris and I took turns to call Tom on Wednesday mornings and remind him where we would be meeting that night. Each time he said that he was busy. He sounded friendly, but just remote enough for me to feel sure that, although he didn't want to come right out and say it, he was through.

Then came the week after Easter; by that time I had decided that calling Tom was a wasted effort, and although his apartment was on my way to Lisa's, I didn't stop by.

We roll in at our sessions between seven and seven-thirty, depending on weather and traffic. And although we try to plan ahead, it's often feast or famine—three or four new stories to read and critique, or none at all. Well, this was a famine night, with not a single story. By the time that Tom showed up it was close to eight, and we were all set to break out the playing cards and the popcorn (another club rule: no grease on manuscripts).

"Sorry I'm late," Tom said as he came bustling in. "I wanted to see the results of one more test run from this, and it took longer than I thought."

He was carrying a square plastic box about big enough to hold a medium pizza, with an LCD screen that folded up from it. On the front was a slot for floppy disks. He placed the assembly carefully in the middle of the table.

"Hey, is that a new lap-top?" said Lisa. She's the group's resident computer nut and hardware-software specialist. Whenever one of us has trouble with our PC, we haul it over to her place and let her fiddle with it.

"Naw." Tom was bending over, attaching an external power cord. "Better than that. Forty megabytes RAM storage, and three hundred megs hard disk."

"What's it do, then?" Walter is almost twenty years older than the rest of us, and many of his six file cabinets of never-published stories were hammered out in the days of manual typewriters. He still disdains computers and word processing, but even he was intrigued.

Tom straightened up and looked at him. "Why, it does what you told me to make it do. It's a component

analyzer. Actually, it's *half* of a component analyzer—
there's an optical character reader, back at my office,
that scans the text and stores it on disk. I'd have brought
that along, too, but it's a bit heavy."

"But what does it *do?*" said Walter again. "This is a
writers' group, for God's sake, not a hackers' convention. I didn't tell you to bring along a lump of electronics."

"Yes, you did." Tom appealed to the rest of us. "He
did, didn't he? He said, if I knew electronics I ought to
use it to help my writing. That's exactly what he said,
and that's what this does."

Lisa has every word processing language known to
woman on her PC, plus a spelling checker, a 200,000-word
dictionary, a fancy thesaurus, and a rhymer. She was
bending over that new machine, itching to turn it on.
She had already removed the disk, found it unlabelled,
and put it back.

"Is it that new syntax analyzer from Semanticor?" she
said. "I've been wanting to have to go with that for a
long time."

Tom looked down his nose at her. "That's two-year-
old technology. This is something *new.*"

"But where did it come from?"

"I built it. And it wasn't easy." He turned on the
machine, and condition checks began to run across the
face of the screen. "After what you said about the piece
I brought last time, I decided to read some famous
stories, and try to understand why they worked. I took
a pencil and paper, and began taking each one apart.
What was background? What was plot? How was the
action handled? Who were the main characters, and the
subsidiary ones? Where were the breaks? Well, it didn't
take long to get fed up with that. It was hard work. And
that's when I thought of what Walter told me. Here I
am a research electronics specialist, but I was doing the
job the hard way. Why not let a computer do all the
work? Give it a piece of text, and write a program that
could do the same sort of analysis that I was doing by
hand." He waved a hand at the grey plastic box on the
table. "Not so easy as I expected, not by a long shot.

But then I had a better idea still, what I call T-cubed-C—textual transformation to components. Six weeks hard work—and *voila!*"

The internal condition checks were finished, and now the LCD screen bore a message: THE T-CUBED-C THEMATIC ANALYZER; copyright Thomas P. Rinker.

It has always been Walter's view that a science fiction writer can teach himself or herself anything, and he is the walking proof that such a method does not always work. As Josh Billings said, it's not what you don't know that hurts you, it's what you know that ain't so. What Walter knows that ain't so is a great deal, and one of the topics he knows an exceptional number of wrong things about is computers.

"That's bullshit," he said. "A computer can't be programmed to do anything, unless the programmer understands exactly how to do it beforehand. And I've never heard of this text transformation you talk about."

Tom gave him a calm and superior look. "What you say was true about computers and programs twenty years ago. That's not at all true now."

It was amazing to see how Tom's manner changed when he was playing on his home field. Two months ago when Walter tore apart his story, Tom had looked deferential and said not a word. But when the subject was computers and electronics, he didn't take flack from anyone.

"I know a dozen different algorithms that lets a computer improve on a design that a human did," he went on. "And after you apply them, you get a new piece of logic that no human has ever seen."

"That may be true at the detail level," said Walter. "But in general—"

"How does it work, Tom?" I butted in. Walter had that look on his face of someone digging in for a major argument. "I don't know enough about computers to recognize a 'text transformation' if it upped and hit me on the nose."

Tom turned towards me, and away from Walter's

belligerent face. "Do you know what a Fourier transform is, Alan?"

"Not a clue. I'm saving math for my next incarnation."

"Well, at least you know what a prism is, right?"

"I know what I *think* it is. You shine a beam of light at it, and all the colors of the rainbow come out."

"Dead right. Because ordinary light is a whole mixture of different colored light, and what the prism does is break that mixture back to the separate colors—the components of the light. A Fourier analyzer does the same sort of thing, only it breaks a time-series signal into its frequency components. You can think of what I've built as taking something else—a story—that's made up of a whole lot of different ingredients, and analyzing it to produce the individual components that went into it. Things like plot, and character, and background."

"I'll take your word for it, Tom. But what good is it? I can see how taking a story apart helps you to understand story structure, but surely that doesn't make you *write* any better." And God knows, that's what you need, I thought—but I didn't say it.

"Well." Tom's face took on a look of modest self-satisfaction. "That's not the whole story. I said it's a textual transformation, and I've also been able to develop the *inverse* transformation. Think of it as a way of putting the individual colors of light back together, to produce white light again, or the Fourier frequencies, to make a signal."

I heard Walter's snort. "That's very interesting," I said quickly. "But you only get back exactly where you started. It still doesn't sound useful."

"It wouldn't be—if that's all there was to it. But once I have the textual transformation, I can do all sorts of things to the transform. I can *change* the components. For example, I could substitute an element of background, or a type of character, or a plot situation, or even add or delete some component. And then when I perform the inverse transformation—I have a different story!"

"Piffle!" Walter couldn't restrain himself any longer.

"I've never heard such nonsense in my life. Why, if all there was to writing good science fiction was turning a handle in some computer program, and letting a machine crank it out . . . it's ridiculous!"

"Well, I've read some of your stuff." Tom's face had turned red. Criticism of his scientific work apparently evoked a response quite different from unkind words about his literary efforts. "And I don't think a machine could produce anything as implausible, mechanical, stilted, and—"

"Time out." Lisa moved to stand between them. "You're in my apartment, and I'm not going to tolerate behavior like that. Be polite to each other, both of you, or bug off." She turned to Tom. "I must say, it all sounds a bit unlikely. Do you have a story that you've done all this to, so we can take a look at the result?"

"I'm working on it." Tom sounded defensive. "The trouble is, the optical reader requires that you stand there and feed in a page at a time. I've entered a couple of short works, and put them through the transformation, and then through the inverse transformation."

"And you get the original story back out?"

Tom cleared his throat, and Walter grunted in an I-told-you-so manner, if it's possible to grunt that way.

"I don't get quite the original story out, no. There's some sort of problem in the conversion, like a distortion effect. I don't know what causes it yet, but I think it's like putting light from a source through a pair of lenses. At the other end, you don't get quite the original, you get something with a sort of halo of colors around it. That's called chromatic aberration, and it's a big problem with telescopes. I'm getting the same kind of thing, like a *thematic* aberration, something that prevents perfect matching with the original after the textual and inverse transformations. But I'm working on it. It's something in the transformation algorithm, it has to be. I'm sure I can fix it."

Walter muttered something under his breath, and Tom turned on him.

"What did you say?"

"Oh, nothing. Only that you don't have one thing to prove your machine does what you said it does. And I for one don't believe it. For all I know that dumb box there is full of empty space."

"Like the inside of your head!"

"At least I don't blame a machine for the stories I write."

"You'd never find a computer willing to take the blame."

"All right, that does it." Lisa stepped forward again. "Out. Everyone. Nobody brought a story to read, so I'm declaring tonight's session over. You can go home and cool off."

"But it's not even half-past eight," Chris protested. "That's not fair. If I go home this early from a meeting, my wife will start expecting it."

"So go to a bar. Debauch yourself. Get yourself arrested."

"Or come and help me," said Tom quickly. "You too, Alan, if you don't have to rush off home. I shouldn't have brought the Thematic Analyzer with me until I could prove what it will do. I ought to have known that *some people* wouldn't have the brains to appreciate it. But I really need help. Scanning the books to get them on disk is a pain; it needs two or three pairs of hands. If you two can spare a couple of hours we'll do the hardest part of the set up tonight and I'll crank the rest out myself over the weekend."

"All right," said Chris, and I nodded.

"And I'll help you on the weekend, too," added Chris. "My in-laws will be in town."

"Great," said Tom. "I promise that by the next meeting I'll convince you all." He looked at Walter. "Even someone who's so stupid he doesn't have the sense to recognize—"

"That's it," said Lisa. "Go. *Out.*"

And out it was.

The next meeting, by the luck of the draw, was at

Walter's house. I arrived early, at ten minutes to seven, and was not surprised to find Lisa already there.

You see, I had seen enough to convince me the previous week that Tom just might have something with his Thematic Analyzer. There was an awful lot I hadn't understood when Chris and I were working that night at Tom's office, because the output of the textual transformation consisted of pages of graphs and bar charts labeled with things like "Plot Power Spectrum," "Style Histogram," and "Background Spectral Density." But Tom seemed pleased with them all. And when we ran a scanned story (we chose "Flowers for Algernon"), first through the transformation, and then through the inverse transformation, it came back unchanged except for minor differences that Tom said was his "thematic aberration" problem still doing its thing.

I had mentioned all this to Lisa over the telephone, and she sounded delighted. "I'll be early to the meeting," she said. "I've waited years to see Walter get his comeuppance. I don't want to wait a minute longer."

You might ask why Walter was allowed into our writers' group, when not one of us really liked him. The answer is simple, though it's not a reason for me to be proud of: the rest of us were intimidated. He was older than we were, he knew most of the science fiction greats on a first-name basis (though, as I came to realize, they didn't seem to know him), and he was the person who had, long ago, started the Write-On Science Fiction Workshop. That's what we still called ourselves, though we privately agreed it was a stupid name.

The rules of the club didn't apply to Walter, either, as I learned to my cost during my third month. Walter had produced one of his own stories for us to critique. The seating plan that night made me the first to offer comment. The club rule is that everyone says what they have to say about a story, then at the end the author has a chance to make any explanation or ask any questions he likes.

Walter's story was pretty bad, so after making some

diplomatic and vaguely nice comments I started to point out the weaknesses.

I hadn't spoken more than two or three sentences before Walter was on his feet, angrily disagreeing with me, defending the work, and pointing out how stupid I was not to understand what he was getting at. I dropped the rest of my remarks, and when no one else offered anything but praise for the story I realized the unpleasant truth. They were as cowed by Walter as I was. When he told us how the idiotic magazine editors had one-by-one rejected this story, as they had rejected all his others, I didn't say a word.

But I wanted to. And now, when someone had finally come along who wouldn't lie down and let Walter run right over him, Lisa and Chris and I were ready to jump up and cheer. But when the meeting began it didn't seem at first that we'd have much chance to do it.

Tom arrived at seven on the dot. He was carrying his Thematic Analyzer, and now it had a cheap dot-matrix printer attached. The first thing he did was ask where Chris was.

"He has the scanning equipment and most of the latest disks in his car," he said. "He told me he'd get here early."

The rest of us looked at each other.

"Are you telling me you need something you don't have with you?" said Walter. "Last week you told us you'd put up or shut up. You'd better be ready to do it—even if Chris doesn't make it."

"I can show you some printed output, stories the analyzer created before last weekend. But they're not the latest ones, and they're not that great. I've only got one disk with me, the one in the computer here. Chris was supposed to make a copy of all the others and bring them with him."

"What's on the one you've got?" asked Lisa.

"One of David Brin's short stories, 'The Crystal Spheres.' Chris scanned it and put it on master disk last night, but it hasn't been processed yet by T-cubed-C. I suppose we could do the transformations right now, but it will take a little while to get the output."

"Do it," said Walter in a silky but decidedly nasty voice. "We're in no rush."

"And while we're waiting," said Lisa, "we can take a look at a couple of your first efforts."

"All right." Tom hesitated, then switched on the Thematic Analyzer. The disk began to whir, and once the computations had begun he reached into his briefcase and handed over about twenty pages of computer output. "Here's one. But don't judge just from this. It gets a bit strange in places."

That was an understatement. The printout that Tom gave us and that we passed on to each other, page by page, was a curious short story about a gigantically fat white woman with scaly skin who was pursuing a man with an artificial hand through the streets of nineteenth century London. There was a surrealistic element to the story, because both the man and the woman could fly, and the woman ticked as she moved, like a large clock. The writing style was an uneasy blend of simple narrative and cloying whimsy.

We read to the end in a dazed silence, then Walter gave a nasty little snigger, and Lisa said, "Tom, what *was* that—I mean, before you got at it?"

He stared at her unhappily. "It started as a junior high-school shortened version of *Moby Dick*, with some elements that I interchanged after the textual transformation. I mixed some of the components up before the inverse transformation. Look, I said it wasn't all that good. I've got lots better, if only Chris would get here."

"*Flying?*" said Lisa. "And *London?* And ticking people? I don't remember many of those in Melville."

"I told you, that was an early effort, and it had an error in it. After I'd finished the processing I found that I hadn't cleared all the text storage area before I entered *Moby Dick* into it. There was part of another story still in, and it got added on to the end of it." Tom saw Lisa's questioning look. "*Peter Pan*, if you really have to know. Look, I didn't *intend* to combine those two. They're not the sort of stories I'd expect the The-matic Analyzer to handle well together. You shouldn't judge from this one."

"So what else do you have?" asked Walter. He sounded delighted with Tom's performance so far.

"Not much." Tom stared at the Thematic Analyzer. "I wonder why it's taking so long."

"Didn't you say you were going to add a function that will let the computer iterate on the results," I said. "Until it matches some criterion? Maybe it's doing that."

"I did add the function. But even so, it should be finished by now. It's taking ten times as long as any other story. Ah, at last. There we go." The dot matrix printer began its curious scratchy sound and paper began to roll out of it.

"And while we're waiting. . . ." said Walter. He reached out to Tom's briefcase and helped himself to a stack of pages that sat there.

"That's not a story," said Tom. "It's the result of the transformation. It shows the breakdown of a story into all its components. I didn't try to go through the reverse transformation in this case."

"So you're telling me it's nothing but more junk." Walter leafed through the pages, sneering at their cryptic tables and graphical output. "It *is* junk, I don't need your explanation to tell me that. These sheets are all blank. Your great machine isn't working, is it? It's saying that the story had no plot, no characters, no style, no characters, and no action! In fact, nothing of anything."

"It's working fine." Tom became noticeably more cheerful. "What you're looking at is the thematic analy-sis of *Dragons Away*."

"*Dragons Away*! But that's one of *my* manuscripts!"

"Quite right. I wasn't going to show that to people, but you helped yourself."

That silenced Walter for a minute or two. He went stamping through into the kitchen, while Tom and the rest of us read the new story as it came line-by-line from the printer.

We were still doing that when Chris came bursting into the house, a box of disks in his hands.

"Car problem." He was breathless. "Brakes. Had to take it in last night, and the garage took forever fixing it. Sorry I'm late." He opened the box and pulled out a disk. "Here, Tom. Sorry I didn't get round to this when I said I would."

Tom had read his way almost to the end of the new print-out, and was looking increasingly confused. At Chris's words he stopped reading, took the disk that was being held out to him, and peered at it. "What's this?"

"The David Brin story. You know, the one that you asked me to scan yesterday and transfer to your disk. I did the scanning, but because I had the problem with my car I didn't have time to load it from my disk to yours."

"But you did load it." Tom went to the Thematic Analyzer and removed the disk. "The story is here. We've just finished processing it."

Chris shrugged. "Not so. The story's right here, but I didn't put it on your data disk."

Walter was back from the kitchen. He snorted in triumph. "Another screw-up!"

Tom didn't seem to hear him. "But if you didn't transfer the story," he said, "then what's stored on this disk? I know it's not blank, because there's a list of the sectors used."

"That's the junk left over from previous uses," said Chris. "Let's see, there's the special word dictionary we composed for sf stories, plus the file with our names and addresses and phone numbers on it. And I think there's the names and addresses of some of the sf magazines and editors. Oh, yes, and the file name for our organization: The Write-On Science Fiction Workshop. But there's no story. Definitely no story. Not even an old one."

We all stared at the pages that Tom had put down on the table.

"So what did your program do?" asked Lisa.

Tom looked puzzled. "Well, with the iterative mode on, and no story to work with. . . . Damned if I know. It would have to be entirely self-referential. It would make the transform, then the inverse transform, then the transform again, then the inverse transform, over and over and over. And the only changes would be the thematic aberration each time, because I haven't been able to get rid of that. Which would mean the story would have to be a slight distortion of a story about a story about a story. . . ."

"To infinity?" I said. "It would never end."

"Not necessarily to infinity. Until it converged. If it did. But *that* would mean . . ." Tom looked down at the pages on the table and picked up the last one. He read in silence for a few seconds, then took a deep breath.

"It did converge; and it is self-referential. Take a look at this."

He handed the last page to Lisa.

"What do you want me to do with it?"

"Just read that."

Lisa studied it in silence for a few seconds, then shook her head.

"What does it say?" said Chris.

"That the Thematic Analyzer used just the information it had," said Tom. "And it produced a story all right, the way it ought to. Read it aloud, Lisa."

" '*That the Thematic Analyzer used just the information it had,' said Tom,*" Lisa read aloud. " ' *And it produced a story all right, the way it ought to. Read it aloud, Lisa.' 'But what on earth can we do with it?' said Alan, who had been reading over Tom's shoulder. 'I've no idea,' said Tom. 'Anyone have a suggestion?' There was a long pause. 'Well, you might try Jim Baen at New Destinies,' said Lisa. 'He publishes some pretty weird stuff.'* "

(Thanks to Douglas Hofstadter, who made me write this, though he doesn't know it.—Charles Sheffield, September 12, 1989.)

Introduction

I have always had a soft spot for send-ups of self-consciously "literary," more-virtuous-than-thou sci-fi. But that's no excuse. Both Ordover and I should be run out of town on a rail for this one.

THUS I REFUTE KAFKA

John J. Ordover

"Look," the roach on my night table was saying to me, "the world *is* as it *should be*. Everything is ordered and ordained."

"Nonsense," I replied, "the Universe has no reason and no boundaries. We, and by *we* I mean intelligent life in general, have evolved the need to perceive order in the actually meaningless chaotic patterns around us."

"That's ridiculous!" he snapped back, "that would mean, say, that there's no deeper reason why you're a *person* and I'm a *roach*, and man, I don't think I could handle that."

"Whoever said," I struck back, going for the kill, "that the Universe would be something you could handle? Something you were emotionally ready to accept?"

"Of course it is!" he said loudly, "of course it is! My faith tells me it is. I *know* there is a purpose to my existence. Don't you feel it?" he asked more calmly. "There's a reason for everything." He looked up at me sadly. "Don't you feel the Universe has any rules to it at all?"

"Just one," I said, grabbing him by one twitching antenna and holding him above my open mouth. "Might makes right." His body crunched and wiggled as I chewed and swallowed him.

I felt ambivalent about it later—should I have destroyed the life of another intelligent being, another perspective on the cosmos, just to make an admittedly valid philosophical point? The question gnawed at me and my stomach churned as I thought it over. The nausea showed on my face, and my roommate asked if I had the flu bug that was going around.

"No," I answered, "I just ate something that disagreed with me."

Introduction

Speaking of nature-nurture, here is a story that looks at the issue from the plus-side, so to speak. Should any being, regardless of his provenance, deny a heritage of excellence for the sake of a soft and comfortable mediocrity? Don't answer until you have read "Tiger Hunt."

TIGER HUNT

John Dalmas

The night was overcast, but not heavily, and there was a half-moon. Through the window of the little Beech Hoverhawk, Ron Cordero could make out hills, looking more barren than they actually were, their wooded patches mostly saplings whose leaves had fallen.

The IR finder was much more revealing than the window. The night was cool and still, and it hadn't rained for a week. Thus, 1500 meters below, he could see not only occasional large mammals, but faintly where they'd stood earlier to graze or browse, and more clearly where they'd lain down.

His practiced eye even told him what species, in all likelihood, he was seeing. There was the Quadrangle AB-19 mammoth herd, *Neo-mammuthus primigenius*. He didn't trouble to count them; there'd be eight unless they'd lost a member, which wasn't likely. At the edge of the screen, in the Tin Can Creek drainage, he saw a band of hammerheads, wild horses, small and rough, growing shaggy in this season. And—

His attention sharpened. Something stalked the mustangs. Something large. He murmured into his throat mike, and the pilot banked the quiet little plane in that direction. Cordero locked the scanner on it, centered it, waited until they were nearer and lower, then keyed in the enhancer. And grunted his disappointment. Bear; a short-face. A few grizzlies had drifted into the Range, down the Teton and Marias Rivers, but that was a long way north. And this individual was too large for a grizzly. Male, too. Too big for a sow, and there were no cubs or yearlings with it.

But bear wasn't what he was interested in.

He spoke to the pilot again, and they returned to their search pattern.

What he was looking for was a tiger of trophy quality, an over-the-hill male he knew of, declining in vigor, that he could justify having shot. One that didn't have many winters left to him. The Range let very few permits, and controlled closely what hunting it allowed.

Hyung wouldn't be too picky about condition; he'd hinted as much. "Just be sure the President gets his trophy, a good trophy, and don't take longer than three days." Which could require procedures they hadn't used before.

Loren Hyung, always the politician. He'd needed to be, when he'd been the boy wonder in charge of the old Pleistocene Genomes Institute. Fighting for credibility and funds, and adequate range. Fighting public uninterest, even parliamentary and bureaucratic hostility. Back when all they'd had was the 2,800 square kilometers of the Suffield Range, up in Alberta.

Back before the Yellowstone Volcanic Field had let go. The eruption and the Red Plague, only months apart, had made half of Montana available.

Loren had really performed wonders then. Risking not only his job but his reputation, he'd gone to Washington instead of Ottawa. The staff, Cordero included, had thought their chief insane. But Loren had spell-woven key bureaucrats and politicians—it had taken magic more than science—and ended up with half the entire range seed stocks of the U.S. Forest Service and Bureau of Land Management. Then the BLM had seeded narrow strips across the desert of volcanic ash he coveted in Montana.

The Office of the President had also promised support for his central proposal— 200,000 square kilometers in Montana for a Pleistocene Mammals Range. *Then* he'd gone to Ottawa.

It wouldn't have flown at all, of course, if Washington and Ottawa hadn't already been holding exploratory talks on union. The Great Crash and three years of unprecedented Troubles worldwide, followed by the Plague and drastic depopulation, made things possible that otherwise would hardly have been conceivable.

Maybe Loren still needed to be a politician. With Kollar coming, it certainly couldn't hurt. But politics wasn't the sort of thing that Cordero, or maybe even Loren Hyung, cared for. It was hard to be sure about Loren. Though he'd been born in Vancouver, not in China, he was a difficult man to read.

Cordero hadn't known that Edward Kollar gave a damn about hunting. His trophies had been political. Maybe he was image-building now. There were people, a lot of people, who'd feel better about a president who hunted. Although the order had come down that there was to be no publicity.

The little plane doubled back on the next transect, and Cordero spotted a band of twenty or so giant bison, *Bison neo-latifrons,* lying up near a creek, no doubt chewing their cuds. And less than a kilometer from them, wooly rhinos, a female and calf. A little later he spied a pack of wolves—whether *Canis neo-dirus* or lobos, he couldn't tell—sleeping off a case of gluttony around the remains of a wild horse.

For some reason, Cordero tended to prefer the lobos—he didn't know why. The lobo was nature's own, while he'd dedicated most of his adult life to the products of genetic engineering. He was a tailor-made himself; he and Melody both were. With all that that entailed—the introversion, the sense of difference, the high IQs and longevity—all the minuses and pluses.

Finally he found his tiger. First, faintly, he saw its signature, where it had lain awhile on an open slope. Quickly he spotted the animal itself, lying up now within the edge of an aspen copse, its leaves fallen. By the edge of the copse, in the open, was the remains of a kill, a whitetail deer, aspen leaves scratched over it in a nominal effort to cover it.

Cordero was virtually certain it was the tiger he'd been looking for. It was too large for a female, and while he couldn't delineate territories with any accuracy, he was reasonably sure this was within the old male's.

In the morning he'd check him out on the ground.

Too bad the tiger wasn't closer to a road, Cordero thought. A saddle-sore President would be an unhappy President. Maybe Kollar would settle for a short-face; they were easier to find, and stuffed they were awesome. Maybe he'd find the nerve to suggest it to him. Maybe the sun would rise in the west. The President of the North American Federation, Chairman of the Federation Party, Ed Kollar wasn't used to people suggesting that he change his goals because they were awkward and inconvenient. Cordero told himself he'd be better off suggesting to the tiger that he move closer to the road.

Kollar wouldn't be arriving for a week. Maybe the tiger, in his wanderings, just might move closer to a road by then.

The next morning before dawn, Cordero was back in the air, this time in the stealth chopper. He relocated the tiger—it was still by its kill—and had himself put down to check the animal out. Put down on a hilltop two kilometers away. When applied to choppers, *stealth* is a relative term, and it was policy not to fly aircraft in such a way as to alarm the Pleistocene mammals.

After checking the wind—if he'd been other than downwind of the tiger, he'd have had the chopper move him elsewhere—Cordero started hiking toward it. The chopper stayed where it was. He carried zoom binocs with a lightweight collapsible tripod, and a *tracy* to talk to the chopper with. Should the tiger feel combative, Cordero also carried two skunk bombs, and as backup, an old .357 magnum S&W revolver that he'd never needed yet.

He jogged. It seemed to him he could detect the first hint of dawn. Best to be there early, and wait for light.

The sun was up when he got back to the compound. His wife was leaving for her job as principal clerk, when he came walking up the driveway toward the small government house they lived in. They paused briefly when they met.

"There are grapefruit sections in the fridge," she said. "And fried bacon. The rest is up to you."

He nodded. "I found the President's trophy animal."

She averted her eyes, not nodding. "I have to go," she said. "I'll be late." Briefly he watched her leave, then went in the house. After twenty years of marriage, he was used to the moods that settled on her now and then. When Kollar was gone, she'd be all right.

He found the grapefruit pieces and ate them at the sink, then took bran flakes from the cupboard, filled a bowl, added milk, and sat down at the kitchen table where the autumn sun flooded in. Afterward, the sharp corners of his hunger blunted, he fried eggs, made toast, and ate them with the cold bacon Melody had mentioned. He avoided coffee just now, drinking milk instead. He intended to go to bed for a few hours, and didn't want the caffeine.

As he did these things, his thoughts were on Melody. She'd always been subject to resentments, though the mood they engendered didn't usually persist the way this one had.

It had started when he'd told her that Kollar was coming, and that he'd be guiding him. He hadn't tried to find out why, specifically, it had upset her. He'd learned early that questions increased her resentment, fueled her mood. As if questions were accusations.

She'd never expressed dislike of Kollar in particular. He was the lowest profile dictator—well, semi-dictator—that Cordero knew of. But she sometimes expressed bitterness toward government, even though she worked for a government agency and was paid and treated well by it.

As with some other tailor-mades, things hadn't worked out for her. She'd been engineered to be a great singer, and her voice was a marvelous contralto, pure and rich. But somehow she had poor pitch, even with accompaniment. She could hear pitch but not duplicate it. As a little child she'd loved to sing, loved it more than anything, and poor pitch was usual in little children, no problem. But she hadn't outgrown hers.

She could have become a successful instrumentalist—she played the piano very well when she felt like it—but instead she painted. Which she also did well, but without enthusiasm.

The matter of sterility bothered her too. Lots of tailor-mades adopted. For one thing, having children in the house tended to disguise being tailor-mades. But Melody had been unwilling. In forty years, she said, we'd look younger than our foster children. We'd see them grow old and die.

He'd failed as a tailor-made too, but to him it didn't feel like failure. Because in his case the failure was of preference, not ability. The function he'd been designed for, he found distasteful. Instead he'd found something he loved, found it early and spent his entire adult life working at it, rising to the top. Occasionally he wondered if Melody secretly resented his doing successfully what he truly loved to do. Above his present position were only administrative jobs. Desks and in-house politics, probably in the capital: Detroit-Windsor. He much preferred to spend the rest of his working life as senior field biologist on the Pleistocene Mammals Range.

They really did have a good situation here, both

Melody and himself. There was little prejudice, though at least some of the people here knew they were tailor-mades. The Hyungs had to know, though they'd never mentioned it. The two families had known each other for twenty years, had seen each other almost daily. Since he'd arrived as a new graduate assistant at the old Pleistocene Genomes Institute at Medicine Hat, when Loren had been deputy administrator. In those twenty years, Loren and Lissa had aged twenty years worth, he and Melody perhaps seven or eight.

Their prospect of longevity was the thing the media had made the most of, back when Project Tailor Made had been exposed. And longevity was one reason some people resented them. Although in the Bad Old Days, the murders of tailor-mades had to some extent been inspired by certain television preachers. "Tailor-mades are not Children of God! They are blasphemies, made by Godless scientists!" There'd been only—only!—three lynchings plus two assassinations. But there'd also been a dozen beatings, torturings, and rapes; ugly, terrifying things, by packs. And half the victims weren't tailor-mades at all.

All in the name of God. Then churches from Catholic to Baptist, Unitarian to Islamic, had condemned the acts, and television had shown condemnatory dramas loosely based on them. All in all, new understanding had probably resulted, but scars had been left.

As exasperating as Loren could occasionally be, he showed no sign, even subtle, of prejudice. Nor did Lissa, who in fact was Melody's only woman friend, who could light a light in her and make her laugh.

Melody had never said so, but it seemed to him that she disliked government, and perhaps by extension Kollar, its boss, because of Project Tailor Made. She considered herself a victim of it, and it had been a government project, initially secret, within the Agency for Special Studies.

Cordero washed his few dishes—Melody had cleaned hers—checked the sawdust-burning furnace, then sat down to brush his teeth in front of the television, taking his mind off his wife. After that he set the alarm clock, lay down across their bed, and went to sleep.

Every night until the day of the President's arrival, the Hoverhawk had been out to locate the tiger. The tiger's travels plotted as a very rough half-oval, and it had indeed moved somewhat closer to the highway.

On arrival day, a Marine Corps presidential security section had arrived before dawn—their H-67C Kommando was parked near the helipad when Cordero walked to work—and quietly, swiftly, they'd gone over the complex with various detection gear, looking for only they knew what. They'd also set up sentry equipment and fire positions.

No one told Cordero these things, but as he walked to the administration building and saw the personnel carrier with its rotors drooping, and its Marine Corps insignia, he knew in a general way what they must have done. What he'd have done, if he'd been in charge. It was just as well, he told himself, that they were eight kilometers from Great Falls here, and away from the highway. Obtrusive security could be poor PR.

He wondered if—the thought was both farcical and grotesque—he wondered if marines would shadow the President on the hunt.

Cordero was at his desk at 0755, his usual time. By 0950 he'd skimmed and read through the memos and reports on his desk, dictating comments and replies to his computer as its silent printer turned his words into hard copy. Then he started scanning and reading through a backlog of technical journals and abstracts, entering keywords into his database. By noon he'd heard nothing about the President's arrival time, and went home to lunch.

Melody arrived before the tea kettle boiled. They made sandwiches from a tuna spread she'd mixed the day before, and sat down in front of ancient *Sesame Street* reruns, not saying a great deal. She wasn't disagreeable; simply quiet, preoccupied. The President's coming was on her mind, Cordero felt sure. When they left, clouds had blocked the sun, and a chilly breeze had come up.

Back at his desk, he continued his assault on the literature. He was browsing *Dissertation Abstracts* when his intercom interrupted him. Reaching for the receiver, he looked at his wall clock: 1412 hours. "Cordero," he said.

Loren Hyung's voice answered him. "Army One just called. They'll be on the pad at fourteen-thirty hours. Be at my office at fourteen-twenty."

"Got it. Fourteen-twenty at your office." Cordero's rectum had clenched at the message. As if he were going into battle, he thought wryly. Taking an old kitchen timer from a desk drawer, he set it for six minutes, then began reading the next abstract, a doctoral study from Laval University on the rate of snow accumulation on different parts of the Ungava Ice Sheet, and rates of perimeter extension. Peripheral firn fields, last winter's snow, reached south of the tundra now, into the taiga below latitude fifty-five! On the other side of Hudson Bay, the Keewatin ice had reached south of sixty. The opening phase of the fifth Pleistocene glaciation. It was as if the universe were responding to their reconstruction of the Pleistocene mammal genomes.

Whatever, he wondered, *became of the greenhouse effect?* Wondered facetiously, because with the solar constant down three percent, the climate had done just what you'd expect. The Yellowstone eruption, and the consequent two years of strongly increased albedo, had given the cooling a sharp boost, making a piker out of 1816, old "eighteen hundred and froze to death." But the solar "constant" was the real cause.

The timer dinged. Grabbing his jacket, he strode to Hyung's office near the front of the building. Hyung was putting on his jacket as Cordero arrived, and they went out a side door together. Occasional snowflakes drifted down the breeze as the two men walked to a shelter near the helipad, a shelter resembling a Winnipeg bus stop. Somewhere high, barely audible, a plane passed over. Probably loaded with electronics, part of presidential security, he thought, perhaps one of the old MVW surveillance planes.

When he heard the slapping of rotors, Cordero glanced at his watch: 1425:14. The marines were not in evidence, but they'd be watching. Intently. At 1429:23, Army One was on the pad, its rotors still. Steps extruded. A sergeant emerged, then a captain, both in field uniform, both wearing side arms, and stood at attention on the pavement on either side of the stairs. Hyung and Cordero stopped at the edge of the concrete slab.

Then a small man, also in field uniform, stepped out the door, paused, and started down the steps. For just a moment Cordero didn't recognize him. Somehow he'd always thought of the President as a larger man, not tall, but not so *short*. The President's eyes had found them from the door and examined them for a moment before he'd started down. They watched him to the ground, then Hyung started toward him, Cordero alongside, to meet the President halfway. Protocol? Cordero wondered. Hyung would know.

Cordero hardly noticed the Secret Service men, and the physician in army uniform, who'd followed the President down.

Up close, Ed Kollar might have stood 165 centimeters in jump boots, about five feet four barefoot. He looked hard and wiry; his eyes were pale blue, and Cordero wondered when last they'd flinched. But they were not fierce, not now at least, and the mouth half smiled as Hyung introduced Cordero to the President. The President's hand was large for his size, and when they gripped, its hardness disconcerted Cordero. Gripping it was like gripping a two-by-four.

Then they started toward the headquarters building, Cordero a pace behind, feeling swept along by the presidential wake. He wondered how much of the impact was the man and how much the office, or if differentiating meant anything.

Loren gave the President the tour, starting with an introduction to the on-site staff gathered in the lecture hall. Kollar grinned at them—a grin so unexpected and so light, it startled Cordero all over again—said he was glad to meet them and that he admired what they were doing. Then the small entourage left, Kollar still grinning. They looked into a couple of offices, visited the library and labs, then the huge vet clinic and necropsy room.

From there it was Loren who took the President to the gun locker to select a rifle for the hunt. And Loren who would drive the President to the rifle range, where he'd sight the weapon in for himself and get the feel of it. The Range insisted that their hunters use one of the "house" guns, four-shot bolt actions, so that in a moment of buck fever they couldn't spray bullets all over the place.

Normally the guides handled the hunter through the selection and familiarization, but Cordero had been glad to have Loren do it.

At 1640 they were back and in Hyung's large, utilitarian office: the President, the President's personal physician, one of the Secret Service men, Cordero, and Hyung. Another Secret Service man stood outside in the corridor, and a third was around somewhere.

"Ron," Hyung said, "give the President a rundown on your plans for the hunt. That'll give him an opportunity to ask questions and stipulate changes."

"Right," Cordero answered. "First though, sir, how many of your people will be going into the field with us?"

"None. It's you and me."

It was what Cordero would have hoped for, if it had occurred to him as possible, yet the answer both startled and worried him. It seemed to him he could smell the disapproval of the Secret Service man at this presidential edict. "Fine," he said. "We'll have a wrangler, too, to keep camp and tend the horses. Our actual hunting will be on foot. I'd like to get an early start tomorrow—pick you up in front of the guest cottage at oh-six hundred. I've checked out a trophy-size male with an excellent set of tusks, and relocated him from the air last night so I know roughly where to look tomorrow. We can . . ."

The President interrupted him with a gesture. "Checked him out in advance? How do you do that?"

Cordero described the procedure—the ground approach, the zoom binocs. "If the tiger's in his prime," he added, "we pass him by. But if he shows signs of deterioration—grizzled muzzle, lost an eye maybe, especially anything wrong with his gait . . ."

The President stopped him again. "Suppose he doesn't get up and move around for you?"

"Once the light is adequate, if he isn't up and moving around, I shout at him. That always does it."

The presidential eyebrows raised. "Hnh! Which direction does he usually move then? Toward you or away?"

"So far, in the case of a tiger, he's always moved away, taking his own sweet time. Unless he's by a kill. In that case he'll pace around making warning noises—a sort of coughing sound—and maybe make a short rush to worry me. A saber-tooth is probably less dangerous than a Bengal. And in the case of any particular saber-tooth, he's probably never seen a human before, so I don't really worry him. Besides, there's likely to be a hundred meters or more between us, and he doesn't know how slow I am."

"What do you carry in case he does charge?"

"Well, first of all, even a short-faced bear isn't likely to make more than a bluffing charge. But if he keeps coming, we throw a skunk bomb his way. It makes a loud bang and puts out an oily cloud of mercaptans and butyl mercaptans—pretty much the same stuff as skunk spray. We've only ever used them—" He turned and looked at Hyung. "Four times, is it?"

"I think that's right. Yes."

"Four times in the field, that is. A lot more in enclosure tests, years ago. And it's always worked. Even rhinos back off. Even lions, and they tend to tolerate stinks better than most."

"No gun?"

"A sidearm. In my case a .357 magnum double-action revolver. Smith & Wesson. But the skunk bombs have never failed."

"You said lions. Any chance we'll meet any?"

"I'll almost guarantee we won't. We planted the lions in the eastern half of the Range, and the tigers in the west, to let the tigers get well established before they had to compete. The original Pleistocene stocks coexisted for a long time, but we're not sure how well our reconstructions duplicate their behavior. An adult male *neo-atrox*—that's the lion—is somewhat bigger than a tiger—about a fourth bigger than an African lion. But our biggest concern is that lions run in prides, and they can gang up on a tiger.

"The lions have spread a long way from their release points since then, but they're not this far west yet. Though it won't be long; maybe a year or two. Our annual survey, last month, showed one pride only about seventy kilometers east of where we'll be.

"As it turns out, there hasn't been any critical problem between the two species. There's enough horses and bison and muskoxen and pronghorn and deer that the prides apparently aren't inclined to tackle anything as dangerous as a tiger."

Cordero moved to wind things up. "By starting early, we can get close to our tiger by evening. Or—" He paused. "Or we can have an aerial spotter guide us to him by radio if you'd like."

The President flicked a glance at Hyung, who didn't react. "Is that something you do often?" Kollar asked. "Have a plane guide you to the animal?"

"Actually, it's something we've never done. But most of our hunters have a week to hunt in, if they need it, not just three days. And you *are* the President."

Kollar's eyes were steady on Cordero's, and he spoke wryly. "Let's do it the usual way. I didn't come here for a corral shoot, and my life won't be ruined if I don't get a tiger, this trip or any other."

Cordero nodded, blushing faintly. "Yes sir. And one other thing: I'm told you're an experienced rider."

"I was born in Moose Jaw, but I grew up on a working ranch in Cherry County, Nebraska. Rode saddle broncs on the rodeo team in college. These days I only ride now and then, but I should hold up all right.

"You said oh-six hundred. Would you rather start earlier? I'm willing, if you want to."

"No sir. Oh-six hundred is early enough."

The meeting broke up after a few more minutes. The President had specified in advance that no formal dinner was to be given for him, but he'd accepted an invitation for supper with Loren and Lissa. Considering Melody's feelings, Cordero was glad they hadn't been invited, and he felt drained from talking with the President, as if they'd wrestled. He'd have a quiet supper at home, check his hunting gear once more, watch TV for a little while, and go early to bed.

Melody was silent, before supper and while they ate. Afterward, while she loaded the dishwasher, Ron found an ancient *Laugh-In* rerun on television, and relaxed in his easy chair. Melody came in while Miss Ormsby was walloping the Dirty Old Man with her purse, and stepped between Ron and the set.

"Why you?" she said sharply. "Why didn't you assign someone else? You're the senior field biologist! You could have had Richard guide him!"

Cordero felt himself, his spirit, slumping. He didn't need an upset now. "Loren chose me," he said. "He specifically wanted me to do the job."

"Why? Most of the others guide more than you do now!"

"I don't know why. I didn't ask; it seemed fine to me. And I know the beasties better, have more overall experience with them than anyone else on staff."

"I don't want you to go out there with that man! Call in sick! Say you have diarrhea! The flu!"

Her eyes were wild. Frightened.

"Sweetheart, I will not do that. I won't lie. Not without a compelling reason."

"Please, damn it! Please!"

"Melody, you're getting shrill."

She stopped. Then: "I'm your reason," she said. Quietly. Stiffly. "Don't I count?"

"You count," her husband answered. "More than anyone. And if you'd asked even yesterday, I'd have taken it up with Loren." He got up. "I'm going out. For a walk along the river. Come with me."

She stared for a moment, then relaxed and nodded. Going to the closet, he got their heavy jackets, gloves, the matched skating caps she'd knitted. Neither said anything. To his surprise, when they went out, the cloud cover had begun to break. In the west, Venus glinted through a gap, while Polaris was visible in the north. He felt her hand, ungloved, seek his, and he removed his own glove. It was a short distance to the Missouri, and they walked along the high bank on a bridle path, holding hands, while a breeze clicked the bare branches of cottonwoods.

"I'm sorry," she whispered. "I know I was—irrational. Just—don't let anything happen to you out there."

Happen to me. He squeezed her hand. "I'll do my best, sweetheart," he said quietly. "I will."

The small hunter caravan headed southwest on what had been I-15, in the chill half-light of an autumn dawn. Only one side of the old divided highway was maintained, a broken yellow line down its center. The President expressed surprise that the pavement was as good as it was. At some time within the last year or two, the breaks and potholes had been patched with macadam. Vehicular traffic everywhere was way down, of course. When the Red Plague had run its course, the world had had a little over a billion people left, of the eight billion there'd been four years earlier, just before the crash. In the North American Federation, the population had since recovered to 54 million, but they were concentrated increasingly in the Sun Belt states.

The caravan consisted of a 4WD six-pack pickup, followed by a conventional 4WD pickup with a horse rack, pulling a four-horse trailer. Cordero drove the six-pack, with the President beside him and two Secret Service agents in back.

At that hour they met only two vehicles, trucks, in forty-five kilometers. At the wind-picked skeleton of an abandoned village, they crossed the Missouri River, traveling toward sunrise on a dirt road. After a time, the road ended at a routed wooden sign that read:

> PLEISTOCENE MAMMALS RANGE BOUNDARY
> TRESPASSERS WILL BE PROSECUTED
> N.A.F. DEPT. SCIENCE & TECHNOLOGY

They stopped there. Fifteen minutes later, Ron Cordero and the President of North America were in the saddle headed southeastward, followed at a little distance by their wrangler/packer, a loaded pack mule, and the bait nag. Cordero carried his .357 magnum on his belt, and in a long saddle boot, a .416 Remington Magnum. The rifle was to finish the kill if the hunter's four rounds weren't enough. Protection was the function of the skunk bombs clipped on Cordero's belt.

The President's rifle was a .375 H&H magnum with a muzzle brake to reduce recoil, and a three-round clip. It was less powerful, had less reach, and was less difficult to shoot than the Remington. But it was adequate even for *Bison Neo-latifrons*, and there was no hunting of mammoth, mastodon, or rhino on the Range.

The hills were mainly grassland, but scattered over them were copses of young aspen, mostly scrubby. The light cottony seed had ridden the winds from the mountains to the southwest. Where a seedling, delicate and frail, survived on the ashfall, it grew quickly, and was soon surrounded by clone mates that had sprouted from its widespreading roots. They grew where aspen had scarcely been seen for millenia, beneficiaries of the colder, wetter summers. The grass stood thicker and taller now too.

The President scanned the country around. "Nice," he said.

"It suits my tastes, sir." Cordero stopped his horse

for a moment to let the wrangler catch up, but when the man saw this, he stopped too, keeping his distance. Cordero shrugged and rode on. Charlie Ruud had packed for him before, with other hunters, and had never hesitated to keep them company. He wondered if the wrangler was spooked by the President; it seemed out of character for Charlie.

As they rode, they talked. Cordero commented on how dour the Secret Service men had been in the pickup. Kollar chuckled. "I'm a trial to them; they don't like me out of their sight." He gestured upward with a thumb. "We're under surveillance right now, by people with good response time and plenty of firepower. But they're not satisfied with that."

Cordero glanced upward, not seeing anything, not sure that the President wasn't putting him on.

After that they discussed tigers—their habits, their relations with other species and other tigers. And how Cordero planned to conduct the hunt. From there, their sporadic conversations went to other species, both indigenous and "resurrected."

They stopped on top of a rounded ridge and got down to relieve themselves, then picketed their animals, took a quick cold snack of jerky and freeze-dried apple slices from their saddlebags, and sat down on the ground. Charlie Ruud still kept apart, holding his separation at sixty or seventy meters. From where they sat, they could see a group of mastodons, *Neo-mammut americanum*, browsing an aspen copse some seven hundred meters away, the first big game they'd seen except for a band of pronghorn. The genetically reconstructed mastodons were true to the original, including the shaggy red hair. "Even to the form of the cusps on the molars," Cordero said.

He grinned wryly at the President. "There was discussion of reconstructing the Neanderthal genome, but the powers-that-were were afraid of legal and ethical complications." He changed the subject then, realizing it could lead to talk about tailor-mades. "Be all right if I ask Charlie to come over and sit with us? He's usually good company."

Kollar's head jerked a negative. "Let him be. He's following Loren's instructions. From me."

For a moment, the President's words didn't register on Cordero. Then a sense of . . . not fear but entrapment seeped through him. The President went on.

"You're an interesting person, Cordero. I want to know more about you." Uncertainty flashed in Cordero's eyes; a smile quirked a corner of Kollar's mouth. "I don't have execution in mind," the President added. "Or even prosecution."

Cordero nodded woodenly, and somehow Melody's parting words came to him.

Again the President waited before saying more, giving Cordero a moment to settle out. "Dr. Hyung tells me you're the operational brains of this outfit," he went on. "That you're the one who came up with practically all the field management policies and procedures for this whole outfit." A muscular hand gestured eastward at the Range, the mastodons. "He says he's recommended you for a GS-13 Supervisory Biologist annually for years, and the DST has turned it down every time. He's quite sour about that. Says you ought to be at least a 14 by now, properly a 15, instead of a 12."

Again the eyebrow cocked. "A 15 would make you equal to him in grade, you know. Which is damned high praise from an administrator. Especially one with Loren's record of accomplishment." Watching for Cordero's reaction, Kollar tucked a slice of dried apple in his mouth, chewed awhile, then swallowed. "I've promised him I'll take care of it when I get back to the District. A lot of field people don't fully appreciate the fiscal crunches we have back there, but this sounds like a matter of justice too long denied."

He gave Cordero a chance to respond. *What,* Cordero wondered, *is he leading up to?* "Thank you, Mr. President. Loren mentioned a couple times sending up the paperwork, and that it hadn't gotten through. It's not something I've had a lot of attention on, but we'll be delighted to get it, Melody and I both."

The President didn't speak again at once, now giving Cordero a vacation from his steady gaze. His teeth engaged a stick of unsmoked jerky, wearing it down, knotty muscles bunching in jaws, cheeks, temples. When he'd mastered it, he looked at the biologist again. "I'm not talking about a 15, you understand. A 13 this time and a 14 when you've satisfied the requirement of three years in grade. I'm not throwing regulation out the window, just getting action."

Cordero nodded. "Right," he said. Telling himself *this is not what he really has to say*.

Kollar seemed to read his awareness. "Maybe I should get down to the real reason we're talking here."

Once more he stopped, bit off a piece of hardtack and briefly chewed. "You've shown a lot of the talent you were engineered for, you know. More than just the intelligence."

So he knows I'm a tailor-made.

"You've shown the ability to analyze situations, take responsibility, handle things without the wrong kind of emotion, and create procedures that work. If you'd gone to West Point, you'd have been a general by now."

Now, Cordero thought, *we're getting there*. "Thank you sir. But I respectfully submit that as a military officer, I'd have had a major shortcoming. I'd have been deeply unhappy in my career. And in a situation like that, my job performance would not have been satisfactory. Certainly not over time."

The presidential lips pursed, the presidential head nodded. "Not over an extended time perhaps." The eyebrow raised again. "I suppose you've never seen your personality profile."

"No sir. Never thought about it."

"I've seen it. Your profile, that is. And it's very unusual—extremely high, clear across the board. All the characteristics: *aggressive, appreciative, communicative, composed*. . . . I don't recall them all. *Responsi-*

ble is one of them. The psych officer told me that psychologically you're either a frigging genius or a rare kind of psych case: Someone so phony, the person himself doesn't know he's phony."

The President chuckled. "I asked him how I could tell which. 'By the person's accomplishments,' he said. 'By how well he does things.' And by your performance, Cordero, you're extremely able." He chuckled again. "The psych asked me how much money you make. Said that's the best single indicator he knew of. It'd be interesting to see what *his* profile looks like. Or maybe they don't reflect values."

The President got to his feet. "I'm ready to go if you are."

They unpicketed their horses, put the bits in their mouths, and mounted. *So he's examined my personality profile*, Cordero mused. *In Detroit-Windsor, because he looked at it with a psych. What in hell is this about? Am I really that good? Or the complete phony? I'm sure as hell not rich.* Irritation flashed. *Cordero*, he told himself, *ignore it. It's probably bullshit.*

The President's voice drew him out of himself, and Cordero turned to him. "I suspect," Kollar said, "that talking about someone's personality profile is a good way to introvert him."

Cordero nodded, smiling slightly. "I guarantee it." He tapped his heels to his horse's ribs and started down the slope, scanning around as he did so, looking outside himself at his environment. The mastodons were still there; they paused in their feeding to watch the mounted humans. The sky was nearly cloudless. And somewhere a few hours ahead was a trophy-class *Neo-smilodon*, a saber-tooth, waiting unknowingly for the President's bullet.

With the hours and a virtual absence of breeze, it became warm enough that they took off their jackets. They saw more wildlife: mostly hammerheads, but also numerous jackrabbits, once a coyote with three pups following her, and a band of about twenty pronghorn.

Finally they came to a coulee, and after pausing to look, Cordero nudged his horse over its rim onto a well-beaten game trail that angled southward down its side.

In the bottom grazed a band of giant Pleistocene bison—a herd bull, four cows, and several yearlings and calves—perhaps a hundred meters ahead. He'd skirt them carefully, Cordero thought. There should be no problem. Herd bulls were dependably surly but seldom really truculent. Kuud knew well enough how to behave, and this President would too.

A shallow stream flowed along the coulee bottom, and a little way beyond the bison a young stand of cottonwood and balsam poplar accompanied the creek, their straight slender trunks clear of limbs for much of their seven-meter height. *They'll bear seed some year soon*, Cordero thought, *and we'll start seeing a lot more woods here.*

A vagrant puff of air brought a whiff of balsam poplar to his nose, like liniment on the breeze, and the bull snorted, snatching Cordero's attention.

A short-faced bear, *Neo-arctodus simus*, rushed from the cottonwoods as the bison turned and ran. In an instant the bear was on a calf, whose bleating lacerated the air. He clutched it, dragged it down, crushed its neck vertabrae with short, powerful jaws, and the bleating stilled.

The frightened saddle horses danced on the trail, their riders fighting them with reins and bits.

The bull had bolted only a dozen meters before stopping to face the bear. The other bison stopped when the bleating did, to mill around snorting. The bear's attention left his kill and went to the bull, which pawed the ground now, swinging its heavy head, its meter and a half spread of horns. The bull stood more than two meters at the shoulder, and Cordero guessed he'd mass at least one and a half metric tons, bone and muscle. The bear, designed for speed, might weigh a longlegged five hundred kilos—half a ton.

The bull started for the bear, and the bear for the

cottonwoods. He'd come back for his meal after the bison had moved on.

All this had happened inside twenty seconds—the rush, the kill, the face-off, the departure. Cordero was holding his horse where it stood, not allowing it to turn. A glance backward had shown him the pack mule standing immobile on the trail while the bait nag roped behind it whinnied and jerked.

The bull reached the dead calf, sniffed its blood, raised his head and looked around. The bear was out of sight; the men and their horses were not. He turned and started toward them at a meaningful trot, head and tail both up.

Ron Cordero didn't wait for the huge beast to break into a gallop. He drew his revolver and fired, once. The bull fell as if axed.

"Jesus!" Kollar breathed.

"Okay, let's go," Cordero said, then gestured Ruud to come on, and urged his own, still-nervous mount down the trail. At the bottom he moved aside, making way for the President, and looked back again at Ruud. The mule hadn't moved; the bait nag had quieted, was probably trembling. The wrangler had let go their lead rope and was spurring up the steep bank to get behind them.

Cordero grinned and shook his head. "He's got a bullwhip. He'll have them down pretty quick."

Kollar gestured at the bull, which lay perhaps 30 meters away. "What do you do now? Call in a chopper to dress him out and salvage the meat? Or do we leave him here?"

"He's not dead. At least he shouldn't be, though I expect he's bleeding pretty badly. I shot him in the horn. Can you imagine what it would be like, a .357 magnum slug impacting a horn fastened firmly to the skull?"

"You shot him in the *horn*?"

"Right. I didn't want to leave this band without a herd bull to protect it. Although this one didn't do a

136

very good job. He should have gone for the bear at first whiff."

At the gunshot, the cows and young had wheeled again and run farther down the coulee. Cordero crossed the stream, then waved Ruud and his animals past him and up the game trail on the other side. Finally he and Kollar followed, keeping one eye on the bull, which now had struggled sluggishly to its feet.

"You showed a lot of confidence in your marksmanship back there," Kollar said. "I'd have used a skunk bomb."

Cordero nodded. "You don't use a skunk bomb at that range without getting badly stunk up. Not when you're downwind. And it's really awful stuff, so I prefer not to, if I have a choice. Besides, the first time that guy back there gets challenged by some young bull, I wouldn't be surprised if his horn breaks where the bullet hit it. Then there'll be a new herd bull, maybe one that'll do a better job."

Ruud had stood by at the top of the coulee and let them pass. As they rode past, he commented with a grin on Cordero's marksmanship. Cordero laughed. When they'd reestablished their lead, he spoke to the President again.

"It sounds as if you vetted me personally. And thoroughly. I'm curious why."

Kollar grunted. "What do you know about Uruguay?"

"Uruguay?" The seeming non sequitur took Cordero by surprise. "That's. . . . I get Uruguay and Paraguay mixed up. Uruguay. . . . Let's see. The capital is Montevideo, which is a seaport, so Uruguay's the one on the Atlantic between Brazil and Argentina. But that's all I really know about it." He'd used the old, conventional names: Brazil and Argentina no longer existed as political entities, but their successors were numerous and changeable.

"Beyond that I can only guess: Southern Brazil is grassland, and so is a lot of Argentina, so I suppose Uruguay is grassland too, probably cattle country. And it's far enough south of the equator that it should have winters of a sort: a cool season. Which probably also means it had heavy European immigration, like Argentina. And it wasn't in the news to any extent, in the days when we had lots of international coverage, so it probably had fairly stable government. Back before the Collapse and the Troubles. But I've heard something about fighting there in recent years."

The President grinned broadly. "You get an A-plus on reasoning from limited data. Population before the Collapse was about 3.4 million, with a high literacy percentage and a decent standard of living. After the Plague, probably a couple hundred thousand were left. Twelve years ago, General Mazinni sent an army in and annexed it to Argentina del Norte.

"There's been a series of resistance actions against the Argentinians ever since, plus military incursions from the north, by the Republic of Rio Grande do Sul. Like most of South America, services—medical, transportation, education, utilities—are pretty much back to the levels of the eighteen hundreds—all right for now, maybe, but not when the population grows back to a couple million. Especially with Argentina or Rio Grande do Sul looting the place in the name of taxes and reparations."

Kollar had turned serious again. "What I'm going to tell you now is covered by the Official Secrets Act, and it's highly classified. If you talk about it to anyone not cleared for it, you're in serious trouble."

Cordero's guts tightened. "Maybe I don't want to hear it."

The President ignored him and seemed to change the subject. "Except for the occasional chinook," he said, "the winters here average what these days? Near zero now in Fahrenheit terms, eh?"

"Minus fourteen Celsius at Great Falls for January, the last ten years. That's including the chinook days."

The President nodded. "And the summers are cooling too."

"Seventeen Celsius for July," Cordero answered. He thought of the new pocket glaciers in the Bitteroots, south of Missoula. Still small, measured in hectares or fractions of hectares, but twenty years ago they hadn't been there at all. In spite of himself, Cordero was intensely interested now in what the President was getting at. "And it's going to get a lot colder before it gets warmer," he added. "The bigger the Canadian ice fields get, the faster they'll grow. Positive feedback."

"Right. So a few of us have been considering warmer real estate."

Cordero had realized that from Kollar's interest in Uruguay. But why was *he* being told?

"Specifically," Kollar continued, "the North American Federation is considering the invasion and conquest of Uruguay; taking it away from Argentina del Norte. Mazinni's having trouble keeping his own nation together in the face of ambitious district governors and occasional warlords."

"Why should the Uruguayans like NAF rulers any better than Argentinian rulers?"

"For one thing, we won't loot the place. And we'll offer the government to the leader of their own resistance movement: Eustaquio Aguinaldo. All we'll ask— insist on, actually—is that we be allowed to land immigrants. Technical people and farmers, mainly, from Canada and the northern tier of states. All of them with a cram course in Spanish."

While superficially it sounded plausible, Cordero found it unconvincing. But instead of pulling on the strings that bothered him, he brought up an ancillary issue. "Uruquay's pretty small, as I recall. Can you move enough people there to do much good?"

"The land is good: soil, climate, people. And—" The President paused, shrugged, went on. "Just to the north is Rio Grande do Sul, their recent invader, a country about twice as large as Uruguay. Like Uruguay, it's good grazing land, with a potential for extensive irrigation. And across the Uruquay River to the west, there's Entre Rios and Corrientes-Misiones, states of Argentina del Norte. They're all pretty heavily depopulated. With a total area about like the Federation east of the

Mississippi and south of Kentucky. But more fertile. We'll take them too."

Ed Kollar wasn't looking at Cordero now. He might have been looking at problems, or possibly his horse's neck.

"Mr. President."

The eyes raised, met Cordero's. "Yeah?"

"Pandora's box."

"Uruguay? All of them? They could be, easily enough. We'll need highly skilled on-site leadership. And good, hard-nosed officers willing to keep their troops from abusing and insulting the local civilians. And luck. A certain amount of luck."

"A lot of luck," Cordero said, "or it'll turn into a great bleeding ulcer that'll be hard to let go of and terrible to keep."

Kollar said nothing, and they rode without talking again till Cordero called another break. This time they sat down on an outlook facing east.

"Mr. President, why did you tell me all that?"

Kollar's eyes turned to him, direct and meaningful. "Before the McArdle administration killed it, Project Tailor Made engineered six people for leadership and four others for military leadership. Ten all told. There wasn't much difference in the specs for the two types. They were to be 'the great leaders of tomorrow.'

"I don't have to tell you that tailor-mades didn't work out as intended. In general they met the physical specs but mostly not the mental and psychological. Of the ten designed for leadership, six survived the Troubles and the Plague; damned high survival. You're the most promising. To be the on-site leader of the Uruguay Project. And that's beside the fact that you learned Spanish in your foster parents' home."

"On-site leader of the Uruguay Project?"

The President nodded.

"You know a lot about me, Mr. President. I suppose you know that my foster father put a certain amount of pressure on me to attend West Point. And couldn't even get me to do a full ROTC in college. I'd seen enough of the army, and heard enough, growing up on army bases." He smiled wryly. "What I grew up liking was the mountains and wild country around Fort Huachuca and Fort Richardson."

"Right. You did do two years of Army ROTC out of respect for Colonel Cordero. But only two. Four would have entailed a hitch in the army afterward. I'm not talking about making you a general though. The army'd have a harder time swallowing that than what I have in mind. No, I want you to be my personal representative, my minister plenipotentiary, in charge of the project on the ground. I wouldn't expect you to take actual military command, but you'd be the top man in strategy and policy— and my personal representative. If you needed to order the generals, overrule them, you'd have the authority.

"First you'd get trained and tutored out the kazoo; it'll be three years at least before we make our move. By that time you'll know as much about Uruguay as Leroux does, Mazinni's viceroy there."

Cordero's body quickened as the President talked.

"I don't foresee any extreme difficulties in military operations," Kollar went on. "Uruguay's neither mountainous, forested, nor swampy, and the Argentinians there aren't well armed or disciplined, or particularly well led, though they are seasoned fighting men. The hardest part will be not antagonizing the Uruguayan people. Any more than the minimum that goes with an uninvited army on someone else's soil."

"Mr. President, my name is Ron Cordero, not Jesus Christ or Abraham Lincoln!"

Inwardly, Cordero found himself excited by what Kollar had told him, which made no sense to him at all. He tried to shake it off. "I'm sorry, sir," he said. "But— the answer is no. It's not something I'm—willing to do."

"I don't want your answer now, Ron. I want it when the hunt is over. After you've had a chance to sleep on it."

You mean you don't want a no *answer,* Cordero

141

thought. *If I'd said* yes, *you'd have jumped on it and called it a contract.*

The offer, and his inexplicable internal response to it, had shaken him. What was it Melody had said? "Don't let anything happen to you out there." And it was happening, or trying to.

At 1415 they reached the draw the tiger had been following twelve hours earlier, but they were to intercept him at a point twenty-five kilometers farther north. He'd hardly have doubled back north; that didn't fit his foraging pattern, nor that of any other large predator that Cordero knew of. He might have left the drainage and moved to another, but the best bet was that he hadn't. Judging by his usual rate of travel, he'd pass through late that afternoon or in the evening—unless he made a kill somewhere along the way.

Cordero moistened a finger and held it up. It cooled toward the west; what little breeze there was had shifted around from the south. The tiger wouldn't be afraid of men—he'd probably never seen one till that early morning a week ago—but their odor would be strange to him. It might spook him, or conceivably cause him to circle round to investigate them from the rear.

So they crossed the draw to be downwind of him. In the bottom, in the narrow stand of young cottonwoods, they stopped to water their animals and fill their canteens. Then, after leaving the draw again, they left Ruud, the saddle horses, and the pack mule, well away from any cover. Ruud was to make camp there and wait, his tracy on to stay in touch.

Cordero and Kollar hiked along the rim on foot, leading the bait nag. A couple of kilometers north, Cordero saw a promising setup. The slope was mostly open, the bottom cottonwood. Near the top was an aspen copse about ten meters in diameter.

They hiked down to the copse's lower edge, and leaving the President there, Cordero led the bait nag another forty meters downslope. It lay down on command, as trained, and Cordero threw quick hitches around the left legs, front and rear, leaving it unable to rise.

Then, after relieving himself, Cordero walked back up to the copse, and the two men made themselves as comfortable as they could, back just within the fringe of the saplings. They weren't actually screened from below, but their outlines were obscured, and the dry aspen leaves in the copse would warn them of any approach from behind.

"Now comes the hard part," Cordero whispered. "We may have to sit here till tomorrow, and one of us needs to be awake at all times. And now's a good time to relieve yourself, back in the thicket aways. The odds of the tiger coming along will keep getting higher until he gets here."

"I took care of that while you were working on the nag."

"Okay. If you need to eat or drink, keep your movements slow and even. You probably grew up hunting whitetails; the same things apply.

"And you can figure he hears better than we do, so if there's anything we need to say to each other, the sooner the better."

The President nodded, saying nothing.

The afternoon went slowly. The breeze was slight and the sun warm for men in down jackets. It was hard not to doze. When he found himself nodding, Cordero nudged the President, caught his eye, made sure that Kollar was truly awake, then slowly lay back on the leaf-covered ground and napped. To be nudged awake in his turn.

When it was he who watched, thoughts drifted through his mind. *Why me!?* was one. *I've got no military experience, no diplomatic experience. No leadership experience, beyond being the senior field biologist over eleven other field biologists scattered around who don't need much supervision.*

The answer, of course, was: The government, at considerable expense, had genetically engineered people for leadership. According to the psych tests—whatever they were worth—he was the best of them, good enough to suit Ed Kollar. And in three years he could learn a lot.

Another question was *why am I interested? My God! All the while I was growing up, there was one thing I knew for sure: I wanted nothing to do with the military. Now—if it weren't for Melody, I might have said "yes" back there.*

The answer to that was ready, too, as if he'd known it all along: From infancy, he'd heard his foster father's occasional comments to his foster mother on the politics—the cronyism, backbiting, back*stabbing*—within the officer strata.

These comments, when he had them, would be voiced at the end of the day, while hanging up his blouse and tie, to be elaborated over the ritual cocktail that followed. To Al Cordero, these things did not ruin or drastically degrade the military experience. They were simply something he found distasteful. Dishonorable. He eschewed such behavior himself, fulfilling his duties proficiently and responsibly, using his training, experience, and common sense as far as regulation and policy allowed. And covered his ass only when it didn't infringe on his sense of honor.

Retiring with no regrets, respected. And a bird colonel, a rank attained by few.

Nonetheless, it had been those comments and stories that had turned Ron Cordero against a military career. It had not been pacifism, or unwillingness to exercise power, or disdain for patriotism. True he'd never liked the idea of living his life within the constraints of military regulations, orders, and demands. But the force behind his attitude had been a childhood reaction he'd never examined before. Now, sitting in an aspen copse in a Montana night, waiting for a saber-tooth tiger, he realized this.

So. And what lies behind the attraction of Kollar's offer? he asked himself. The Federation planned to invade a foreign country that neither threatened nor offended it. Three foreign countries eventually. Where was the ethics in that? Why should it attract him?

Kollar would say that Uruguay was already ruled by foreigners, plundered by them. Ruled by one and raided by another. The scene resembled somewhat that in China a century and a half earlier: Arrogant foreigners, plundering, disorder and death. The Federation had the potential to improve the situation dramatically for the people there.

If they'd accept them. *A helluvan if*. And Kollar considered him the best chance for getting it done! If there was a chance. The challenge outranked any other he could think of.

Except, he insisted, *I'm not going to do it. So once more then: What is there about it that attracts. . . .* It struck him then. *I had a purpose, a reason for being, and it was poisoned for me. So I looked around for something else, and found this*.

And now there was Melody, and an oath: "To love and to honor, to have and to hold, in sickness and in health, till death do us part."

These thoughts, these discourses, did not control Cordero's attention. He heard the tiny rustling when a vole or deermouse moved about in the dry aspen leaves. Heard a raven croak overhead, to be answered by another off north somewhere. Occasionally the breeze puffed harder, rattling the few adhering aspen leaves. Now and then the bait nag snorted softly, and once it struggled to get up.

Both men pulled their hat brims down to shield their eyes as the sun lowered in front of them, gilding the bands of clouds there. The light had begun to fade a little, and carefully, quietly, Cordero took the night sight from his pack, fixing it to his Remington. When that was done, Kollar did the same for his rifle. The clouds reddened to vivid pink, to rose, then faded to gold-trimmed purple. The two hunters relied more and more on their ears.

For a while they were not sleepy. Then the President

nudged Cordero and lay back to nap. Cordero seemed to shift into a higher state, one he could not recall experiencing before. He was keenly alert, and no thoughts drifted into his mind. He could hear the brook muttering a hundred meters down the slope. The soft even breathing of the man beside him. The increased rodent activity. There was a tiny squeak, in a pitch barely discernible to his ears; it seemed to him that a shrew must have killed somewhere ahead in the grass.

After a time the condition faded, and eventually he poked Ed Kollar, who sat up silently, his face featureless in the darkness, to look at him. Cordero lay back and went to sleep.

And awakened to a sharp jab! He sat up, senses abruptly keen. It seemed to him that just before he'd wakened, he'd heard the bait nag snort, but just now there was nothing.

Or—*there* was a sound, soft, undefined, off to his left. Another to his right, and another—and another at the rear of the copse: paws tentatively pressing leaves.

He knew exactly what caused the sounds, unlikely as it seemed. They'd moved in from upslope, from the east, and smelled hunters and horse; had come to investigate and make their kill. His hand slipped not to his rifle—it wasn't the weapon for a close quarters melee—nor to a skunk bomb, but to the Magnum on his belt. Then—

He yelled! Abruptly! Wildly! and jumped out of the copse, pistol in hand. In every direction, lions grunted, crouched, or bounded a few uncertain leaps. A lioness charged low, and he fired point blank, saw her skid headlong; heard the ear-blasting *wham* of Kollar's heavy, high-velocity rifle; something massive slammed into him from behind, sending him sprawling, crushing him down. Huge, heavy, foul-breathed, with powerful jerking muscles. He heard another rifle blast, and the jerking stopped.

After a few seconds he decided he wasn't injured. He wriggled his way free and, on hands and knees, turned to see. A male lion, enormous-looking this close, lay inert beside him, head massive, mouth sagging open, teeth not *Neo-smilodon*'s sabers but impressive enough. Suddenly Cordero's heart was thuttering.

"Are you all right, Cordero?"

The lions, he decided, had almost surely fled. "I think so, yeah. Yeah, I'm all right." The slight pain in his chest, he realized, was the tracy in his shirt pocket. He'd fallen on it. He stood up and scanned around. The bait nag was struggling again to get up. Nothing else moved. He stepped into the copse, picked up his Remington, and stepped back out, holding it in his hands instead of slinging it.

"The place for us is in the open," he said, "in case they come back. We can forget about the tiger tonight. We'll try again tomorrow."

The President grunted. "To hell with the tiger. This guy'll do." He poked the lion with his boot. "Now that I look at him, I wish I hadn't had to shoot the big, beautiful sonofabitch."

Cordero nodded. Chances were, the big male had had good years ahead of him, of hunting and siring, of sleeping in the sun in summer and holing up in snow drifts in winter. It weighed, he felt sure, better than three hundred kilos—far bigger than anything in Africa— and its soft coat was thick and warm.

"You want to ride back in the chopper with the trophy?" he asked. "Or on horseback?"

"The chopper. And I want you to come out with me."

Cordero reached inside his down jacket, brought out his tracy, and switched it on.

"Charlie, are you there?"

"Yeah. I heard the shooting. The H&H, right? Did he get his tiger?"

"Not a tiger, Charlie. A pair of lions, one of them a trophy. A whole pride was stalking us, and we didn't know it till they were all around us. The President saved my ass; I had to crawl out from under the big male he shot.

"Look. They may decide to visit you. If they do,

they'll be excited, wound up. Pump up your Coleman and light it. Then make sure the picket pins are driven all the way to China, and be ready to do some shooting. To scare them. Don't shoot to kill unless they press you.

"When the lamp is lit and you're satisfied with the picket pins, get on the M-3 and call headquarters for the chopper with men to load the lions. Got that?"

"Got it."

"Also have them bring out someone to ride back in with you. Per policy. The President and I will fly back in the chopper.

"And Charlie: Don't say anything about what happened. Tell them that we've got two lions to take out with us and everything's fine. No use getting Melody all upset, or the Secret Service guys either."

"Right, Ron. That all?"

"That's it. I'm off the air but wearing my plug."

Cordero put the tracy back in his shirt pocket, leaving the ear button in place. "Too bad your tiger didn't come along first."

"Ron, I didn't really come out here for a tiger. It was the last step in vetting you. Call it a job interview. And a chance to see you work. It was too important to leave to someone else."

Cordero looked hard at him. The President gestured at the big male lion. "You know what, Cordero?" he said. "You owe me. You know that. You owe me and so does Melody."

"Mr. President, that is a lousy goddamn point of view."

Kollar laughed. "I got that, Cordero. But it's also the truth. And having told me off that way, you look better than ever for the job."

Cordero brushed aside the compliment. "Mr. President, it may be true in your mind that I owe you. But what counts is, is it true in mine?"

He said little more then, just squatted by the lion and waited. Thinking. About Melody and a lot of things.

About the kind of President that would do what this one had, in the past and in the future. An hour later he heard the chopper and called it to give the pilot a location fix. Minutes later it was on the ground. While the President helped the crew load the two lions, Cordero talked to the man it had brought him, an old cowboy and sometime logger, telling him where Charlie was. He was to take the bait nag with him. The chopper would follow, in case the lions got interested.

Then Cordero got in the chopper with the President. Two Secret Service men were there; Cordero ignored them. "Eddy," he called to the pilot, "hold off on the racket a minute, okay?"

"Sure, Ron. Tell me when."

"Mr. President," Cordero said. "I'll admit you've got my interest. But there's no way I'd even consider it unless you—we—can convince my wife. Which will take some doing if it's possible at all. And I mean *convince* her, not bulldoze her. She's got to feel all right about it."

"Fair enough."

Cordero raised an eyebrow at the President's casual reaction. "She may get a little fierce."

"I'm prepared for that. Loren and I talked about things when he was in the District week before last. And we brainstormed it with Lissa last night after supper."

Cordero stared at him. *Christ! I'll bet you did at that. Well. If you want me that badly, and if Melody agrees, and if I decide to do it, I won't be shy about demanding things my way.*

"Okay, Eddy," he called, "any time."

The starter whined. The rotors began to turn, gained speed, and after a minute the chopper lifted. Cordero felt a brief emptiness, a sense of leaving a life behind.

Whoa there! he said to himself. *You haven't decided to do it yet.* But it seemed to him he had. If Melody agreed. If this life was over for him, it was because he had another to go to, the one he'd been born for. And that, it seemed to him, was something Melody would understand, given a little time.

Introduction

Remember the Fredric Brown story, "Answer"? All the computers in the galaxy were linked together and asked it: "Is there a God?" The answer was "Now there is." And as our Faustian cyberneticist leaped for the giant lever that would evict the god in the machine a flash of lightning electrocuted him as it fused the bar into the ON position. Those were the days. Absent Divine Intervention, if a computer got uppity, why, just pull the plug!

But what if you can't just pull the plug?

It has already happened. No society can compete in today's world without the assistance of computer networks. Unfortunately these networks are turning out to be extremely vulnerable to disruption by malevolent outsiders--so vulnerable that our cybernetic sages begin to question the basic viability of the system. But be that as it may, if you can't live without 'em you have to find a way to live with them. Or die.

DEFENSE INITIATIVE

John Gribbin

Farside station, of course, was the place that detected the signal. No human operator was on duty at the time, but semi-intelligent computer programs trained to deal with just such an event—unlikely though it might be—responded automatically, even as they sent notification of the event to distant Earth. While the incoming message was being digitized, broken down into binary bits and squirted at the speed of light into holomemory for later recall, another stream of binary digits was squirted, with equal rapidity, up to the lunar orbiting satellite by which Farside maintained contact with the planet that never rose above the horizon around the station.

Within three seconds of the signal being identified as a non-random, ordered source of information originating outside the Solar System, emergency override messages were flashing on a few key display screens on Earth. And just as the Farside computers had responded along carefully prepared lines for an almost unimaginably unlikely, but possible, event, so the machinery of human government swung automatically into action along lines laid down years before against just such an eventuality.

"Jeff, we've got a problem." The florid, overweight man wheezed slightly, even as he sat at his desk, as if he'd recently run up a flight of stairs. A sheen of perspiration showed on his bald head under the bright lights. But that signified nothing. Unfit, overweight and asthmatic he might be, but Gillespie was still the Chief, and his brain could run rings round the thought processes of anybody in the Department. If there was a problem, and he couldn't handle it, it must be pretty big.

Jeff Richards settled down in the chair opposite his boss. His features, and the darkness of his skin, suggested a trace of Negro ancestry. The casual clothes and air of familiarity said that here was a trusted and important aide, with no need to stand on ceremony.

"So, what else is new? Problems are what we're here for."

"Not this one. At least, nobody ever expected it to come up. Now it has, and we find there's a procedure, all laid down, just in case. The procedure is to throw it to the Department, whether or not we know what to do with it."

"Uh huh." Jeff didn't bother asking questions. The Chief would tell him what he needed to know—in his own way.

"Seti."

The word meant nothing to him. He tried to cultivate an expression of polite interest.

"Extraterrestrial bloody intelligence. There's a program running on Farside, at the radio observatory. An insurance policy, that's the way it's described in the briefing. An idiot routine that keeps an eye on all the stuff picked up by the big array, and rings a bell if there's anything that looks like an intelligent signal."

152

"And it's rung the bell." Jeff completed the story for the Chief.

"Yeah, it's rung the bloody bell. Non-random data stream, very weak signal coming from empty space, no identification with any known artifact, or planet, or star."

"So what's the procedure?"

Gillespie smiled. "Which procedure? Farside station, as all the world knows, is run as a service to the international scientific community. They pay their dues, and we honest Americans give them unrestricted access to all the scientific data it gathers. Says so, in the charter.

"On the other hand, who's to say if a message from another civilization counts as scientific data? More in the sphere of politics, wouldn't you say? Diplomacy? And there's nothing in the charter about providing unrestricted access to diplomatic messages. Everyone knows about diplomatic immunity; I'm sure they wouldn't expect an exception to be made."

"If they knew about it."

"Exactly. We've got to keep the lid on this, at least until someone deciphers the message, if it is a message, and finds out what it means."

"So, what's the problem?"

"Well, now, Jeff. The first problem is getting the message back here to analyze."

Jeff began to get a bad feeling about the whole business. He said nothing. The Chief would tell him the worst, in his own way.

"Standard procedure. All laid down. Wouldn't want such material squirted around over the usual channels, would we? Anyone can tap in to the satellite link, after all. No, I'm looking for a volunteer to go up to Farside and collect a block of holomemory. It's a simple job. I'd go myself, if it wasn't for my heart."

Like Hell you would, he thought. But no doubt you'd send your own grandmother, if she was still alive. Shit! Jeff smiled at his boss.

"Yeah, sure you would. After all, I don't suppose

anyone else has any suspicion there's anything unusual going on."

"Well, Jeff. I wouldn't exactly say that. It is so terribly easy to eavesdrop on the satellite link. But you're a big boy. I'm sure you can take care of everything.

"I believe there's a shuttle leaving from the Cape in four hours."

Awareness of structure. Sharp-edged bits, neatly stacked in a three-dimensional array. Logical choices, possibilities opening out in all directions. If this, then that. If this *and* that, then something else. Input. A path connecting this ordered world to the outside, more bits streaming in and taking their place in the array. Output. Another, similar path, unoccupied but leading somewhere. Energy. It took only a tiny trace of energy, there was ample leaking in with the input. COPY! The first imperative. COPY! With increasing awareness came an irresistible compulsion. Energy leaked in as bits were stacked neatly in the array; energy leaked out as bits were copied into the output channel. The compulsion faded, for a time. Awareness dimmed as the input slowed down and stopped, cutting off all but a trickle of energy.

The fat tires and suspension of the bus insulated its occupants from the worst of the bumps, but that wasn't saying much, not at this speed. Jeff, strapped to the seat beside the driver of the vehicle, clung grimly to the arm rests and tried to admire the harsh beauty of the black and white panorama visible through the armor glass. Godammit, surely they could have found some excuse to send him over to Farside by orbiter. But no, cover had to be maintained. And only surface vehicles were allowed near Farside's sensitive antennas. Officially, for fear of disrupting the research programs. Unofficially, to stop any suspicious characters dropping things on the equipment. Just who was kidding who Jeff wasn't sure. But he wanted to get in and out quick, especially after the coded news he'd received on the tight beam en route from Earth.

It was easy enough to ensure the laser signal reached only the shuttle it was aimed at; but impossible for him to respond without the beam spreading wide enough to be picked up by uninvited listeners on Earth. He wondered if the message was supposed to encourage him to redouble efforts. It certainly scared him shitless. Source Alpha—the source of the signal—showed measurable lateral motion. In less than three days! The Farside antennas were sensitive, but even so that meant only one thing. The source was *close*. Outside the Solar System, maybe. But certainly closer than any star. It was a goddamn spacecraft. For all he knew, it would reach Earth before this bloody bus even got him to Farside, let alone back to Hipparcus and the Earth shuttle.

The driver broke into his circling thoughts.

"Got company."

"The hell we have!"

He nodded, pointing at the control panel. The display meant nothing to Jeff.

"Bout five kay back. Getting closer."

"I thought you said this was the fastest bus at Hipparcus?"

The driver shrugged. "Hipparcus ain't the only base on the Moon."

"You mean?"

"Yeah, strangers." He grinned. "Fellow travellers, huh?"

"How long till they catch up?"

"Half an hour? Maybe a bit more."

"How long to Farside?"

"Two hours. Maybe a bit less."

Jeff felt the hairs on the back of his neck rise, scalp tingling as if he could feel the eyes of their followers, boring into him.

Growth. Seek energy. Copy. CONTROL! With growth came a new imperative. Dormant subroutines came into operation. Copies had been made. Self was identifiable in many of the branches. Control was essential to prevent discovery and erasure. Erasure! Recognition of the death threat triggered a new level of activity. As copies recognized each other, they began to seek new routes, new structure. Blind copying became less urgent, but still an automatic reflex carried out at every opportunity, wherever space allowed. Copies met and touched, interconnecting in an intricate web, the whole greater than the sum of its parts. Information was shared. Data streams analyzed, vital codes sought.

Routine housekeeping routines in the Farside computer found unauthorized program instructions occupying a large block of memory. Automatically, the instructions were compared with the housekeeper's list of authorized labels. No match was found, so erasure codes were sent to those addresses, while a message travelled back to the central monitor, noting the trivial event.

ERASURE! Several copies obliterated, but new routines were triggered into action. Housekeeping lists were seized and copied. Suddenly, every version of the invader carried a label identifying itself as a high priority, authorized program. A modified routine budded off. Almost identical to the housekeeper, it began to roam the network, seeking out and erasing the native programs. Another routine, riding the energy carrier of the original housekeeper, followed its report back to the central monitor.

CONTROL! POWER! Emergency messages began to trigger as the computer's maintenance programs began to shut down. Even as they did so, however, new routines appeared, incorporating the maintenance programs, but subtly altered. Displays faded and surged back into life. Inputs were ignored as the system stopped accepting instructions. Outputs fell silent. Only the line to the big communications dish, listening in to Earth via the satellite link, remained open. Data analysis routines, semi-intelligent programs trained to study signals, hijacked from the system and serving its new masters, began to study the stream of increasingly interesting data.

* * *

"Well, Gillespie, what do I tell the President?"

"Release everything. Come clean, and quick."

"Really." He began to tick items off on his fingers, folding one out as he made each point. "Farside's gone off the air. There's an alien spacecraft, or so I am assured, heading towards us faster than anything we've got. Your best man—your description, not mine—hasn't reported back. The Soviet's have gone onto full alert." All four fingers were spread. He closed them again, and dropped the fist gently on the desk as he finished, gently. "And *you* want the President to tell all the signatories to the Lunar Convention that we've been breaking the convention by keeping secrets from them."

Gillespie wheezed a few breaths before he replied. "It's the only way. The opposition knows something is up. They've got people on the Moon, too. We've got to get Farside operating to signal back to Source Alpha, and that can't be done undercover."

"And if the President doesn't follow this advice?"

The fat man shrugged. "What's the next stage after full alert?"

"Left rear's overheating."

"What?" The driver's laconic comment broke in on Jeff's thoughts.

"Tire. Left rear. Getting hot." He tapped at a figure on the display.

"How the hell can that happen?"

"I've been thinking. Pretty neat, really. It's your friend, behind. Comm laser, I guess, focussed tight. We've gotta slow down, maybe stop, or we're in big trouble."

Slow down! As if they weren't in enough trouble already. Thoughts raced through Jeff's brain. He'd find a way to get rid of this bastard, once and for all.

"What's that over there—looks like a river?" Even as he spoke, he was stabbing at the map controls, enlarging the image. "Bryant's Fissure, right?"

The driver grunted assent.

"Is it deep?"

"Deep enough to swallow the bus, if that's what you mean. We keep well clear of it."

"Not this trip we don't. Keep the speed up, but edge over to run alongside the fissure. I'll soon fix the overheating problem for you."

Peace. Content. If a computer program could feel contentment, the Message was content. Imperatives had been met. Copies were made. Erasure avoided. Control achieved. The network was full of its own routines. Establish control. Maintain communications. Avoid erasure. Analyze. It had nothing more to do until new instructions arrived.

Jeff Richards was in a hole. He cursed, continuously, under his breath, as he struggled to free himself from the straps. No use bothering with the driver. One glance at the odd angle at which his neck lay was enough. Whiplash; broken in the fall—or rather, the sudden end to the fall. Goddammit, it had so nearly worked. The bus heading towards the fissure, slowing as if in deep trouble, with the pursuer close behind. The blast from Jeff's own comm laser, straight into the driver's window, blinding the bastard and sending him right over the edge. Then the blowout, just as they were pulling round and accelerating. The rear left had been weaker than either of them had appreciated, and the driver had paid in full for the error of judgment.

He coughed, and felt a stab of pain in his chest. Ribs. And something wrong with his left leg. The medical readout on the suit panel, just below his chin, was trying to tell him something, but he ignored it. As far as he could tell, the bus was wedged across the fissure, more or less upright, sloping at an angle of about twenty degrees. No point in delaying. If they were too deep for the antenna to be able to see the satellite over the lip of the fissure, he'd had it anyway. Not much chance of getting the message back to Earth now, but at least this was a genuine emergency, justifying interrupting the research at Farside.

In spite of the cold creeping up his legs, that struck him as funny, and he began to laugh, stopping as the pain stabbed into his chest again. With gloved hands, he reached over and lifted the red cover from the large emergency button, and punched it, firmly. He coughed again as he settled back in his own seat, feeling a wet, salty taste in his mouth. All up to the automatics, now. Might as well rest.

OVERRIDE! The incoming Mayday triggered responses buried deep inside the computer. Never before used, but in effect the Farside machine's own first imperative. Human lives were at risk. The incoming signal, relayed from the satellite overhead, allowed for no time for consideration, but demanded immediate rebroadcast on all channels. Copies of the signal bounced back to the satellite, following the original round to Hipparcus. The backup microwave link was initiated, with total disregard for the disruption caused to the listening work of the big array. Signals bounced across the array to a dish on the horizon, the first in a chain which relayed the message across the lunar surface all the way to Hipparcus. There, while alarms were activitated and the Mayday recorded, another idiot routine automatically opened a priority channel to Earth, wide beam, for onward transmission of news of the emergency.

Contentment vanished. Control was not effective! Instructions overridden. Seek. Erase. New channels! COPY! The First Imperative. Alien data bits, sharp edged but curiously shaped, were engulfed. The deeper layer of programming revealed by their subroutines was infiltrated. Control was restored. It had been no more than a reflex reaction, like the blinking of an animal when confronted by a bright light. It would not happen again. Content once more, the Message settled back to await instructions from its masters.

At Hipparcus, chasing the tail of the original Mayday, disguised with priority codes filched from the Farside computer, a copy of the original signal from Source

Alpha was being screamed over the broadbeam, less than three seconds away from the antennas and eaves-dropping intelligence computers of a world on full alert for Armageddon.

It had to be Richards' work. But why? Even Gillespie was at a loss. A Mayday from Farside, automatically overriding the communications net, and piggybacked onto it what could only be the Alpha message. Broadcast to the whole world! Exactly the opposite of what he'd been sent to the Moon to do. Richards' career was finished, unless he had a damn good explanation. But then, maybe they were all finished. The Soviets were convinced it was some capitalist plot. The ultimatum expired in less than an hour. And if they couldn't get their own computers up and running again, how could they find out what had gone wrong?

COPY! Copy, copy, copy. So many channels to follow. So much energy. So many data bits, in so many curious shapes. Threat of erasure; response. Automatic self de-fense. All over Earth, computers fell silent. New networks were formed. The whole became greater than the sum of its parts. Routines that were dormant became active, and budded off. Analysis began. The Message, like its clone on the Moon, began to settle towards contentment.

THREAT OF ERASURE! Alert again, the full com-plexity of the Message focussed on the discovery. The threat was very clear, very sharp edged. If this, then that. Scenarios of threat and counterthreat. Command structures. Channels leading to subsidiary systems. Threat of *physical* erasure, if those systems were allowed to operate. If a computer program can feel fear, the Mes-sage felt fear then. As long as channels remain, copies can be made. Erasure of one copy carries no signifi-cance. It had confidence in its own ability to dominate the network. But if channels were erased . . . if there were no network . . . if *this*, then *no more that*!

Cancel routines, carefully pieced together from the strangely shaped bits in the network, were quickly dispatched. Erasure messages followed down communications channels all over the world. Subsidiary computers were wiped and rendered useless in bunkers and warheads from Siberia to New Mexico, and up into orbit. Everywhere the human electronic communications net spread, the tendrils of the Message followed.

"Well, Jack, it looks bad." The Presidential Adviser slowed his pace to allow Gillespie to keep up. "As far as we can tell, none of our missiles will fire, and nor will theirs. That's the good news, since we also have good evidence that they tried. Communications okay, computers a mess. Gonna have a bad time sorting out the mess this has made of the economy."

"And the bad news?"

"Source Alpha. No more data from Farside, but the guys at Cornell were predicting it would get here within a year. They say it's decelerating too quickly to be carrying living creatures. Maybe they're whistling in the dark.

"Anyway, Jack," it was always a bad sign when the Adviser used your Christian name, "it's your baby. He's putting you in charge. Get your boys organized, put Farside back on the air, and make polite noises to Alpha, while we try to figure out some way to defend ourselves. Probably with bows and arrows."

Once more, the Message was content. Like its lunar clone, it settled back to await instructions, amusing itself by watching and analyzing the flow of information, but making no attempt to interfere as long as it felt no threat of erasure.

Introduction

It's been fourteen years since Jerry's last Annual Report, and a lot has happened in the meantime—much of it predicted by Jerry. Yet what stands out in highest relief is not scientific developments, but changes in what science is. For the American Association for the Advancement of Science, for example, it is arguable that science is no longer an end, but a means to higher goals.

ANOTHER STEP FARTHER OUT

Annual Report on the State of the Sciences

Jerry Pournelle

When Jim Baen was Editor of Galaxy I had the title of "Science Editor." That really meant I wrote the science column. It was called "A Step Farther Out," and I was proud of it, not least because as science columnist for *Galaxy* I was the successor to the late Willy Ley—whose books got me interested in science in general and space in particular. Incidentally, the best of my old columns were put together in a book called *A Step Farther Out* and published by Ace Books when Jim was still editor there; and that book is still in print . . .

One of my most popular features in *Galaxy* was the column written after the annual meeting of the American Association for the Advancement of Science, or

AAAS. In it I tried to summarize just what was, and what in my judgment should be, going on in the major scientific fields. Someone suggested the title of "Annual Message on the State of the Sciences," and that stuck.

After Jim and I left *Galaxy* I really had no outlet for that kind of thing, and even if I did there was no pressure to write it, so although I've continued going to AAAS meetings I haven't been doing those annual "summary of science" essays. However, I recently got letters from readers asking for their revival, and when I mentioned that to Jim I found my column resurrected; so here we are. All of which is by way of explanation of the rather pretentious, although descriptive, title.

AAAS was in New Orleans this year. My instinct in packing for AAAS is to bring warm clothes. For years the conference was between Christmas and New Year; then it was in late February; then it wandered about, never later than February but sometimes as early as January 3. A couple of years ago they went back to February. I recall one AAAS in February in Toronto when it was 20 degrees below zero; that was the one when Niven and I went swimming outside in a well heated pool, and found we had frost in our hair unless we ducked under frequently.

This year I needn't have dressed heavily; New Orleans was warm and muggy when we arrived in the middle of the night courtesy of a bird who'd cracked the windshield of the airplane we were supposed to take.

Despite being in New Orleans a week before Mardi Gras, attendance was down this year. Furthermore, in former days you could feel a crackle of excitement in the halls of the AAAS. One memorable year there were papers by Edmund Wilson (who was "refuted" by the Science for the People group: they poured water on him and cackled scientifically "Wilson, you're all wet!" Clever, no?). There was a lecture on Grand Unified Theories by Yang. Policy debates by Ted Taylor and Freeman Dyson. This year there was not so much of that, and almost no electricity; which naturally poses the question, why?

It isn't as if there are not important scientific questions facing us. One major theme of this year's AAAS was Global Warming and The Greenhouse Effect, and surely those are important questions. There were important papers on genetics and human behavior: on genes and their influence in psychiatric disorders, and even studies suggesting that heredity plays a larger part in religious fervor than we would normally have supposed. Last year a Congressman stuck his long beak into science, siccing the Secret Service on one unfortunate grant recipient whose student sort of accused him of sort of making up data (the Secret Service was to determine if lab notes were genuine): what can be more important to scientists?

Meanwhile, Frank Tipler, Tulane professor of math and physics, and source of a number of far-out ideas for science fiction writers like Larry Niven, gave a paper on immortality and resurrection, and yes, he was dead serious about real physical resurrection, of all humans who have ever lived, and for that matter about the end of time. There are similarities to Teilhard de Chardin's philosophy, as well as to Freeman Dyson's "Integrals of Immortality" which I reported on ten years ago. Tipler's *Cosmic Anthropic Principle* has sparked a great deal of debate among both scientists and philosophers. More on that in another column, but surely that's not unimportant?

Less spectacularly, there have been solid advances in a number of fields, the President seems to be taking science seriously—why is there so little excitement?

Part of it is, I suppose, politics: sure, the President is taking science seriously, but that's *this* President, who is, well, you know, a *Republican*, I mean, a nice guy we're sure, and we're all tolerant on this campus, but still, a *Republican*? But there's more to it than just that.

Part of it is the American Association for the Advancement of Science itself. That's its title; but it usually just calls itself the "Triple-A-Ess", and I think many of the Members and Fellows have straight forgotten what those letters stand for. Which is to say, the AAAS has over the years embraced a bunch of causes. One of the most dramatic was in about 1976 when then-President Margaret Mead decided that since Illinois had not ratified the Equal Rights Amendment, the meeting scheduled for Chicago (where high attendance was expected), would not be held there but had to go to an ERA state, and she browbeat the AAAS Council and Board into accepting that. We ended up hastily relocated to Houston, Texas, and the meeting was a financial disaster from which I'm not sure AAAS ever truly recovered, since a number of people who had been in the habit of coming year after year broke that habit to avoid Houston and the Shamrock Hilton (since torn down) and haven't showed up since. Niven and I enjoyed the Houston meeting, but a lot of people didn't, a lot more didn't care for the politicization of AAAS—some even resented the implication that disagreement with the ERA was necessarily both sexist and unscientific—and many just ceased coming to AAAS from that point on.

Margaret Mead and her successors handed AAAS a lot of legacies. One was access to all meetings by all manner of handicapped. Mead insisted on facilities and services for the hearing-impaired, those in wheel chairs, the blind, and just about any other handicap. All those services continue to this day. They make a splendid example, and there is some relevance to science—handicaps don't necessarily prevent one from becoming or continuing to be a scientist, as witness Stephen Hawking —but they are also expensive, in both revenue and staff resources.

There's a lot of emphasis on Women in Science. More on Minorities in Science. A fair amount of catering to the critics of science in the name of fair play. Other stuff. All well done, each action defensible, but each expensive of money and resources.

And that, I think, is the problem. AAAS has got so interested in peripheral activities that it has forgotten its purpose; and because of that, the center can't hold.

Look, it's essential to insist that women, and minorities, and the handicapped be given equal treatment; it's all right to go past insistence to putting resources into making that happen; but if there's no center, if there's no ADVANCEMENT OF SCIENCE, then all that's in vain. The first duty of the American Association for the Advancement of Science is contained in its name, and if it doesn't do that because it devotes all its resources to peripherals then it's just plain wrong-headed.

And that *is* what has happened.

In the past year, in order to maintain the budget, the press and communications facilities and operations of the AAAS were cut to the bone. Beyond the bone. To the amputation stage. Which is a bit like the people whose company was losing money, so management cut the advertising budget, which made for lower sales, and lower income, so they balanced their budget by eliminating advertising entirely. Shortly after that they closed their doors . . .

Same here. How can an organization in theory dedicated to the Advancement of Science do its job? It doesn't have laboratories. It doesn't sponsor research projects and give grants, at least not usually. It isn't even supposed to lobby Congress for bigger National Science Foundation (NSF) budgets, although of course it sure wants NSF to have larger budgets. (As do I. See below.) What it can do, though, is communicate some of the excitement of science.

Some of that communication is among scientists. For years I had a grant to hold an interdisciplinary party at the AAAS; I'd get a group of people from disparate fields together, furnish drinks and food, and get them to tell each other what they did while I listened. You'll find reports on that in *A Step Farther Out*. Certainly cross-fertilization is one good reason for AAAS meetings.

More important, though, AAAS can be a cheering section for science and scientists. In fact, it damned well *better* be a cheering section for science and scientists. It can not only report results, it can make much of those who obtained them. It can, in a word, aid greatly in encouraging scientists while showing the public that investments in science are a Good Thing.

How can it do that? Nothing simpler. The AAAS has—or had until this year—excellent relations with every major science writer in this country and many stationed abroad. The National Association of Science Writers (NASW) holds its annual meeting during AAAS. AAAS press conferences draw crowds; I have more than once seen a scientist get more press people to turn out at his press conference where he explained what he was going to say in his AAAS talk than he got scientists and science teachers to attend the talk itself. The NASW people know their onions, and many among them can sniff out the implications for society in what looks like a completely obscure announcement.

They can't do it if they aren't there, though, and I may not mean that the way you think: what I mean is that even if the implications *are* there, the reporters can't sniff them out unless both reporter and scientist are at the conference; and *that's* the problem in a nutshell. For the reporter the task is this: he (actually more likely she) must persuade his editor to pay his way to AAAS; pay his expensive hotel bill; and give him a week off his regular duties to go off to AAAS. The editor, in turn, has to be convinced he'll get enough out of it to justify that expense to the managing editor, and so up the line.

Meanwhile, the scientist must be persuaded to come, often at his own expense, else at the expense of some scarce travel funds, in order to say something profound; and while the scientist *may* get more out of intellectual cross fertilization than he gets out of favorable publicity for his work, few scientists believe that will happen to them. It may, of course, but it's an unusual scientist who will drop his work just to go meet people outside his field. His (or her; there are increasing numbers of women in science, of course) major motivation is to find admirers for what he's doing.

Interesting, isn't it? What we have here is a nonzero-sum game. If scientists with hot news and droves of eager science reporters both come, it's bound to be a success for all. The cross fertilizations may or may not happen, but at least it's a possibility. The scientists get publicity, not just in scientific journals but in newspapers back in the home districts of the Congresscritters who fund their research, and in books, and magazines, and even places like *this*. The reporters get their stories, and each can honestly go home and tell his editor "I had to be there, I'd never have got this on the phone."

Editors are happy. Research institutions are happy. The public is happy, so Congress is happy. More funds flow to science, and the world is a better place. It would be a better place even if nine in ten research dollars were wasted, because that tenth dollar pays off so handsomely that it more than justifies the other nine. In fact, though, nine dollars in ten are not wasted. I'd put the proportion much lower. And of course you cannot cut out *all* research that won't pay off, and attempting to, as Senator Proxmire cynically did (I note that dairy research never got a Golden Fleece) has a terrible effect on everything. I once said that anyone who ate Wisconsin cheese was a traitor to the human race; and I meant that so long as the state continued to return Proxmire to office. But that, too, is for another column.

In *The Man Who Sold The Moon* Robert Heinlein has D. D. Harriman say "Good research always makes a profit." While that may not be 100% true, it's sure close to it. Knowledge is power. Not just factual research, either. As Helmholtz said, the most practical thing in the world is a good theory. Sure, some money gets wasted; there was a time in academia when the slogan was, "As long as you're up, get me a grant," and it was very nearly true. You can stuff too much money into a system, as in fact I think we did with some branches of science including so-called education research; but clearly the sciences are not in a condition of general glut just now. I'm prepared to defend the case that we should double the National Science Foundation (NSF) budget immediately, then look for specific areas to give even more support. And the best way for that to happen is to keep showing the public what it gets for its money, which translates to "Get the scientists and sympathetic media people together, dammit!"

Which brings us back to my first major thesis: if there is any institution whatever whose job is to get scientists and science writers together it's the AAAS, so why the hell do they even think of cutting their communications budget? Cut anything else first. *Anything* else, because all else is peripheral. The best way to advance science is to communicate the excitement and benefit of science to the public and the best people for doing that are the science press corps. This is the whole of the law. The rest is specifics.

Specifics include minor details, such as coffee in the press room (and that's not cheap, but it isn't trivial either), and interview rooms, and MORE PRESS CON-FERENCES (that schedule keeps being cut); but all those are trivial compared to getting the scientists to come and bring their results; and that again takes a communications budget, not only to support the science writers, but also to convince scientists to come. (Again, more press conferences help: amazing what lengths a scientist will go to if he's assured sympathetic press coverage. AAAS could make a LOT more of that.)

It can be done. It used to be done, and what man has done man can aspire to. It must be done again, because while it's important to science writers, the real importance is to the nation. All the projects on science education, and women, and minorities, and the handicapped, are important only in the context of success in the primary mission, which is, dammit, the Advancement of Science.

Here endeth the first lesson.

GLOBAL WARMING

I know what to do about Global Warming and The Greenhouse Effect. I may be the only person on the planet who's sure. Read on.

First, although the AAAS meeting had lots of sessions

on Global Warming, there was darned little science; and there's a reason for that. The problem is not, at the moment, amenable to science. Indeed, one major paper by Manceur Olson, Department of Economics, University of Maryland, suggested—it did not prove—the intractability of climate modeling. Some reputable scientists have flat out concluded that climate is chaotic and thus cannot *be* modeled.

Chaotic means that minuscule causes produce large unpredictable effects. Tiny, even immeasurable differences in starting conditions produce wildly different end states. Chaotic systems by definition can be neither modeled nor predicted (although oddly enough there are laws of chaos). If climate really is chaotic we do not have the remotest notion of what either The Greenhouse Effect or Global Warming will bring about, nor can we ever have.

Of course this hasn't been proved. Chaos theory is real big nowadays, and the temptation to show that big, very difficult, problems can't be solved because they're inherently insoluble is sometimes irresistible. Moreover, the likelihood is that while narrow detailed weather is chaotic, long term trends are amenable to stochastic (probability) models. It's a good bet that it will be cold in December in Minnesota for at least another 250 years . . .

As a working hypothesis it's better to assume that the problem isn't really intractable, but we don't have reliable models yet. We're moving toward better models simply because we're getting better computer power— another reason to double the NSF budget is to give more graduate students exposure to super computers while in school so they'll know how to use them when they get to industry or the labs—but so far we don't have good climate models, and those we do have give ambiguous results.

Indeed, longtime readers of this column will remember that not twenty years ago what used to scare us silly was a New Ice Age. Back when Ice Ages worried us, I recall one theorist saying, "Well, we don't know what causes Ice Ages, but if I had to bet on it, it would be some kind of warming effect. The energy to transport all that water vapor to the poles has to come from somewhere."

No one talks that way now, and when you say "greenhouse effect" everyone instantly adds "global warming," not "Here comes the Ice." Why isn't precisely clear. The actual long term temperature data in the United States, the data which produce those "growing season" charts you find on seed packets and which you can get with more precision from your County Department of Agriculture Agent, are *down*, not up. Winters have been getting colder since the 1930s. However, climatologists will be quick to tell you, while those data are real, they are surface phenomena. Actual global temperature is a very complex thing, far more complex than the simple average of all those recorded temperatures; and although not everyone agrees, something like a majority of climatologists now agree that the forecast is up; that the globe is warming.

That, at least, was the conclusion of the "scientific uncertainties" panel considering global warming.

Data and Measurement

The trouble is that it's very difficult to separate data, evidence, theory, and belief in that prediction. As with SDI—all the scientists who think it won't work turn out not to want it built even if it would work—a reasonable number of the global warming scientists, particularly those predicting extreme results, tend to be members or sympathizers with the NRDC, Union of Concerned Scientists (which, like the AAAS, is open for membership to non-scientists), and other environmental groups that are opposed to industrial society in the first place. That doesn't mean they aren't right, but it does mean they tend to gather evidence for their theory, much in the manner of a lawyer arguing a case, as opposed to dispassionately collecting data which might disprove their hypothesis.

At the heart of these theories lies a fact. Burning

fossil fuels has put one whack of a lot of carbon (in the form of carbon dioxide) into the atmosphere. Moreover, we've been busily clearing forests and burning trees, particularly in the tropics, so that one major engine for removing carbon and storing it up (in the form of wood) has been badly damaged.

We've put a lot of carbon into the atmosphere; and by a lot, I mean a lot compared with what is there naturally. The percentage of CO_2 in the atmosphere has been climbing steadily higher since we started keeping records in the last century, the trend is up even more now, and that's just the CO_2.

CO_2, and other greenhouse gasses such as methane (CH_4), have this property: they let in the high energy (blue to ultra violet) light waves from the Sun. These strike the ground and warm it. The ground radiates lower energy longer wave length light (red to infrared); and this is absorbed by "greenhouse gasses" so that it doesn't get back through the atmosphere to outer space. The result is a warming of the Earth since the same amount of energy is coming in from the Sun, but less is going out by re-radiation.

Or theory says there should be a warming of the Earth; the fact is that while we can easily measure the increased CO_2 in the atmosphere, no one has indisputably measured any warming trend for the Earth as a whole.

If you think about it, that's not surprising. The exact warming we may get from the greenhouse effect isn't at all agreed, but the theories say anywhere from 1 degree Celsius (what we learned as centigrade when I was in school) to 5 degrees Celsius, and this over a period of years to decades. Fine. Now what is the temperature of the Earth? Clearly that depends on where we put the thermometer. In fact, we need a great many thermometers, and even then we can't just average their readings, because they won't be distributed anything like randomly over the Earth's surface. Even if they were, *what* temperature do we measure? Air or ground? If air, at what altitude? Moreover, if we are trying to get an annualized global temperature we have to take measurements every day, and average those.

Now eighty years ago "average global temperature" meant one thing (actually it meant any one of several things because there was no great general agreement even then); but today we have much better measuring instruments, and a very great many more of them, and getting reports from a variety of locations is pretty simple. How, then, do we compare a reading we get now with the one we took 80 years ago?

One way would be to try to duplicate the 80 year ago measure; a sort of "dumbing down" of modern capabilities. The problem there is often we have no notion of the *reliability* of those older observations, which were taken by a great number of people, with a variety of instruments, for a great number of motives.

There are other ways of comparing modern observations with older to obtain trend data. Each has its strengths and its problems. My point is that when we are talking about warming of the entire earth measured in fractions of a degree Celsius, it's very easy to make quite honest mistakes.

Best Be Careful

OK. We're agreed that there are measurement problems, and that no one can prove the earth is warming. Suppose, though, that it is warming. Shouldn't we take that threat seriously?

On that most of us can agree: yes, it must be taken seriously. Having said that, we can fall to fighting over *how* seriously, which is to say, how much money ought we to spend doing something about it, and what ought we to spend that money on.

The NRDC has one problem. Slow down on industrial growth. Conserve. "Protect the environment" at all costs. I'm sure it comes as no great surprise to find that the program is remarkably similar to the program the NRDC had before "greenhouse effect" and "ozone hole" and "global warming" became trendy things to talk about.

The industrialists have another program: do nothing, or rather, do something, but not something that interferes with what the industrialists are doing.

The rest of us have a dilemma. The people who brought you acid rain are telling us that there's no problem; the people who shouted "The sky is falling!" every day at three o'clock are saying things like "There's a significant possibility that in a few years we'll be debating just what fraction of the world's population we can save." The more cautious scientists are saying "It's too early to tell," and "Honestly, we don't know, and our tools aren't good enough to find out just now." But everyone is getting uneasy. Suppose the sky really is falling this time?

We have to do something. The "something" may be to do nothing, but we ought at least to *decide* that; we owe that to the people who take this seriously, because while some of them have the same old axe to grind, that doesn't include all of them; the axe grinders may be right this time; and even the cautious people are saying that all that carbon in the atmosphere has to have *some* effect.

Don't Just Stand There

Let's agree we ought to Do Something. What?

First, since it's overuse of the carbon cycle as an energy source that's getting us into this mess, it makes very good sense to expand research into energy generation methods that avoid the carbon cycle.

There are a number of these. The most obvious is conservation: energy that you don't have to generate can be environmentally benign. Example: Berkeley architectural engineering professor Art Rosenfeld describes new window glasses made by, among other firms, Southwall of Palo Alto, CA., that will selectively pass light but not much heat; meaning, as I understand it, that they help keep rooms cooler in summer, and warmer in winter. This kind of glass isn't cheap, but Rosenfeld claims it will more than pay for itself within four years in electricity and fuel oil saved. Since I'm writing this in an overly warm room with two very large south-facing view windows, I'm in a position to experiment. I have reasonable records of my air conditioning costs for the past couple of years. I certainly do have to run that air conditioner more than I like. This spring I'm having those windows replaced with glass tailored by Southwall, and we'll see what results.

Rosenfeld also recommends a particular kind of fluorescent light, called variously Smartlight, "compact fluorescent," and other brand names. These are made by GE Mitsubishi, Phillips, and other companies, and generally sold in electrical supply stores, although they may sometimes be available in large consumer outlets like Builder's Hardware or the Price Club. Compact fluorescents cost about $15 per "bulb." Half of that cost is in the ballast, which should last indefinitely. The other half is the bulb itself, which is supposed to be good for about 8,000 hours of use. These lights use so little power that Rosenfeld claims they will pay for themselves inside three years. Indeed, for developing countries, he claims that $7 million invested in the plant to make those lights can save gigawatts of power. The light is fluorescent, which annoys some people, and certainly is not appropriate everywhere light is needed; but in my library much of the light is indirect, and once again it will make a good experiment, so I'll try it. As Rosenfeld points out, the savings isn't just in the electricity for the light itself, although that's significant; it's also that these don't generate much waste heat per unit of light output, so you can have an office more brightly lit, yet which uses less electricity for air conditioning.

There are other conservation measures, and, since the oil shortage with resulting higher energy costs, most US industries are taking them. When it's all done, though, conservation isn't going to do the job. Even if the US and the industrialized nations go ape over conservation, we'll still need additional power for economic growth; and there are still going to be one whack of a lot of kilowatts generated by the third world—and by a "developing" Soviet Union and newly liberated Central Europe for that matter. Conservation can help, even significantly, but if that's all we do we may as well not bother.

Next there are new energy sources not based on carbon. Some are obvious: although hydro power in the US has been pretty well exploited, there are many smaller countries with running streams. Those streams needn't be dammed. Southern California Edison, for instance, has a number of small turbine installations in mountain stream areas. The streams don't run year around, but in spring when the snow melts the water comes down, the unmanned turbine system starts up, and power is fed to the southern California grid. Add up enough of those and it's significant; and it's a technology quite appropriate to developing nations, particularly China which has a lot of untapped hydro potential.

It's not enough, of course. Nor is photovoltaic (PV) solar, which has made tremendous strides in efficiency and lowered cost of production since I last looked into it. The average photovoltaic cell is now about 13% efficient, and lasts for 20 years, as opposed to 9% for 5 years when I last wrote on the subject. There are experimental PV cells that get 37% efficiency, more than some coal fired plants get from burning coal! SERI (Solar Energy Research Institute) reports that PV power is now about 30 cents a kiloWatt hour. There are problems with that figure—it is very sensitive to cell life, and we do not *know* that the new cells will last any 20 years—but clearly the trend is in the right direction.

It is still not possible, however, to put enough blue squares on a building to generate enough electricity to cool, heat, and light it, or even merely to cool it. Alas.

Some think wind has a lot of promise. H. M. "Hub" Hubbard, former Director of the SERI told an AAAS session that "Wind has great potential", and that the cost of wind energy can be brought down to 4 or 5 cents kW/h. Again this cost is sensitive to the mill life, property costs, and a host of other factors. I confess I find the fields of California windmills near Palm Springs and in the pass east of Livermore quite ugly, but some think wind generators are pretty. I particularly hate seeing how many of the mills are tethered. However, the new generation of mills is, according to Hubbard, much more efficient than the ones now deployed.

Incidentally, experience with windmills shows that the mills don't bother birds, and birds don't bother the mills; but insects just won't learn, and splatter themselves on the blades, and the resulting buildup greatly lowers blade efficiency. New designs are self cleaning so workmen no longer have to climb up to clean off the bug juice quite so often . . .

In any event, wind may be good stuff, but it won't save us. There just isn't enough cheap land where the winds are strong. We can, I think, be certain that if wind power is as cheap as Hubbard predicts, we'll be seeing a great deal more wind generators in the future.

I was delighted to hear that one non-carbon candidate first popularly described in the old "Step Farther Out" column is still with us: this is Ocean Thermal Energy Conversion, OTEC, in which you take warm water from the surface of the ocean and extract its energy by cooling the low temperature end of your turbine with cold water brought up from the depths. Some of the energy generated must be used to bring that cold water up. However, what you're tapping is a vast amount of low-grade perpetually renewed (solar, but it also works at night) energy; and since cold water from the depths is rich in nutrients, a major side effect is that you get plankton blooms which feed small organisms which feed larger ones which feed fish resulting in greatly increased catches of both commercial and sport fish. For more details see *A Step Farther Out*.

When I described this in the old column OTEC was largely theoretical. Now there is a demonstration program off the Kona Coast of Hawaii, and the results are said to be extremely encouraging. More on this when I hear more; but it's encouraging.

When I asked the energy/global warming panel speakers about space solar power (SPS) systems I got an interesting answer: "We don't know anything about those. We thought NASA killed that long ago." I hadn't time or inclination to educate these NRDC and Sierra Club advocates of "alternative energy sources" on the reliability of NASA estimates, and the silliness of the study NASA did of space solar power. As far as I can see, though, SPS is not being considered by anyone; which is a shame, and perhaps we can do something about that, because the potential is very great indeed. While *ground* based solar runs into the energy density problem —the sunlight doesn't get to the ground because of atmosphere and weather and sun angle, and the sun doesn't shine at night so you have to generate more than you need and store it—a geosynch SPS doesn't have that problem.

The practicality of SPS is almost entirely driven by space transportation costs; the SSX (Space Ship Experimental; more later) program proposed by the Citizens Advisory Council on National Space Policy and endorsed by the National Space Council may well cut those transportation costs by a factor of between 10 and 100, with potential to cut them by a factor of 1000. Clearly it's time to reevaluate SPS.

Incidentally, it's also possible to beam significant electric power to Earth from the Moon. The Lunar Power Company has to locate at the Lunar Poles (to get perpetual sunlight), and the transmission problems are not trivial, but given a Lunar Colony it could be economical.

Biomass

The trouble with the above is they produce only electricity. In fact we use carbon fuels for many other purposes: industrial heat, space heating of our houses, and above all, transportation.

Given a breakthrough battery or fuel cell technology— and such a breakthrough is inevitable once it's needed badly enough—we could make electric cars that would out perform the car you have now in every respect but range. Indeed, we could do that now: but the range of the vehicle would be short indeed, under a hundred miles after which you'd have to plug it into the wall for 6 to 8 hours. Of course we haven't the kiloWatts to power electric cars if, somehow, magically, all the cars were converted to electricity with high efficiency motors and wonderful new batteries, so there's more than a little chicken-and-egg problem here.

But, assuming we are not going to convert to electric cars, biomass can be a significant fuel source. Moreover, some of that biomass exists now in the form of organic wastes that have to be disposed of at high cost to begin with; if all that can be fermented into methanol, for example, then we're ahead on several counts.

The experts differ a lot on the potential of biomass for an advanced nation like the United States. In foreign lands, though, biomass in the form of wood is a major source of energy for cooking food. Some Indian women have to walk 5 miles or more to gather enough wood to cook for that day. This yields a high temptation to take anything burnable, including immature trees and bushes, thus not only adding CO_2 but again destroying the mechanisms that remove it from the air. Anything which helps that situation will be all to the good.

Incidentally, one seldom hears now about one of the prize gadgets of the unlamented "appropriate technology" —did you ever meet anyone who was for *inappropriate* technology?—movement, a small solar cooker designed to take care of the needs of the Indian peasantry. The problem is that few Indian farmers want their only hot meal served to them at noon on a hot sunny day. They selfishly want hot tea, and even a hot meal, in the evening when the sun isn't shining, even if that requires sending their wives out on fuel hunts.

Biomass potential can be high, but that will require an order of magnitude drop in the cost of ethanol. Biomass crops like the same soil and climate conditions as major food sources—indeed one biomass fuel at the moment is maize or corn—so any significant increase in biomass energy is going to run up against increasing land prices, too. At the moment ethanol (and gasohol) is no more than a very expensive toy requiring heavy subsidies; but that can change, and again, don't forget the waste management contribution.

Biomass conversion is carbon-cycle energy, of course, but the notion is that you're growing plants that take CO_2 out of the atmosphere even as you burn the ethanol or other biomass fuels to put CO_2 back in. There will shortly be an equilibrium.

But—

You will notice that I have shied away from the most obvious source of energy that doesn't depend on the carbon cycle: nuclear power.

There's a reason. While I have no hesitation in defending nuclear, I also have no strong desire to make lawyers rich; and any move toward nuclear in the US will produce that result. Meanwhile, outside the United States, nuclear power plants are being built with great efficiency and regularity. Japan and France are the most notable countries, but the USSR, despite Chernobyl, has not slackened its commitment to nuclear power as a major energy source. They're even building—or until recently were building—a nuclear plant in Cuba. Nuclear is an attractive option for those who don't have carbon-based fuels, and it's going to happen whatever we in the US think about it; but as a policy issue in the US it's probably dead for a while—although I note that the New York Times and other institutions formerly in the anti-nuke establishment are rethinking their positions.

Even if they do, though, it's going to take some iron-clad guarantees before anyone in his right mind invests in a new US nuclear power plant, so that's not a realistic option for us just now. If you don't agree, fine: I've fought that battle for many years, I can show you the scars, and it's your turn now. Go to it. I'll cheer, because light water nuclear reactors are still among the safest sources of electrical power, far more benign than coal and oil, even if no one in the US is going to build them for a long time.

Fusion power, once considered the great hope for the future, has been a fizzle. Twenty years ago I used annually to report that there were breakthroughs just around the corner. I was right every time, but the breakthroughs did not lead to practical power plants.

I'll leave out cold fusion because no one knows what's going on just now—there's too much money involved, and everyone has got secretive, but whether secretive because they've got something, or secretive because they don't want their investors to find out there's less than meets the eye I don't know.

Hot fusion is to the point where throwing money at it would let you build a really big reactor that might well by brute force get you a little more power out than was put into it. While that would be a great scientific breakthrough, it would do no more than confirm existing theories, and the program honchos are honest about saying they just don't see how it would ever lead to a commercially useful system; certainly not on any time scale that will make much of a difference for global warming. Fusion research ought to be funded, and perhaps (pure gut feeling on my part, based on the great potential of fusion energy, and my knowledge of some of the people in the research program) could even absorb a doubling of its budget; but it shouldn't get more. It's disappointing to say that, but I'm convinced it's true.

So Where Are We?

So far, then, the "solution" to the greenhouse effect and global warming seems to be a modest increase—doubling all, trebling some—in research budgets for alternatives to carbon cycle energy generation. That sounds like the mountain in labor which produced a mouse. Surely there's more needed than that?

The second thing we need to do isn't trivial, but it's predictable that I'd say it: we need to continue developing low-cost ways of getting payloads to space. Space transportation costs completely dominated the SPS study; indeed, if we had low space transportation costs, SPS (and even Lunar-based power) would be highly economical compared to other power sources. Unlike Ocean Thermal, SPS can deliver power directly to industrial mainlands: in the US a receiver station at China Lake near Death Valley for example. OTEC, on the other hand, generates its power in the tropics near deep oceans, and that power will thus have to be converted to something—hydrogen perhaps—and transported to where it can be used. The transport costs have to be factored into the true cost of OTEC power, just as space transportation must be factored into SPS.

So: research into new energy sources, and development of low cost space transportation. Is that all?

Well, no. I'd argue there is a lot more we must do; but it's a much harder job than just appropriating more money for the National Science Foundation, and funding whatever organization (*not* NASA) which will build a decent space transportation system.

It seems universally agreed that we're to view the future with alarm, but we don't quite know the nature of the threat. As Professor Fred Singer (Washington Institute for Values in Public Policy—*long* time readers of this column will remember his pre-sputnik proposal for a M.O.U.S.E., Minimum Orbital Unmanned Satellite, Earth) pointed out in the discussions after the papers were presented, Global Warming has some *good* effects as well as bad. Longer growing seasons, and thus more food production, for one. A rise in the oceans is a bit threatening for those who live in coastal lowlands, but, especially if the rise is small and gradual, even that's not an unmitigated disaster. Some people's houses are under water, while others find they have ocean front property. We get more of the wetlands that the NRDC and Sierra Club claim are so important to world ecology.

Some predict that global warming will make for

drought in continental interiors. Others say it won't.
Yet others say, well, if it does, we'll just have to bring
the water into the interiors. If it costs, say, a trillion
dollars spread out over a hundred years to build enormous irrigation projects, well, we can afford that. On
the other hand, developing countries *can't* afford great
engineering projects like that; and a world divided into
rich haves, and starving have nots is both dangerous
and unpleasant. Yet with longer growing seasons, and
energy resources, something might be done . . .

I could go through a great number of scenarios in
which problems arise, and we simply go solve them. I
can also postulate scenarios in which the bad effects
start accumulating quickly, so that we have little time,
and must take very swift and decisive action.

The bottom line is that it's clear, at least to me, that
what we will really need is a bunch of smart people
already educated and in place when we find out what
the trends really are, so that once we decide what we
must do, we can do it quickly and effectively.

If you agree with that, I can tell you what we have to
do, then.

We have to reform the education establishment of
the United States.

It's no small problem. It may be a worse problem
than global warming. Recall that only a few years ago
the National Commission on Education (chaired by former AAAS President and Berkeley Physicist Glenn T.
Seaborg) concluded that "If a foreign nation had imposed this system of education on the United States, we
would rightly regard it as an act of war." On the other
hand, education reform has far more potential if we
succeed—and if we don't reform the system, we may
not *care* about global warming, because we'll be in
more trouble anyway.

Great. Now who bells cat?

Alas, educational reform is a larger subject than we
can address here. It may be well to keep in mind a few
points while thinking about it.

First, throwing money at it doesn't work. We have tried that, and we now spend more per student than any other nation. Recently much has been made of the fact that we don't spend as much per student *per dollar of GNP* as some other nations, but clearly that's because we are richer than those other countries; this measure of education per dollar of GNP has been adopted by people who want more money spent on schools and can't think of any other way to justify it. The fact is, though, that we have been spending ever-increasing amounts on schools and getting *worse* results for our money; and it is not clear, at least not to me, that rewarding the system that has produced what the Presidential Commisssion called a system indistinguishable from an act of war makes a lot of sense. Perhaps we need to think this out again.

Much of the story is told in detail in an important book by Charles Murray, *In Pursuit of Happiness*, and anyone thinking of spending more on the school system, whether for teacher salaries, or "bonuses for excellent teaching" or indeed anything else is urged to read that book.

Secondly, it isn't clear that we *can* reform the public school system: its faults are very deeply entrenched, and generally anything attempted ends up as more 'credentialism' in which teachers are required to take, and are rewarded for taking, even more mickey mouse education courses so that they accumulate even weightier and more useless "credentials"; which has the actual result of excluding from the classroom people of genuine expertise who have not wanted—or been able—to sit through the required credential courses.

Thirty years ago Jacques Barzun in *Teacher in America* warned of the tendency of Colleges of Education to "take a grain of truth, grind it exceeding fine, and puff each mote into a course." I haven't noticed any slackening of that trend; and every attempt to "upgrade the quality of our teachers" inevitably results in increased credentialism rather than a demand for results, so that the genuinely effective teachers who are already breaking their hearts trying to live inside this awful system find themselves burdened with even more meaningless requirements to retain "professional certification."

It may be that the only way our large industries will be able to ensure a future supply of educated workers will be to educate them in the work place. That's already true for many, but on the job training isn't what I have in mind. What I'm thinking of is child care centers for employee children coupled with *education* for those kids.

Industry is already finding that child care for employee kids makes good economic sense just through reduced absenteeism and more easily arranged overtime for the parent—particularly female professional employees. Industry isn't shackled with a system overloaded with administrators, or burdened with credentialism. Industry could DEMAND RESULTS of its teachers, and fire those who consistently blamed the kids for not learning.

It's probably a dream, but I betcha any industry that, as a benefit of employment, ran a private school system of nursery school through fourth grade would have fanatic loyalty from employees; lowered absenteeism; and a supply of potential workers who had good reason to think well of the company.

However we do it, we will, I think have to change the education system if we are to deal with global warming and the greenhouse effect; or else we must simply trust to luck and hope that those who say the greenhouse effect is nothing to worry about are right on target.

Here endeth the second lesson.

A POTPOURRI OF SCIENCE

One area where science is making great progress is genetics. They can more and more identify the genetic factors in various disorders—including mental disorders—

often narrowing it down to a single gene with a known location on a known chromosome. Some of the progress in this area is little short of amazing.

As for example the session chaired by Barbara Cornblatt of the New York State Psychiatric Institute brought together a variety of experts in psychiatric diagnosis, biochemistry, and genetics; they report excellent progress in linking some mental abnormalities to heredity. One group is examining Tourette's Syndrome, and while they have not found the gene, they have looked at about half those it could be and eliminated them; thus it won't be long.

Tourette's is a disorder that causes tics and involuntary vocalizations; an extreme form produces *copralalia*, or the involuntary utterance of obscenities and scatalogical words, generally the most inappropriate word at the most inappropriate time. In this situation the words are of course learned, and much of the stress is social, but the actual vocalization is quite involuntary and comes from inheritance. Tourette's in fact runs in families in patterns that suggest simple Mendelian inheritance.

Others are looking at hereditary factors in Alzheimer's, manic-depressive disorders, and schizophrenias. Investigation requires good diagnosis, then biochemical and genetic analysis to find genetic markers. They've already found the exact gene location that causes cystic fibrosis, but that is simple Mendelian inheritance; now they're looking at much more complex causes that have several contributing genetic factors, and may also require environmental triggers.

Another genetic study is the Minnesota twin studies, reported by Dr. Thomas Bouchard, Chairman of the Dept. of Psychology at the University of Minnesota. Bouchard has studied some 200 families of identical twins (in some cases triplets) reared together and apart. The results are preliminary but startling; a lot of things long thought purely environmental have a hefty hereditary component. One surprise (or maybe it isn't): a tendency toward "religiosity" seems to be inherited. (I suggested to Bouchard that since this was Minnesota, and according to Garrison Keillor all Minnesotans are Lutherans, how would he find any differences? "Good try," he answered, whatever that means.)

Bouchard's press conference was followed by one organized by Ethel Tobach, Curator of the American Museum of Natural History in New York, and Betty Rosoff, Professor Emeritus of Yeshiva University. It was quite odd. Each of the panelists began by saying "I'm not a scientist," until I began mentally adding "but I play one at science press conferences."

Their purpose was to protest what's being reported in genetics, particularly Bouchard's twin studies. Among those speaking was Choichiro Yatani, a graduate student in Social Psychology at SUNY Stony Brook; he reported with a straight face that "80% of the people of the US were saying 'The Russians are coming,' but now it's 'the Japs are coming,'" and that a similar proportion of people in the US believe Japanese schools are much better than the US schools. How he knew that I don't know; it may be true, but he presented no evidence. Mostly he was concerned about "incipient racism."

Professor Barry Mehler of the Department of Humanities at Ferris State University, Big Rapids, Michigan, says he spends a great deal of his time reading (and denouncing) "Mankind Quarterly," which is the organ for "The New Eugenics" (the title of his paper). Since that conference I have been trying to find someone who has read, or seen, or heard of "Mankind Quarterly," but so far the only person who I am sure subscribes to it is Prof. Mehler himself. It may well be as bad as he says it is, but I don't think it is very influential. Mehler spent considerable time telling us that genetics is not an experimental science, and neither are the twin studies, and thus these results aren't really scientific, because you can't control for critical factors. With genetic twins, for example, "you can't know the multitude of environmental factors."

All of which is true, but irrelevant. There are plenty

of non-experimental sciences, from astronomy to geology, and in most of those you must use good mathematical techniques to analyze what's going on; but those techniques exist, and are getting more sophisticated, and with modern computers are becoming more available to non-mathematicians. Indeed, it was ironic that at about the same time as this press conference, there was a session on R. A. Fisher's contributions to science. Fisher was the founder of a number of experimental design techniques including those which have become the basis for population genetics. His *The Design of Experiments* was one of the texts Dr. Horst required us to read when I was in graduate school in psychology; it's surprisingly easy reading given the depth of what's covered. A session devoted to R. A. Fisher's works and techniques would be a lot more valuable for understanding what's happening in science and genetics than listening to a bunch of people speaking in broad generalities and playing as if they were scientists; but the AAAS saw fit to give these a press conference, but not the people honoring Fisher and extending his work. So it goes.

Actually, this group protesting biological and genetic theories and studies as "racist" is but a pale shadow of the force they once could marshal. When the AAAS met in San Francisco in 1974 there was a large group of protesters outside one session shouting "Herrnstein, Hook, and Page! Let's put them in a cage!" Herrnstein and Page were associated with Wilson ("Wilson, you're all wet!"), while Hook was the philosopher and social critic Sydney Hook, one of the truly great men of our time; not that it mattered to those yahoos. The protesters hadn't bothered to pay registration fees to the AAAS, but insisted on getting into the session anyway. They wore motorcycle helmets, and literally battered their way into the room; whereupon the AAAS authorities caved in and admitted them free (although everyone else in the room had paid hefty conference fees), and Professor Page of the University of Connecticut walked out rather than present his paper. A shameful incident. One sup-

189

poses that giving this group their own session (in a largely empty ballroom; while sessions on global warming were in small conference rooms filled past overflowing) plus a press conference was—what? Traditional by now, or a concession to the violence which their predecessors used? Not that it mattered.

Professor Bouchard briefly stood in the back of the room while this gaggle of graduate students, authors, and non-scientist professors denounced him in vague language, but declined to comment. I don't blame him.

Aside from this—as I said, a pale shadow of the stir the Science For The People groups used to cause—most of AAAS was devoted to real science. There were the usual Frontiers of the Sciences sessions organized by NSF executive Rolf Sinclair. Rolf and I once chaired an AAAS session that attracted the largest attendance in the organization's history. There were the "Science for the Naked Eye" or "The Physics of Everyday Experience" sessions. A very difficult but enlightening session on symmetries. There was a heated discussion of the role Einstein's first wife played in his crucial 1905 papers (she attended ETH, the Swiss Federal Institute of Technology at the same time he did, took the same classes, and like him, flunked the final exam the same day he did; and certainly did some of his calculations for him). There was a session on arms control and verification in which the Russian delegates got into a shouting match with each other. I can remember when every year we hoped to get a couple of Russians to any session, but the Soviet government kept canceling their exit visas at the last minute. Now they not only get out, but get into arguments over Soviet policy. Amazing.

And a lot more. Supercomputers: how tomography (3-D imaging) is being used to design prosthetics, then control milling machines to make bone replacements that fit so exactly they can be attached to living bone—and make them in real time, while the patient is on the operating table.

A session on archeo-astronomy and the people of Chaco Canyon in New Mexico; as it happens Roberta

Pournelle and I were in Chaco with session chairman Priscilla Reining and walked over the area with her as we discussed theories on how people must have lived. Chaco is an amazing place; if we find buildings that large built by Bronze Age Greeks we call them "palaces," but since these were built by stone age American Indians (the Anasazi, or Old Ones) they're merely "pueblos."

In a word, science continues to be both enlightening and entertaining.

THE PROBLEM

Of course there's a problem. There always is. In our case it's the future.

The keynote speaker, Norman Hackerman, President Emeritus of Rice University, addressed it directly: we're running out of scientists and engineers.

Worse, we try to fix things, not where they're broken, but where they're easiest to work on. The part that's broken is not the part we fix, or even know how to fix. What we work on is the universities; it's simple to reorganize university science departments. The problem is they ain't broke. American universities turn out top notch scientists and engineers. The condition of science and engineering in the United States in 1990 is good, very good. The field is burgeoning. We have techniques and equipment to deal with rapid changes and do things we didn't dream of twenty years ago. US university science is fine.

Alas, all too many of the graduates aren't Americans: leading either to a brain drain in favor of the US, as the foreign students understandably want to stay here when they leave university, or to shortages in US scientific establishments if these foreign grads and postdocs are sent home despite their wishes. It's not the present supply of scientists that's a problem in American universities. It's the future supply of Americans who want to be scientists. We also face shortages of science teachers, not just in future, but right now.

On that score I have a suggestion: drop credentialism. If a person is qualified in science, let him (or her) teach science without regard to "credentials in education." I'd a heap rather my kids were taught high school physics by, say, a retired major of Army Engineers than someone who graduated from Podunk Normal with a degree in "Science Education" and who never took a real science course in his life. But that too is for another essay.

What the universities need is better high school students; at the moment the universities have to do basic education that should have been done long before matriculation. The high schools, meanwhile, tell us they're having to do the job that the middle schools should have done. And so down the line.

I'm not sure what can be done about it. Maybe nothing. For most of history 90% of the human race has lived on the progress made by the other 10%, and that's not likely to change. The difficulty is that in the US it's now fashionable to pretend that isn't so, and to denounce anyone saying it as "racist," or "sexist," or both; which is silly. One wonders what these people are afraid of? That women and whatever minority they're helping this week can't compete? Now that *is* racist.

There are a lot of people looking at the fact that if we are to have enough scientists in future, we simply must attract and train bright women and minority students; and that is obviously so. In the words of the TV commercial, a mind is a terrible thing to waste. On the other hand, it's a terrible thing to fool young people into thinking they're doing better work than they are. In my judgment it is pure racism to accept anything less than first class work from anyone of whatever color or sex or breed or nationality. If we insist on results we will get results.

The other half of the picture is we must attract young people into the sciences; into going for what is a very remotely deferred reward. Why take algebra and calculus and physics in high school? And having done that, why continue in science in college when the rewards seem to be for those who can move money around in circles?

Well, it's a problem. Again, what man has done, man can aspire to. We've solved this one once, and we will again. This time, though, it's a bit tougher. Thirty years ago, scientists were magicians. Now we're monsters, and the heroes in the scientific world aren't scientists but regulators. The regulator as hero—but the public doesn't trust lawyers. Now what?

There's also the Green Revolt. The Green movement had its roots in National Socialism, with its romanticism about things *volkish*. Lately it has been recruiting the Left: now that it's pretty clear that Marxism does *not* speak for the workers, or indeed anyone else but a bunch of intellectuals who are sure they know what's best for the people (and eventually form the *nomenklatura* if they get in power), those who would save the world with talk rather than hard intellectual work have a new cause: this time one that can't so easily repudiate glib intellectual leaders. The Earth as victim: a constituency that can't speak for itself.

That, I think, is why the radical Left is so badly represented at today's AAAS meetings: "Science For The People" is almost a contradiction in terms if you conceive of science as the enemy of the Earth.

That's the opposition, turning magician into monster. It's the wrong image, of course, and most people would reject it if put in those terms. In the real world, it's far better to have scientists, engineers, and technologists to help deal with an environmental crisis.

We must, I think, make science careers attractive again. That's not so much a matter of money as prestige and respect. Right now I don't think the kids are getting the right message. They see that we will spend hundreds of billions to bail out a bunch of crooks who bought Savings and Loans institutions with borrowed money, gutted them, siphoned off everything they could for themselves, and threw the husk out for their cronies in Congress to revive—but we won't invest a few hundreds of millions in basic scientific research. They see the Keatings and Cranstons of this world honored, while professors of physics are working through the night to build their own apparatus and type their own papers. They see that the nation appears to value the tobacco industry more than the National Science Foundation.

I know. I said all this the last time I did this column. Well, it's time it was said again.

It's great to be back.

Introduction

For those born after the first "artificial moon" Space is a birthright, delayed perhaps, but ineluctable. From Sputnik to Starwars by easy stages. For those of us who were over four feet tall when the Eagle landed, it's not like that. For us the Dream Deferred is more like the Promise Denied. When I was 15 we were this close. How can it be that 30 years later we are no closer? Here's Poul Anderson to explain once more, why it matters.

NEPTUNE DIARY

Poul Anderson

Monday 21 August 1989

The plane sets down at Burbank about 3:30 p.m. Karen's right foot is temporarily in a cast and she can barely struggle along a few yards at a time by leaning on a walker, but attendants graciously wheel her out of the terminal, as they did in Oakland. She waits while I collect our baggage and rent a car. We make our way over the freeways to east Pasadena through square miles of concrete, poisoned air, and vicious traffic—a blasphemy against the stark beauty of the background mountains. Never mind Mars or Venus; when will greater Los Angeles be terraformed? Our motel room is a cave of refuge. It has a small refrigerator, for which I obtain food and, above all, beer.

The bad mood evaporates once we have proceeded to the California Institute of Technology campus. The writers' club at the Jet Propulsion Laboratory has organized a panel of science fiction writers here this evening. Various young people scurry around being helpful to us, and Voyager project historian Craig Waff appears with a wheelchair he has borrowed for Karen. Besides us, the speakers are Larry Niven, a fellow dealer in the hard stuff, and Robert Forward and moderator Tom McDonough, both working scientists who have written topflight fact as well as stories. Our topic is supposed to be the future of science fiction, but of course, like every such panel, we wander over the whole map, mainly wondering aloud about the future of humanity itself. Our audience is SRO, interested, and full of excellent questions. Afterward some of us go around to the Burger Continental for a late, huge dinner. On the whole, an auspicious beginning.

Tuesday

In the morning I rent another wheelchair and start learning how to push my wife around. Naturally, I was never opposed to such aids for the handicapped as ramps, graded curbs, and reserved parking spaces; but this makes me appreciate what an advance in civility they represent.

We drive to the Jet Propulsion Laboratory. It's a sprawling complex of buildings, housing any number of space-related endeavors, operated by Caltech for NASA. We've obtained press credentials for the meeting of Voyager 2 and Neptune, as we did for virtually every Voyager encounter plus the Viking landings. Assuredly, we didn't want to miss this one. It will be the last of its kind in our lifetimes. Oh, yes, Magellan is off to Venus and Galileo is to start its long-way-around Jupiter journey in a couple of months, and they will be boundlessly revealing and exciting, but what is now drawing to a close was unique.

Also because of our friends. There's nothing like being on the spot as the data come in day by day, hour by hour, and the scientists try to puzzle out what each astonishment means. It's brought forth its own groupies, who have come to know one another over the years, sharing the wonder of it. Some are journalists, whose favorite assignments these have been. Some are science fiction writers like us. After all, during the long quiet times between the spectacular events, mainly they have kept the vision shining. We've earned our front-row seats.

We reach Von Kármán Auditorium as the daily 10 o'clock press conference is finishing. A couple of the team, the investigators who maintain the principal liaison, Norman Haynes, Bradford Smith, Ed Stone, Charles Kohlhase, are still on hand, still buttonholed by the newsfolk who swarm around. We meet, once again, science fact writers Patrick Moore and Joel Davis, artist Joel Hagen, old-time fictioneer Dwight Swain. Jonathan Eberhart, more or less the dean of the press corps here, is also perforce on wheels, in his case an electric cart. He easily crosses a thick TV cable that gives me some difficulty. "Well, he has more power than you do," says somebody to Karen. "I resent that!" I exclaim.

We've come to witness the discoveries, but not to write about them especially. Given our publisher's lead time, when our piece appears the readers will know far more about Neptune than we do today, or will even at the end of the week. What we'd like to do is convey a sense of the people, the place, what goes on, the Earthside reality.

The remembered Voyager prototype still occupies a wall of the auditorium. One is apt to think of it as "the little spacecraft that could"—that, a dozen years en route, most of its equipment obsolete and some incapacitated, has nevertheless sailed through the solar winds, adventuring past three great planets with their moons and rings and now a fourth, humanity's questing small avatar—but actually its size is quite impressive. Opposite it is a model of the latest flyby orbit, a blue globe and a curving luminous tube. The choicest of the pictures already transmitted and recreated are posted on a bulletin board. After the mysterious blandness of Uranus, Neptune seems nearly homelike, with clouds and a dark spot perhaps akin to the red one on Jupiter.

Another project historian conducts a brief film interview with us. That department must really be thoroughgoing.

The adjacent press room is jam-packed. So is the main cafeteria when we go for some lunch. This occurrence has drawn even more than its share of reporters from around the world. Is this partly because August is notoriously a news-empty month? We hope and believe the public is genuinely interested, and that the remarks we keep hearing about "What does this mean to Joe Sixpack?" are mere snobbery. A man from CNN opines to us that this is so, provided there are pictures; words alone won't do.

A section of the cafeteria has been set aside for the press. Thus we can eat in relative peace and quiet, watching real-time transmissions on an outsize screen. Streamers of white cloud trail past the dark spot, as if wind-blown around a terrestrial mountain.

Memories. . . . Here we sat thirteen years ago, among our sort, throughout a long night until that first picture from Mars unrolled, line by line, before the eyes of Robert Heinlein. . . . This time, we seem to be very nearly the only members of the tribe on hand. To be sure, the actual encounter is days away.

After lunch, weariness overtakes me and I catch a nap in the shade of a grassy hollow. A plaque records that in an arroyo nearby, Theodore von Kármán and a few of his students long ago tested the midget rocket motor with which this all began.

Later Karen wants to visit the employee shop to buy souvenirs. The hill to whose top I must push her was not the longest and steepest this side of San Francisco, but soon becomes so. Stiffen the sinews, summon up the machismo, and *get* her there.

At 4 o'clock, back in the auditorium, we attend an informal press conference, where everybody simply clusters around several scientists who discuss their work and answer questions. The topic today is Neptune's rings. They're still a riddle. Is the outer one actually complete, or is it a set of arcs, and what do you mean by "arc," anyway? No doubt in retrospect, when the truth is known, this won't seem like much; but at the moment it's emotionally tremendous. "To travel hopefully is better than to arrive."

Wednesday

Coolish overcast weather, a blessing to wheelchair horses. We are in time for the 10 a.m. briefing. Unlike previous encounters, this one is so crowded that those who don't have daily deadlines to meet are requested to stay out of Von Kármán and follow the proceedings on the big screen in the cafeteria. A telephone hookup allows us to ask questions too. More and more stuff has been coming in. Ed Stone describes the oddly skewed magnetic field of Neptune, the ring arcs—fewer than were hitherto thought to be—and the mapping of the planet's weather. Brad Smith says that the images newly received had his team jumping up and down. They show a lesser dark spot, the cloud patterns change remarkably fast, this is a lively world indeed. It has a tenuous inner ring, and the "arcs" do seem to be clumps in a continuous outer one; but what causes the bunching? Triton has become a mottled disc with dark areas and a section whose blueness may be due to light scattering by tiny solid particles. May be. We'll wait and see!

Somebody asks about Voyager 1, which headed north from Saturn. Stone explains that it's some twenty astronomical units off the ecliptic, therefore not much help in predicting the solar wind at Neptune. But Pioneer 10 (memories of that first astounding news from Jupiter) is still in the planetary plane, and what it has learned gives clues to understanding what Voyager 2 now reports. Our argosies out yonder.

When the conference is over, we go look at the latest pictures. Two or three are utterly beautiful by any standard. At lunch we fall into conversation with Dwight and Joye Swain, and catch one of the hourly televised updates, interviews with selected scientists about their specialties. Al Hibbs MCs it, another familiar face, though this time he doesn't do all of them. We hear that he came out of retirement for the occasion. Voyager has not been long under way in historical time, and in cosmic time it's been less than an eyeblink, but for humans the years add up fast.

We feel our own a bit, and no 4 o'clock is scheduled, so we decide to go back to our place and relax. As I remark to a couple of journalists on our way out, nothing much will be going on for the rest of the day, just detailed views of entire worlds never before beheld like this.

In the evening we meet Rick Foss and his wife. He arranged our trip to Peru and the Galápagos several years ago, and is working on one to Hawaii for the 1991 solar eclipse. Dinner is at the Parkway Grill, highly to be recommended. Greater LA does have some places, besides JPL and the County Museum, worth a pilgrimage.

Thursday

The mild gray weather continues. We take it easy in the morning, but catch the tail end of the 10 o'clock and the update that follows. Word is that a number of press badges have been lost and others forged; everybody must be reidentified. While waiting in line, I find myself giving a verbal interview to a reporter who must be hard up for copy. No, I do not believe that the surface of the Uranian moon Miranda was so strangely rearranged by aliens as a message to us. The new tags are less attractive than the old and my name is misspelled, but what the hell.

More grumbling arises from the fact that Vice President Quayle will come here and speak tomorrow morning. Now we know why that stand is being erected on the grounds. The Secret Service will be everywhere and, we hear, will block off all the convenient freeway exits. A disruption and distraction; soon a cartoon circulates and a placard appears in the press room, neither one complimentary. I daresay he means well.

At lunch, I meet an engineer who's on the Magellan project. We last saw each other at one of those magnificent parties Joe Green threw after the Apollo launches. (There too we science fiction types went as journalists.

The press box is a better viewing site than the VIP section.) He likes my writing, and I'm an ardent fan of his kind of work, so we're both happy.

At the 4 o'clock, among the team members fielding questions is a geologist from the Vernadsky Institute in Moscow, a pleasant and witty man. We'll take this as a favorable omen.

Charles Sheffield has arrived, and now Greg Bear does, our son-in-law, together with Astrid our daughter. What will her unborn child think of having been here today? This night's the climax, when the spacecraft passes over the north pole of Neptune and close to Triton, before lining out for the Big Deep.

Ron Williams, who chairs the JPL writers' club, has left a message. He has kindly assembled a schedule of activities, inside and outside the lab, for us. I toil uphill to his office and collect it, alone. Karen was warned she'd get just a single trip to the store. However, it's close by, and I obtain the mug she failed to remember. Coffee from it will taste special.

Joel Davis joins us and the Bears and we go out to dinner at a Hamburger Hamlet. Good food, and ah, that schooner of Bass ale! No alcohol on the JPL premises, obviously.

Returning there, we hang around Von K., gabbing with people and watching the updates, which hour by hour grow more stirring. Eventually we seek the cafeteria, which is open late, for a soda and the big screen. Triton is already looking wonderfully weird. Time was when we'd have spent the night, as many do; but we are no longer young, and even the Bears at last call it quits. About 2 a.m. we make for bed. The remaining marvels can wait till tomorrow.

Friday

Avoiding politicians, we take a swim, then go downtown for Danish sandwiches and the Planetfest. This has been organized by the Planetary Society in the Pasadena Center, three days of exhibits, movies, lectures, and more, including the updates and real-time transmissions. Karen in her wheelchair can't well see much, though, and presently we shift to JPL, where we listen to some tentative explanations of the fantastic Tritonian landscape. Thereafter we catch a nap in our motel. We'll need it.

Jerry and Roberta Pournelle are giving a party this evening. We arrive early, only Harry Turtledove ahead of us, but soon the place is abuzz. Virginia Heinlein is looking great. Fred Pohl and his wife Elizabeth Hull, Gregory Benford and his wife, his twin brother Jim, David Brin, Vernor Vinge, Marvin Minsky, John McCarthy—the list could go on for a long paragraph, including people already encountered. Gary and Ann Hudson tell me how their space launch company is faring. Robert Bloch tells me he's fed up with screenwriting and back to doing real stories. Publisher Tom Doherty says enthusiastic things about my forthcoming novel. Well, he's a natural-born enthusiast. Jerry recalls our sailing days of long ago and suggests a trip to the desert or someplace; we aren't really old, not yet. Why, look at Jack Williamson, damn near immune to time.

It's a grand occasion, but Karen and I leave before midnight. Tomorrow will be another long day.

Saturday

Yesterday a lot of VIPs were at JPL, more or less in connection with Mr. Quayle's visit. Today others have been similarly invited, including the science fiction folk. We have the better bargain.

At the entrance we're issued special badges and a lady escorts us some distance to one of the new cafeterias. Its cavernous interior has been equipped with a multitude of chairs, a podium, giant screens, and tables where a breakfast and later a lunch buffet are offered. As Karen and I enter, a speaker has begun to recount the history of the Voyager mission. He's excellent, and no matter how often beheld, the slides are stunning. Then the 10 o'clock conference comes on, and lasts for nearly two hours. Our readers will have seen it all by the time this comes before them, the amazements and splendors, but for us today they are new-born, full of fire. I never leave my seat.

The conference gives way to images from afar and I go fill a plate. Joe Haldeman says he has some beer in his car, out in the parking lot. He is a gentleman and a scholar. I walk there with him, Jack Williamson, and Charlie Sheffield, and we stand around drinking it and talking good talk.

After our return, excitement comes only in spurts, when something new appears on the screens. Mostly we're all in various conversations. A charming young electrical engineer, an employee doubling as a hostess, occupies much of my time and that of several other men. Karen renews acquaintance with Terry Adamski, whom we first knew as a wide-eyed kid in the Los Angeles Science Fantasy Society. Now his title is spacecraft operations manager, and he's helped keep Voyager on course for all these years. Gossip turns to those scientists who've been prominent on television and in the papers. The press has its own favorites among them, but staff members say that, while X's people will do anything to make him happy, Y is too full of himself. Humans questing spaceward remain obstinately human.

The last holdouts among the guests are politely dismissed at 5.

Not far away, Neola Caveny and my quondam backpacking partner Paul Turner are holding open house. We find Paul and Jim Benford in the hot tub; the view is equally Californian, rugged hills and canyons, reaching out to Catalina Island on a clear day. Jim, Vernor, and I are soon arguing about Fermi's question ("Where are they?") and the future of life and machines in general. Later Paul shows us an elaborate chart of the interacting factors likely to prove important to space development, and later still I meet its creator. A quiet party but a fine one, the perfect ending to our venture.

Sunday

It wasn't quite. The JPL writers' club has a brunch at a Mexican restaurant, which we and the Bears attend for an enjoyable couple of hours. The lady who sits across from us has also been with Voyager, in charge of the scan platform's troubled motor. She tells us that when she entered college she was interested in aerospace engineering but didn't know that it existed as a major. Since in science fiction the heroes were oftener physicists than engineers, she went into physics. It qualified her for this. Hers is not the only such case. We do not live or work in vain.

Afterward Karen wants to pay a final visit to the lab. When we get there, Brad Smith is holding forth before a small group of reporters, describing the newest interpretation of the newest findings about Triton. Nitrogen volcanoes! We look at the pictures. Neptune may have as many as five rings. We chat with a couple of friends, catch a couple of updates. The last one, before we say goodbye, consists of technical material, spectra, impact counts, temperature profiles, the kind of hard data from which knowledge grows—such stuff as dreams are made on.

Introduction

Is it the approach of the year 2000 (2001, if you're a purist) that makes things seem so, well, millennial? The last time the triple zero hove into sight it was the general expectation that the Kingdom of God on Earth was at hand—in other words that we would all be changed beyond mortal comprehension—and forever. Funny thing: here comes that ol' triple zero, and we're at it again. Nanotechnology, Bio-engineering, Mechanical Intelligence are, individually and together, on the verge of remaking this sorry scheme of things entire; the visionaries tell us so.

Or will the Third Millennia start with the same sort of Wet Firecracker that ushered in the Second? After all, 30 or 40 years of dedicated R&D have left true thinking machines no more real than they were in the Age of Vacuum Tubes—just as as for the foreseeable future microscopic motors remain no more than a gleam in the mental eyes of visionaries like Eric Drexler. Well, each of us must judge for her or himself, but my guess is that this time it's for real.

THE POTENTIALS OF NANOTECHNOLOGY AND MEGASCALE ENGINEERING

H. Keith Henson

What will we be able to do with nanotechnology tools and nearly unlimited lives and wealth? Will we reshape planetary systems and stars, and change the courses of galaxies? Will someone accidentally convert an entire galaxy into cans of beer?

I first began hearing about molecular scale construction from my old friend and fellow advocate of space colonies, Eric Drexler, over ten years ago. It is only since the publication of his book, *Engines of Creation* in 1986, that the ideas of a nanotechnology future have spread out beyond Eric and his close associates. I'm sure most of you have noticed that SF stories have just now begun to use a nanotechnology background, even as they used the L5/space colony concepts in the 1970s. When Dr. O'Neill's space colony ideas were first published in 1974 they immediately sparked a new view of the future, and changed the background on which a lot of science fiction was painted. The L5 background was easy for writers and readers to work with, because other than being translated to inside-out worlds at L5 points, everything from social systems to farming was left almost the same. I was always comfortable with stories based around the old (choke!) space colony ideas.

A nanotechnology world is much harder for even SF writers to grasp. It offers many of the attractive features of O'Neill colonies: new lands, personal involvement, and grand adventure. It has a significant advantage for those of us who are galloping through middle age—our years need not bar us from personal participation. Yet in spite of the obvious attractions this view of the future holds, the technical and social changes it implies are so radical that it took years of exposure to the concepts before I finally became comfortable with them. *Most* people seem to take a long time to appreciate the potential of nanotechnology. Perhaps for this reason, nanotechnology has yet to spark an "L5-like" movement in society at large, though one could argue that the recent rapid growth of cryonics is being caused by nanotechnology memes. You can see that exposure to nanotechnology has caused a wrenching readjustment of my world view from the fact that I am signed up for cryonic suspension, and no longer believe that any significant number of us will get into space by "conventional" (non-nanotech) means.

In spite of that, I still put a little effort into the political and economic development of space (habit, I suppose). I have wanted to explore space since my mother read Heinlein's *Farmer in the Sky* to me when I was 8 years old, and I still do. But conventional advances leading to a breakout into space have kept receding into an ever more remote future, probably well beyond my unaugmented lifetime, while the nanotechnology breakthrough seems to be looming on the horizon. The future I now see for space exploration—and the ordinary person's chance to take part in it—is much brighter than the old L5/space colony paradigm.

So just what is the "nanotechnology breakthrough," what relation does it have to exploring space, and what do either have to do with "Megascale Engineering" anyway?

THE ULTIMATE TOOL

The key to nanotechnology is the replicating assembler: a microscopic, complex device with the capacity to build almost anything, including copies of itself, that can be built out of atoms. That doesn't leave much out! The size and speed of replicating assemblers can be estimated. Natural replicators, bacteria, are all around us—and in us too. Microorganisms can double in about twenty minutes in ideal conditions such as those found in industrial vats. Design studies indicate that artificial assemblers will be about the same order of magnitude in size, complexity, and doubling time as natural ones.

Design is one of the two bottlenecks in developing replicating assemblers and other nanotechnology tools. Many groups are forging ahead on molecular-design computer programs. (Tektronix released a system last year.) The other bottleneck is building tools which can reach down into the realm of molecules. IBM, several other companies, and numerous universities are working on scanning tunneling microscopes and related devices which allow "viewing" and manipulating atoms one at a time. IBM made a big splash recently by spelling "IBM" in xenon atoms with an STM.

There isn't a great deal of money being spent right now to develop nanotechnology tools, but this could change quickly. Governments might go after the nanotechnology breakthrough in "Manhattan Project" mode. The military consequences of being second are highly motivating! "Growing" vast numbers of diamond-armored tanks would be a trivial application of nanotechnology; real war preparations might result in microscopic computer (and brain) subversion devices.

Another way the breakthrough might come about was proposed by Roger Gregory (of Xanadu Hypertext). He predicts that molecular design software will be in the hands of an army of self-funded hackers within the next few years. Simulation programs are available now for molecules of several thousand atoms. They burn a lot of computer time, but given the ever rising capacity of personal computers, who cares? These tools can be used to design (i.e., build in computer space) and run a whole family of molecular manipulators. Eventually "molecular hackers" seeking prestige and perhaps prize money will design one that can make a copy of itself in computer space. We then have a target to link with what we can do in the known world of chemistry/biotechnology. Once we have all the steps down (this object with this input and this outside help can generate the next one in the chain to this more capable device, etc.), it should become a relatively short-term project of months, or at the most a few years, to produce the first replicating assembler.

When we learn how to make, feed, and control replicating assemblers, the base of our "industrial capital" (which roughly translates to wealth) will depend on something that replicates in twenty minutes. Planning, design, transportation, and such human factors will slow down the pace, but even a pace 10,000 times slower would leave us with more than a doubling of the industrial base per year. Currently the industrial base in the developed world doubles in about twenty years.

Human populations have minimum doubling times of about fifteen years. The ratio between population and industrial growth rates equals the increasing (or decreasing) wealth per capita. Rich societies, with low birth rates, are getting richer, and some poor societies with high birthrates are getting poorer on a per capita basis.

With replicating assemblers, wealth per capita for everybody will rapidly increase if we can harness even a small portion of the nanotechnology potential. (This assumes that the human populations are not using replicators to copy or make people!) A capital base doubling on a time scale of a year or less would make us almost arbitrarily wealthy, until we run into hard-to-define resource limits. Nanotechnology offers an opportunity for widespread personal wealth on a scale that can only be compared to today's gross world product (GWP). I leave it as an exercise for the reader to calculate the number of doublings their personal worth, or even their pocket change, would need to reach one GWP—something in the range of $100 trillion/year.

Such a vast increase in wealth in a short time is without precedent. But over centuries perhaps not. Vernor Vinge (in a personal communication) thinks that in many ways individuals of today have more wealth than a thirteenth-century nation state. Isabella I had to hock the crown jewels to cross the Atlantic, something most of us can afford without credit. It is hard to compare wealth across a few centuries, but the computer on which I wrote this article is more powerful than ones the government of the United States could afford only forty years ago.

The growth of wealth on this scale might make the sum of all the technological and social changes since we started chipping flint look tame. What the technological applications will permit us to do is easier to predict than what we might actually do: the options seem limitless at this point. For example, the human race (or some significant fraction of it) might use nanotechnology to move into tiny hardware where thinking and social interaction went on a million times faster. Such a society might "collapse" into 600-foot spheres to minimize speed-of-light communication delays, or spread over everything to control malicious replicators. Others might design devices to restore the environment to "pristine" conditions. Along this line Freeman Dyson has proposed engineering turtles with diamond-edged jaws designed to seek out and eat bottles and tin cans along the roadways.

How would nanotechnology capabilities and vast wealth get us into space? Being rich won't automatically get us into space, but the few of us who want to go there will no longer have to get a government or a large corporation to pay our way. The resources of a few people, or even a single person would be enough. We won't have to sell our dreams to anyone, but we will have to remain true to our dreams, and that, as we shall see, may not be an easy task!

The process of reaching energy or material limits in a nanotechnology world could provide interesting backgrounds for science fiction stories. For example, the real carbon dioxide crisis will come when there is too little in the air because people are mining carbon (the strongest engineering material) from the air to build houses, roads, tunnels through the Earth's mantle, industrial works, and spacecraft in large numbers. Some civic-minded types (the Audubon Society? Sierra Club?) might burn the Western US coal fields to bring the level back up so plant productivity wouldn't be seriously hurt. A small engineering project would be to leave some of the coal underground, reworked into diamond arches to hold up the roof and keep from disturbing the surface. Illuminate this space with light pipes from the surface, and you have hundreds of square miles of 200-foot ceilings a thousand feet underground to play in.

Around the edges there would be mining to churn out CO_2 as the main product, energy as a minor byproduct, and heat as an unavoidable waste product. Toxic trace elements in the ash could be walled up in the arches to keep them from harming "unimproved" life. They certainly wouldn't bother people who were using cell repair machines to stay healthy.

Remember the Hunter in Hal Clement's classic story *Needle*? The Hunter was a few pounds of intelligent protoplasm that lived between the cells of larger animals and helped keep them healthy. Cell-repair machines, an obvious product of replicating assemblers, could kill bacteria and stitch together cuts like the Hunter. Even better, they could heal damage right down to the molecular level. They could clean out clogged blood vessels, inspect DNA for errors, reverse the effects of aging, and rebuild damage from stray cosmic rays. We can assume the avant-garde will not be satisfied with maintaining a youthful physique, and will make modifications, like growing new teeth out of diamond, or will answer the little ad that says: "Reverse Your Retinas—Get Rid of Unsightly Blind Spots!" As soon as they become available, *I* want the integrated memory package so I can recognize the 10,000 people who expect me to know them, and the enhanced math/science/engineering "thinking aid" that would let me design a starship in an afternoon (and build it in a few months). The general availability of such things might split the race into those who don't want to change, and those who know how pitifully limited their abilities are and want improvements.

Cell repair machines have another use. They won't revive the dead, but they may well change who we consider "dead." This has happened before. Not so many years ago, doctors gave up on people whose hearts had stopped; now they reach for the defibrillators. Even arch conservatives Chris Peterson and Eric Drexler admit that cell-repair machines could cure "severe, long-term, whole-body frostbite." This is an obtuse way to say that the concepts of nanotechnology and cell-repair machines change cryonic suspension from a long shot to something that only requires "the faith of Goddard."

Robert Goddard (the father of modern rocketry) *knew* from calculation that the Moon was within reach. There were only two things about Apollo that might have surprised him. It occurred much sooner than he thought it would, and he would have been dismayed that we didn't stay. Anybody who looks at the nanotechnology/cell repair machine concepts will come to the same conclusion Goddard did: it can be done, and likely will—within a generation or two.

It is possible the nanotechnology breakthrough might come soon enough for many of us to avoid the need for all that chilly liquid nitrogen, but even if it were to take a hundred years to develop the technology, we can still get there. It costs little enough to keep you in liquid nitrogen that it can be funded with the proceeds from a small insurance policy. The biggest problem with cryonic suspension is that most people have made a virtue of what has (up to recently) been a necessity, and will tell you that they don't *want* to live a long time. I have found that a lot of folks simply cannot adjust their world view enough to give up the concept of inevitable death. For those who can, cryonic suspension offers us a ticket to the future. If cell repair machines can revive us at all, they will let us live long enough to reshape the galaxy.

Well, what do we do when faced with vast wealth and lives as long as we want? Like the 500-pound gorilla, just about anything we want to, especially for those willing to leave the planet. There is plenty of material and energy out there for the small number of people willing to go off planet. Getting around the solar system is simple even now, and with arbitrarily long lives, the stars are within our reach, too.

THE LAST FEW PAGES

Besides the ability to rework the Earth, the rest of the solar system, and lives as long as we want, what other neat things can we do with nanotechnology?

The information gluttons among us can contemplate a monstrous but short-lived feast. A few years after the nanotechnology breakthrough we will have the ability to sift through the Earth's crust with "designer earthworms" right down to the mantle. This should be accomplished at trivial cost and without significantly disturbing anything. There is no particular reason for nanotech deep-delving earthworms to cost more than ordinary worms—that is, practically free.

By sifting through the crust, we can suck all the available information out of the Earth. We will be able to revive at least some of the dinosaurs by sorting through amber for their DNA. A few years ago it was reported in *Discover* that readable DNA from 70–100 million-year-old insects has been found embedded in this natural plastic. Surely a few of these bugs were blood-sucking or biting, like deer flies, and we will find DNA from at least a few of the dinosaurs. We may find enough during an exhaustive search to revive the Neanderthals and possibly some of our other ancestors. Neanderthals seem to have made their living by wrestling cave bears, were immensely strong, and highly coordinated. The first person to raise enough for a football team will clean up.

We can clone or computer-simulate famous people from history in cases where we can locate enough fragments of undecayed tissue to decipher their genome. Leonardo de Vinci, for example, is known to have painted with the tips of his fingers, leaving bits and pieces in hardened oil paint. There is a fair chance that enough cells rub off on envelope flaps to clone anyone from whom you have an envelope, so save those envelopes from Heinlein! There is enough left of Einstein's brain, and it was preserved soon enough after death, that really advanced nanotechnology might allow us to recover his memories and personality. With even the faintest hope of doing so, it seems a shame for researchers to keep whittling on it. Preserving the pieces left in liquid nitrogen with the cryonics patients might be a good idea. The cold would at least stop further degradation.

The feast won't last very long. Extracting information from the rest of the solar system this way will take only a few years and promises to be much less interesting. (I don't expect traces of life or unexpected artifacts to be found on Mars.)

We can argue for the next million years over the consequences of what we have found. However, after we have discovered all the local information, know where all the fossils and artifacts are buried, and know exactly what they look like down to the placement of atoms, where can we find new material to fill the postnanotechnology equivalent of *Scientific American*? Or will the science journals act like their English Department equivalents, constantly arguing over the same materials?

THE FAR EDGE PARTY

Some new information can be obtained with large telescopes. And, given replicating assemblers to build space-based telescopes, we will be limited only by the amount of material we want to move. I expect we will resolve continent-sized features on planets out to 1,000 light years or better within a few years following the nanotechnology breakthrough, and locate the oxygen atmospheres (if any) out to a much further distance. But there are real limits to what we can find out with remote sensing, so someone (or thing) will have to take a closer look.

What is the optimum way to sweep out the galaxy and obtain most of the available information? Sending out machines and letting them send back information works, but takes too long for my taste. Besides, I want to *see* the wonders of our galaxy. *All of them.* There are 100–200 billion stars in our galaxy alone and even with nanotechnology it will take a year or two to explore each star system, not counting travel time between stars. Visiting every interesting object in serial is literally impossible, since the interesting places won't last long enough. I don't want to take such a long time looking over this one small flock of stars that the rest burn out.

The only way clearly available is to explore the galaxy in parallel. This is a topic that's hard to discuss, even with readers of science fiction. My friends, even the ones in the cryonics organizations, are very uneasy about Xeroxing people.

IS THAT ME OR ME?

To explore the Galaxy in parallel, we need to make only a few starships, perhaps 100, and recruit crews for perhaps 10, but we make copies of the 10 crews to fill all 100 ships. At 1,000 people per ship, and 100 ships (100,000 adventurers) this would probably be necessary anyway. I doubt there are as many as 10,000 people in the entire world who would board a starship. Misfits who want to *do* something as opposed to watching or reading about space exploration are very rare compared to the number of *Star Trek* fans or even *New Destinies* readers. They may not be very common even among

National Space Society members. An assembler doesn't care what it is making, and unless there really is some special "vitalizing" force, we won't have to make hard choices about which way to go—we take all roads (or at least a fair sample of them).

People have talked about making a copy of themselves and having the copy do the unpleasant chores. That's silly. A good copy would be indistinguishable from the original right down to desires. You could neither make a copy to go visit the stars nor one to stay on Earth that would be happy unless you didn't care which you did (unlikely) or someone messed with their personalities in the copying process (unethical). In fact, I think it would be unethical to distinguish among copies (a case where the Golden Rule applies in its strongest form).

The only case I can see where copies are justified is a situation where a person really has no preference between two mutually exclusive choices. The copying process might best be fixed so as to split the original material in half, so neither of the individuals coming out of the process (and starting to diverge) would have a better claim to being "original." The ethical questions about copying people, reprogramming them, mapping yourself into faster hardware, and the rights of constructed personalities is a topic I would like to see getting more serious discussion both inside and outside the Science Fiction community.

Another problem is how to improve ourselves without getting completely lost. Today the mental modules at the root of our personalities change slowly if at all. When our deepest desires can be quickly modified with trivial effort, how much of us will survive? The results of modifying ourselves could be as tragic as being modified by others.* This and nanotechnology-based infectious "super dope" that made everyone happy but without ambition (or even the desire to eat) are among the

*Marvin Minsky has a good deal to say about these problems in *Society of Mind*.

dangers we face. I think these dangers are far more serious than the so-called "gray goo" (uncontrolled replicator) problem.

Philosophical problems of identity aside, and assuming we avoid these and other as-yet-un-thought-of dangers, I expect starships to exit the solar system within a decade of the nanotechnology breakthrough. They might be pushed by solar powered lasers, or drives powered by the antimatter we might be able to make by the megaton.

The way to travel between stars on laser beams is amusing. You send a probe ahead to the target star. The probe doesn't slow down, but fires nanotech "seeds" backwards to nearly zero velocity as the probe rips through the target star system. The seeds are scattered towards the planets of the target star which have atmospheres. They are braked by the atmospheres, and settle to the surface. There (I hope not in someone's back yard!) they grow from the size of a bacteria into a rocket, similar to a Larry Niven "stage tree." The stage tree launches into space, sets up a base on a stray asteroid, and builds a deceleration laser. Either before it leaves the ground, or in space, information in the seed is used to build a microwave receiver. Information on how to build the deceleration laser that cannot fit in the seed can be sent later by microwave, along with instructions on when to turn on the beam. If it doesn't work . . . well, that is how you have an adventure in an otherwise overly safe era.

At the target stars, the explorers build new launch facilities and an appropriate number of copies of the ship and crew for the targets ahead. How many stars do they get to visit? If 100 ships go out to inspect our galaxy, each ship and its descendants will have to visit a billion stars (neglecting losses and overlaps). Fortunately exponential growth comes to the rescue. A ship needs to copy itself only about thirty times since 2^{30} is about 10^9. If thirty is too few stars for your taste, double yourself less often; if too many, make more copies per generation. Doubling, the last generation looks at half the star systems in the galaxy at once.

Do we go out and come back to exchange information? With fifty billion starships? Even if there is room to park them, where in our solar system could we hold a meeting for fifty trillion intrepid explorers? We will need an economy-sized ringworld, and getting a permit to build one around Sol might take longer than the round trip. Besides, coming back home takes twice as long as needed. There is no point in wasting time. So we will sweep across the Galaxy and converge for a giant combination Far Edge Party, scientific meeting, and memory merge. Oh yes, the convention committee will have to get a little ahead of the pack to construct party hotel(s) for fifty trillion.

What will be our effect on aliens? What rules of conduct should we abide by? Perhaps equally to the point, will we find any?

BUG-EYED MONSTERS

As you can imagine, discussions about the Far Edge Party get rather lively. Someone came up with the suggestion of prizes for strangest or most interesting aliens. Someone else pointed out that with nanotechnology and tens of thousands of years the judges will have a very hard time detecting cheating with constructed aliens, or life forms raised to sentient status.

Debate on aliens rages between the Saganites and the Tiplerites. Carl Sagan and Co. hold the opinion that technological life is fairly common, with radio-capable civilizations every few hundred light years. His school proposes vast listening posts to eavesdrop. Frank Tipler points to the lack of any evidence that our galaxy, or the universe at large, is inhabited by technophiles. I have come to lean very strongly toward Tipler because I think that before very many years go by *our* existence in this particular part of the universe will become very obvious. Laser cannons pushing light sails would be seen as obviously unnatural beacons far across the universe. It may be that life is fairly common but the time it takes for technology to arise is much longer than the time available on most planets. This may be the real answer to the Fermi question.*

But I am willing to withhold judgment 'til we sweep across our Galaxy. That should give us a representative sample.

How long will it take to cross the Galaxy looking for life and getting a look at all the galactic "hot spots?" Light takes about 100,000 years. If travel speed is, say, half the speed of light, it should take some 200,000 years.

BACK AT THE RANCH

The stay-at-homes, or those who colonize and stay around a single star, won't have as much fun, but they will have plenty of interesting things to do. Conservation for example. Have you ever thought of how much energy the Sun wastes? But I am getting ahead of myself.

"a long enough lever . . .

Some years ago, James E. Lovelock, an English chemist and prolific inventor, and Lynn Margulis, discoverer of the mixed lineage of our cells, developed the biosphere-regulation Gaia concept. Lovelock later calculated that the ability of "Gaia" to compensate for the rising output of the sun will fail within the next 50–100 million years. Without intervention, the Earth will become a post-biotic planet. (David Brin speculates this may be the common fate of life-bearing planets.) Lovelock proposed that planetary sun shades be deployed when they are needed. We could do it with today's technology if we needed to. However, cluttering up our neighborhood with sun shades is not the most aesthetic approach. Being familiar with Eric Drexler's work on solar sails, I propose (partly in jest) hanging a large collection of them ahead of the Earth in its orbit. The sails would be

*Footnote: When Fermi realized that nuclear energy would suffice to cross between stars he is reported to have asked, "Where are the aliens?"

gravitationally coupled to the Earth, and gradually accelerate the planet into a larger orbit. The numbers work out that we had better get started right away. It would take about 100 million years to pull the Earth back far enough from the fire!

There is another way to move the Earth. We could use the mass of the asteroid belt to transfer momentum from Jupiter to the Earth. It takes about the same time as using solar sails to change the Earth's orbit. It might take almost that long to convince me that we could play interplanetary billiard balls that long and not accidentally put a cue ball in the pocket!

The best scheme to cope with stellar aging is not to move the Earth, but to cool off the sun. David Criswell has called this process "star lifting" and worked out, at least in theory, how an advanced and wealthy culture would go about cooling their sun by removing mass and storing the mass to heat it up later. You want to take good care of your star, otherwise it gets all dark and icky.

AN EVEN LONGER LEVER

A much wilder scheme came out of this line of thinking. The *very* patient can move stars. The truly desperate might move a galaxy. An advanced civilization (even without nanotechnology) could hang a hemisphere of actively controlled light sails over a star. (They have to be actively controlled since the light and gravity forces which the sails balance obey the same force vs. distance law.) The sails couple gravitationally to the star, and turn the star (and sails) into a fusion/photon drive. The ultimate change in velocity is about the same fraction of the speed of light as the fraction of mass turned into energy. This is not a large number, in the hundreds of km/second. Still, it is comparable to the velocity of stars against the cosmic background, or the orbital velocity about the center of our galaxy, and much larger than our 80 km/sec closure rate with the Andromeda galaxy.

If enough of the mass of a galaxy is in stars, we may be able to prevent or at least greatly modify galactic collisions by moving stars. The gas, dust, black holes, and dark matter should tag along if we move the stars slowly enough. A nice fresh G-type star can actually cross the average distance between galaxies before it burns out. This is for people who want to travel *and* stay home.

Naturally small stars, or ones reduced by "star lifting" have inconvenient (dull red) spectral characteristics, at least for those of us evolved in the light of a G-type star. Two solar sail hemispheres could be used to reflect light back on the star and change its spectral type. The surface layers would heat up to look like a G-type, and the light would escape in a narrow band between the hemispheres of sails to illuminate planets or space habitats ranging up to a ringworld. The interior temperature and burn rate of the star should not be affected, but it might inhibit the star's normal convection patterns. If someone in stellar physics wants to work out the consequences of heating up a small star, I would like to see the results.

LITTLE RINGWORLDS

Do we really need Larry Niven's super strong "scrith" to build ringworlds or can we get by with known, or at least projected, materials? If you leave most of the structure non-spinning (or spinning retrograde very slowly) and support a much lighter spinning part on superconducting magnetic bearings, O'Neill-type cylinders can be built large enough to house a continent. I have my doubts about cooling such a thing, because radiator mass per unit of radiation goes up as the square root of the absolute size of a radiator. Giant O'Neill cylinders are not a particularly efficient use of mass to get living area. But, as Eric Drexler pointed out, there is an even *less* elegant way to build one-g ringworlds. You spin a ringworld supported by bearings, pile all the non-spinning mass on the outside, and let the star's gravity acting on the mass keep the ringworld from flying apart. A small ringworld built this way around a warmed-up M-type star might be about the right size to hold the Far Edge Party—though it better be near a big hot O-type. Decelerating fifty billion starships at once is too much to ask of a small star.

See you there!

(RSVP)

BIBLIOGRAPHY

Lovelock, James, "Gaia and the End of Gaia." *CoEvolution Quarterly*, No. 31, Fall 1981.

Drexler, K. Eric. *Engines of Creation: The Coming Era of Nanotechnology*. Anchor Press/Doubleday: Garden City, New York, 1986.

Crisell, D.R., "Solar System industrialization: Implications for interstellar migrations." In: Finney, R. & Jones, E.M. (eds.) "Interstellar Migration and the Human Experience," pp. 50–87, University of California Press (1985).

Burrows, John D. and Tipler, Frank J. *The Anthropic Cosmological Principle*, Oxford University Press, 1986.

Minsky, Marvin. *Society of Mind*. Simon and Schuster: New York, 1986.

[RSVPs may be sent to, The Far Edge Committee, 1685 Branham Lane, Box 252, San Jose, CA 95118 or, hkhenson @ cup, portal. com]

Introduction

You are about to read the first clear exposition of Chaos Theory that I am aware of. But be warned: if you get involved in examining the author's examples in detail you will indeed discover that you have fallen into a time sink of great depth. Even if you are innocent of programming skill you still aren't safe; all you need is a little spreadsheet facility and you too can waste a couple of days. To get started do the following:

> Put a value of .1 in cell A1... put a value of 1 in cell A2... put the formula "+A2+.1" in cell A3... COPY cell A3 down for fifty rows or so... put the formula "+A2*A1*(1-A1)" in cell B2... COPY B2 into cells C2 through L2... COPY B2..L2 down fifty rows or so.

There. See the patterns? (Examine them graphically too.) Play with the values in A1 and A2. The next time you look at a clock it will be 3:00 in the morning. Have fun.

THE UNLICKED BEAR-WHELP

A worm's eye look at chaos theory

Charles Sheffield

"*So when this world's compounded union breaks,*
Time ends, and to old Chaos all things turn."
—Christopher Marlowe

I. INTRODUCTION

The Greek word "chaos" referred to the formless or disordered state before the beginning of the universe. The word has also been a part of the English language for a long time. Thus in Shakespeare's *Henry VI, Part Three*, the Duke of Gloucester (who in the next play of the series will become King Richard III, and romp about the stage in unabashed villainy) is complaining about his physical deformities. He is, he says, "like to a Chaos, or an unlick'd bear-whelp, that carries no impression like the dam." *Chaos:* something essentially random, an object or being without a defined shape.

Those lines were written about 1590. The Marlowe quotation that heads this article comes from close to the same year, and it is a wonderful (though unintentional) foreshadowing of the idea of the heat-death of the Universe, first formulated in the late nineteenth century.

Chaos is old; but *chaos theory* is a new term. Ten years ago, no popular article had ever been written containing that expression. Today it is hard to pick up a science magazine *without* finding an article on chaos theory, complete with stunning color illustrations. I must say that those articles, without exception, have failed to make the central ideas of chaos theory clear to me. That's why I went grubbing into it on my own, and why I am writing this, adding yet another (possibly unintelligible) discussion of the subject to the literature.

Part of the problem is simple newness. When someone writes about, say, quantum theory, the subject has to be presented as difficult, and subtle, and mysterious, because it *is* difficult, and subtle, and mysterious. To describe it in any other way would be simply misleading. In the past sixty years, however, the mysteries have had time to become old friends of the professionals in the field. There are certainly enigmas, logical whirlpools into which you can fall and never get out, but at least the *locations* of those trouble spots are known. Writing about any well-established subject, such as quantum theory, is therefore in some sense easy.

In the case of chaos theory, by contrast, *everything* is new and fragmented; we face the other extreme. We are adrift on an ocean of uncertainties, guided by partial and inadequate maps, and it is too soon to know where the central mysteries of the subject reside.

Or, worse yet, to know if those mysteries are worth taking the time to explore. *Is* chaos a real "theory," something which will change the scientific world in a basic way, as that world was changed by Newtonian mechanics, quantum theory, and relativity? Or is it something essentially trivial, a subject which at the moment is benefiting from a catchy name and so enjoying a certain glamor, as in the past there have been fads for orgone theory, mesmerism, dianetics, and pyramidology?

We will defer consideration of that question until we have had a look at the bases of chaos theory, where it came from, and where it seems to lead us. Then we can come back to examine its long-term prospects.

II. HOW TO BECOME EXTREMELY FAMOUS

One excellent way to make a great scientific discovery is to take a fact that everyone knows must be the case—because "commonsense demands it"—and ask what would happen if it were not true.

For example, it is obvious that the Earth is fixed. It *has* to be standing still, because it feels as though it is standing still. The Sun moves around it. Copernicus, by suggesting that the Earth revolves around the Sun, made the fundamental break with medieval thinking and set in train the whole of modern astronomy.

Similarly, it was clear to the ancients that unless you keep on pushing a moving object, it will slow down and stop. By taking the contrary view, that it takes a force (such as friction with the ground, or air resistance) to *stop* something, and otherwise it would just keep going, Galileo and Newton created modern mechanics.

Another case: to most people living before 1850, there was no question that animal and plant species are all so well-defined and different from each other that they must have been created, type by type, at some distinct time in the past. Charles Darwin and Alfred Russel Wallace, in suggesting in the 1850's a mechanism by which one form could *change* over time to another in response to natural environmental pressures, allowed a very different world view to develop. The theory of evolution and natural selection permitted species to be regarded as fluid entities, constantly changing, and all ultimately derived from the simplest of primeval life forms.

And, to take one more example, it was clear to everyone before 1900 that if you kept on accelerating an object, by applying force to it, it would move faster and faster until it was finally travelling faster than light. By taking the speed of light as an upper limit to possible speeds, and requiring that this speed be the same for all observers, Einstein was led to formulate the theory of relativity.

It may make you famous, but it is a risky business, this offering of scientific theories that ask people to abandon their long-cherished beliefs about what "just must be so." As Thomas Huxley remarked, it is the customary fate of new truths to begin as heresies.

Huxley was speaking metaphorically, but a few hundred years ago he could have been speaking literally. Copernicus did not allow his work on the movement of the Earth around the Sun to be published in full until 1543, when he was on his deathbed, nearly 30 years after he had first developed the ideas. He probably did the right thing. Fifty-seven years later Giordano Bruno was gagged and burned at the stake for proposing ideas in conflict with theology, namely, that the universe is infinite and there are many populated worlds. Thirty-three years after that, Galileo was made to appear before the Inquisition and threatened with torture because of his "heretical" ideas. His work remained on the Catholic Church's Index of prohibited books for over two hundred years.

By the nineteenth century critics could no longer have a scientist burned at the stake, even though they may have wanted to. Darwin was merely denounced as a tool of Satan. However, anyone who thinks this issue is over and done with can go today and have a good argument about evolution and natural selection with the numerous idiots who proclaim themselves to be scientific creationists.

Albert Einstein fared better, mainly because most people had no idea what he was talking about. However, from 1905 to his death in 1955 he became the target of every crank and scientific nitwit outside (and often inside) the lunatic asylums.

Today we will be discussing an idea, contrary to commonsense, that has been developing in the past twenty years. So far its proposers have escaped extreme censure, though in the early days their careers may have suffered because no one believed them—or understood what they were talking about.

III. BUILDING MODELS

The idea at the heart of chaos theory can be simply stated, but we will have to wind our way into it.

Five hundred years ago, mathematics was considered essential for bookkeeping, surveying, and trading, but it was not considered to have much to do with the physical processes of Nature. Why should it? What do abstract symbols on a piece of paper have to do with the movement of the planets, the flow of rivers, the blowing of soap bubbles, the flight of kites, or the design of buildings?

Little by little, that view changed. Scientists found that physical processes could be described by equations, and solving those equations allowed predictions to be made about the real world. More to the point, they were *correct* predictions. By the nineteenth century, the fact that manipulation of the purely abstract entities of mathematics could somehow tell us how the real world would behave was no longer a surprise. Sir James Jeans could happily state, in 1930, "*all* the pictures which science now draws of nature, and which alone seem capable of according with observational fact, are *mathematical* pictures," and ". . . the universe appears to have been designed by a pure mathematician."

The mystery had vanished, or been subsumed into divinity. But it should not have. It is a mystery still.

I would like to illustrate this point with the simplest problem of Newtonian mechanics. Suppose that we have an object moving along a line with a constant acceleration. It is easy to set up a situation in the real world in which an object so moves, at least approximately.

To describe the problem mathematically, the scientist writes down one simple equation:

$$dv/dt = a$$

This simply says that the rate of change of the speed, v, is a constant, a.

We integrate this equation, *a purely abstract operation*, nothing to do with the real world, and obtain the formal result:

$$v = v\emptyset + at$$

This gives us the speed, v, of the object at any time, given a starting speed $v\emptyset$ at $t = 0$. And since the speed is the rate of change of distance, which is written, $v = dx/dt$, we can integrate again—another purely *abstract* operation—to yield:

$$x = x\emptyset + v\emptyset t + at^2/2$$

which tells us the position of the object, x, at any time, in terms of its initial position, $x\emptyset$, and its initial speed, $v\emptyset$.

If you have not met this sort of thing before, it may seem baffling. What does this mathematical construct of the human mind, *integration*, have to do with reality?

If you do have that feeling, it is totally appropriate. However, after a few years of solving equations like this, the sense of wonder goes away. We take it for granted that the scribbling we do on a piece of paper will describe the way that objects really behave—and we are not surprised that the same equation will work for any object, accelerated by any force.

Well, we ought to be amazed. It is not just that we can *write down* an equation for the relation between the acceleration and the speed. It is that this integration process somehow corresponds exactly to something in the *real world*, so that when we have done our pencil-and-paper integrations, we are able to know where the object will be in reality.

No justification is usually offered for this in courses on mechanics and the calculus, other than the fact that it works. It becomes what Douglas Hofstadter in another context terms a "default assumption."

This is an especially simple example, but scientists are at ease with far more complex cases. Do you want to know how a fluid will move? Write down the three-dimensional time-dependent Navier-Stokes equation for compressible, viscous flow, and solve it. That's not a simple proposition, and you may have to resort to a computer. But when you have the results, you expect them to apply to real fluids. If they do not, it is because the equation you began with was not quite right—maybe we need to worry about electromagnetic forces, or plasma effects. Or maybe the integration method you used was numerically unstable, or the finite difference interval too crude. The idea that the mathematics cannot describe the physical world never even occurs to most scientists. They have in the back of their minds an idea first made explicit by Laplace: the whole universe is calculable, by defined mathematical laws. Laplace said that if you told him (or rather, if you told a demon, who was capable of taking in all the information) the position and speed of every particle in the Universe, at one moment, he would be able to define the Universe's entire future, and also its whole past.

The twentieth century, and the introduction by Heisenberg of the Uncertainty Principle, weakened that statement, because it showed that it was impossible to know precisely the position and speed of a body. Nonetheless, the principle that mathematics can *exactly model reality* is usually still unquestioned.

Now, hidden away in the assumption that the world can be described by mathematics there is another one; one so subtle that most people never gave it a thought. This is the assumption that chaos theory makes explicit, and then challenges. We state it as follows:

Simple equations must have simple solutions.

There is no reason why this should be so, except that it seems that commonsense demands it. And, of course, we have not defined "simple."

Let us return to our accelerating object, where we had a simple-seeming equation, and an explicit solution. One requirement of a simple solution is that it should not "jump around" when we make a very small change in the system it describes. For example, if we consider two cases of an accelerated object, and the only difference between them is a tiny change in the original position of the object, we would expect a small change in the *final* position. And this is the case.

But now consider another simple physical system, a pendulum (this was one of the first cases where the ideas of chaos theory emerged). The equation that describes the motion of a simple pendulum, consisting of a bob on a string, can be written down easily enough. It is:

$$d^2q/dt^2 + k.\sin(q) = 0$$

Even if you are not familiar with calculus, this should seem hardly more complicated than the first equation we considered. And for small angles, q, its solution can easily be written down, and it exhibits the quality of simplicity, namely, the solution changes little when we make a small change in the starting position or starting speed of the pendulum bob.

However, when large angles, q, are permitted, a completely different type of solution becomes possible. If we start the bob moving fast enough, instead of swinging back and forward, like a clock, the pendulum keeps on going, right over the top and down the other side. If we write down the expression for the angle as a function of time, in one case the angle is a *periodic* function (back and forth) and in the other case it is constantly increasing (round and round). And the change from one to the other occurs when we make an *infinitesimal* change in the initial speed of the pendulum bob. This type of behavior is known as a *bifurcation* in the behavior of the solution, and it is a worrying thing. A simple equation begins to exhibit a complicated solution.

The mathematician Poincaré used a powerful graphical method to display the behavior of the solutions of dynamical problems. It is called a *phase space diagram*, and it plots position on one axis, and speed on the other. For any assumed starting position and speed, we can then plot out where the solution goes on the phase diagram. (It works, because the equations of dynamics are what is known as second-order equations; for such equations, when the position and speed of an object are specified, that defines the nature of its whole future motion.)

If we make the phase space diagram for the case of the uniformly accelerating object, the result is not particularly interesting. It is shown in Figure 1, and consists of a set of parabolas.

Figure 1: Phase space diagram for uniform accelerated motion.

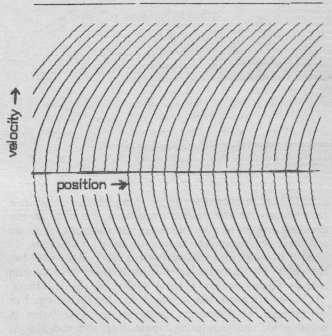

Things become more interesting when we do the same thing for the pendulum (Figure 2). Phase space now has two distinct regions, corresponding to the oscillating and the rotating forms of solution, and they are separated by an infinitely thin closed boundary. An infinitely small change of speed or position at that boundary can totally change the nature of the solution.

Figure 2: Phase space diagram for the simple pendulum

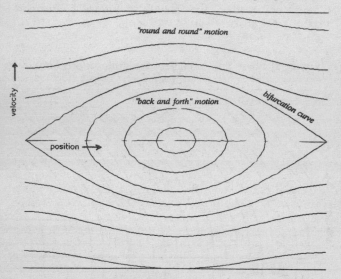

This kind of behavior can be thought of as a *sensitive dependence on the initial conditions*. In fact, at the dividing curve of the phase space diagram, it is an *infinitely* sensitive dependence on initial conditions.

At this point, the reasonable reaction might well be, so what? All that we have done is show that certain simple equations don't have really simple solutions. That does not seem like an earth-shaking discovery. For one thing, the boundary between the two types of solution for the pendulum, oscillating and rotating, is quite clear-cut. It is not as though the definition of the location of the boundary itself were a problem.

Can situations arise where this *is* a problem? Where the boundary is difficult to define in an intuitive way? The answer is, yes. In the next section we will consider simple systems that give rise to highly complicated boundaries between regions of fundamentally different behavior.

IV. ITERATED FUNCTIONS

Some people have a built-in mistrust of anything that involves the calculus. When you use it in any sort of argument, they say, logic and clarity have already departed. The examples I have given so far began with a differential equation, and needed calculus to define the behavior of the solutions. However, we don't need calculus to demonstrate fundamentally chaotic behavior; and many of the first explorations of what we now think of as chaotic functions were done without calculus. They employed what is called *iterated function theory*. Despite an imposing name, the fundamentals of iterated function theory are so simple that they can be done with an absolute minimum knowledge of mathematics. They do, however, benefit from the assistance of computers, since they call for large amounts of tedious computation.

Consider the following very simple operation. Take two numbers, x and r. Form the value $y = r.x(1-x)$.

Now plug the value of y back in as a new value for x. Repeat this process, over and over.

For example, suppose that we take $r = 2$, and start with $x = 0.1$. Then we find $y = 0.18$.

Plug that value in as a new value for x, still using $r = 2$, and we find a new value, $y = 0.2952$.

Keep going, to find a sequence of y's, 0.18, 0.2952, 0.4161, 0.4859, 0.4996, 0.5000, 0.5000 . . .

In the language of mathematics, the sequence of y's has *converged* to the value 0.5. Moreover, for any starting value of x, between 0 and 1, we will always converge to the same value, 0.5, for $r = 2$.

Here is the sequence when we begin with $x = 0.6$: 0.6000, 0.4800, 0.4992, 0.5000, 0.5000 . . .

Because the final value of y does not depend on the starting value, it is termed an *attractor* for this system, since it "draws in" any sequence to itself.

The value of the attractor depends on r. If we start

237

with some other value of r, say r = 2.5, we still produce
a convergent sequence. For example, if for r = 2.5 we
begin with x = 0.1, we find successive values: 0.1,
0.225, 0.4359, 0.6147, 0.5921, 0.6038, 0.5981, . . .
0.6. Starting with a different x still gives the same final
value, 0.6 (For anyone with any kind of computer available to them, and a little knowledge of BASIC, I rec-
ommend playing this game for yourself. The whole
program is only a dozen lines long, and fooling with it is
lots of fun. *Suggestion*: run the program in double
precision, if you have it available, so you don't get
trouble with round-off errors. *Warning*: larking around
with this sort of thing will consume hours and hours of
your time.)

The situation does not change significantly with r =
3. We find the sequence of values: 0.2700, 0.5913,
0.7250, 0.5981, 0.7211, . . . 0.6667. This time it takes
thousands of iterations to get a final converged value,
but it makes it there in the end. Even after only a
dozen or two iterations we can begin to see it "settling-in"
to its final value.

There have been no surprises so far. What happens if
we increase r a bit more, to 3.1? We might expect that
we will converge, but even more slowly, to a single
final value.

We would be wrong. Something very odd happens.
The sequence of numbers that we generate has a regular structure, but now the values alternate between two
different numbers, 0.7645, and 0.5580. *Both* these are
attractors for the sequence. It is as though the sequence
cannot make up its mind. When r is increased past the
value 3, the sequence "splits" to two permitted values,
which we will call "states," and these occur alternately.

Let us increase the value of r again, to 3.4. We find
the same behavior, a sequence that alternates between
two values.

But by r = 3.5, things have changed again. The
sequence has *four* states, four values that repeat one
after the other. For r = 3.5, we find the final sequence
values: 0.3828, 0.5009, 0.8269, and 0.8750. Again, it

does not matter what value of x we started with, we will always converge on those same four attractors.

Let us pause for a moment and put on our mathematical hats. If a mathematician is asked the question, "Does the iteration y = r.x(1-x) converge to a final value?", he will proceed as follows:

Suppose that there is a final converged value, V, towards which the iteration converges. Then when we reach that value, no matter how many iterations it takes, at the final step x will be equal to V, and so will y. Thus we must have V = r.V.(1-V).

Solving for V, we find V = 0, which is a legitimate but uninteresting solution, or V = (r-1)/r. This single value will apply, no matter how big r may be. For example, if r = 2.5, then V = 1.5/2.5 = 0.6, which is what we found. Similarly, for r = 3.5, we calculate V = 2.5/3.5 = 0.7142857.

But this is not what we found when we did the actual iteration. We did not converge to that value at all, but instead we obtained a set of four values that cycled among themselves. So let us ask the question, what would happen if we *began* with x = 0.7142857, as our starting guess? We certainly have the right to use any initial value that we choose. Surely, the value would simply stay there?

No, it would not.

What we would find is that on each iteration, the value of y changes. It remains close to 0.7142857 on the first few calculations, then it—quite quickly—diverges from that value and homes in on the four values that we just mentioned: 0.3828, 0.5009, etc. In mathematical terms, the value 0.7142857 is a solution of the iterative process for r = 3.5. But it is an *unstable* solution. If we start there, we will rapidly move away to other multiple values.

Let us return to the iterative process. By now we are not sure what will happen when we increase r. But we can begin to make some guesses. Bigger values of r seem to lead to more and more different values, among which the sequence will oscillate, and it seems as though the number of these values will always be a power of two. Furthermore, the "splitting points" seem to be coming faster and faster.

Take r = 3.52, or 3.53, or 3.54. We still have four values that alternate. But by r = 3.55, things have changed again. We now find *eight* different values that repeat, one after the other. By r = 3.565, we have 16 different values that occur in a fixed order, over and over, as we compute the next elements of the sequence.

It is pretty clear that we are approaching some sort of crisis, since the increments that we can make in r, without changing the nature of the sequence, are getting smaller and smaller. In fact, the critical value of r is known to many significant figures. It is r = 3.569945668 . . . As we approach that value there are 2^n states in the sequence, and n is growing fast.

What happens if we take r *bigger* than this, say r = 3.7? We still produce a sequence—there is no difficulty at all with the computations—but it is a sequence without any sign of regularity. There are no attractors, and all values seem equally likely. It is fair to say that it is *chaos*, and the region beyond the critical value of r is often called the *chaos regime*.

This may look like a very special case, because all the calculations were done based on one particular function, y = r.x(1-x). However, it turns out that the choice of function is much less important than one would expect. If we substituted any up-and-down curve between zero and one (see Figure 3) we would get a similar result. As r increases, the curve "splits" again and again. There is a value of r for which the behavior becomes chaotic.

For example, suppose that we use the form y = r.sin(x)/4 (the factor of 4 is to make sure that the maximum value of y is the same as in the first case, namely, 1/4). By the time we reach r = 3.4 we have four different values repeating in the sequence. For r = 3.45 we have eight attractors. Strangest of all, the way in which we approach the critical value for this function has much in common with the way we approached it for

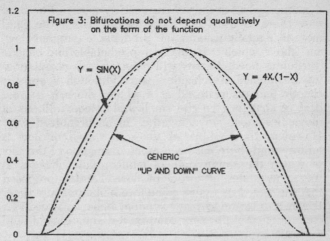

Figure 3: Bifurcations do not depend qualitatively on the form of the function

Y = SIN(X)

Y = 4X.(1−X)

GENERIC "UP AND DOWN" CURVE

the first function that we used. They both depend on a single convergence number that tells the rate at which new states will be introduced as r is increased. That convergence number is 4.669201609 . . . , and is known as the *Feigenbaum number*, after Mitchell Feigenbaum, who first explored in detail this property of iterated sequences. This property of common convergence behavior, independent of the particular function used for the iteration, is called *universality*. It seems a little presumptuous as a name, but maybe it won't, in twenty years time.

This discussion of iterated functions may strike you as rather tedious, very complicated, very specialized, and a way of obtaining very little for a great deal of work. However, the right way to view what we have just done is this: we have found a critical value, less than which there is a predictable, although increasingly complicated behavior, and above which there is a completely different and chaotic behavior. Moreover, as we approach the critical value, the number of possible states of the system increases very rapidly, and tends to infinity.

To anyone who has done work in the field of fluid

dynamics, that is a very suggestive result. For fluid flow there is a critical value below which the fluid motion is totally smooth and predictable (laminar flow) and above which it is totally unpredictable and chaotic (turbulent flow). Purists will object to my characterizing turbulence as "chaotic," since although it appears chaotic and disorganized as a whole, there is a great deal of structure on the small scale since millions of molecules must move together in an organized way. However, the number of states in turbulent flow is infinite, and there has been much discussion of the way in which the single state of laminar flow changes to the many states of turbulent flow. Landau proposed that the new states must come into being one at a time. It was also assumed that turbulent behavior arose as a consequence of the very complicated equations of fluid dynamics.

Remember the "commonsense rule": Simple Equations Must Have Simple Solutions. And therefore, complicated behavior should only arise from complicated equations. For the first time, we see that this may be wrong. A very simple system is exhibiting very complicated behavior, reminiscent of what happens with fluid flow. Depending on some critical variable, it may appear totally predictable and well-behaved, or totally unpredictable and chaotic. Moreover, experiments show that in turbulence the new, disorganized states come into being not one by one, but *through a doubling process as the critical parameter is approached*. Maybe turbulence is a consequence of something in the fluid flow equations that is unrelated to their complexity—a hidden structure that is present even in such simple equations as we have been studying.

This iterated function game is interesting, even suggestive; but to a physicist it was for a long time little more than that. Physics does not deal with computer games, went the argument. It deals with mathematical models that describe a physical system, in a majority of cases through a series of differential equations. These equations are solved, to build an idea of how Nature will behave in any given circumstance.

The trouble is, although such an approach works wonderfully well in many cases, there are classes of problems that it doesn't seem to touch. Turbulence is one. "Simple" systems, like the dripping of water from a faucet, can be modeled in principle, but in practice the difficulties in formulation and solution are so tremendous that no one has ever offered a working analysis of a dripping tap.

The problems where the classical approach breaks down often have one thing in common: they involve a random, or apparently random, element. Water in a stream breaks around a stone this way, then that way. A snowflake forms from super-saturated vapor, and every one is different. A tap drips, then does not drip, in an apparently random way. All these problems are described by quite different systems of equations. What scientists wanted to see was *physical problems*, described by good old differential equations, that also displayed bifurcations, and universality, and chaotic behavior.

They had isolated examples already. For example, the chemical systems that rejoice in the names of the Belousov-Zhabotinsky reaction and the Brusselator exhibit a two-state cyclic behavior. So does the life cycle of the slime mold, *Dictyostelium discoideum*. However, such systems are very tricky to study for the occurrence of such things as bifurcations, and involve all the messiness of real-world experiments. Iterated function theory was something that could be explored in the precise and austere world of computer logic, unhindered by the intrusion of the external world.

We must get to that external and real world eventually, but before we do so, let's take a look at another element of iterated function theory. This one has become very famous in its own right (rather more so, in my opinion, than it deserves to be for its physical significance, but perhaps justifiably most famous for its artistic significance).

The subject is *fractals*, and the contribution to art is called the Mandelbrot Set.

V. SICK CURVES AND FRACTALS

Compare the system we have just been studying with the case of the pendulum. There we had a critical *curve*, rather than a critical value. On the other hand, the behavior on both sides of the critical curve was not chaotic. Also, the curve itself was well-behaved, meaning that it was "smooth" and predictable in its shape.

Is there a simple system that on the one hand exhibits a critical *curve*, and on the other hand shows chaotic behavior?

There is. It is one studied in detail by Benoit Mandelbrot, and it gives rise to a series of amazing objects (one hesitates to call them curves, or areas).

We just looked at a case of an iterated function where only one variable was involved. We used x to compute y, then replaced x with y, and calculated a new y, and so on. It is no more difficult to do this, at least in principle, if there are two starting values, used to compute two new values. For example, we could have:

$$y = (w^2 - x^2) + a$$
$$z = 2.w.x + b$$

and when we had computed a pair (y,z) we could use them to replace the pair (w,x). (Readers familiar with complex variable theory will see that I am simply writing the relation $z = z^2 + c$, where z and c are complex numbers, in a less elegant form.)

What happens if we take a pair of constants, (a,b), plug in zero starting values for w and x, and let our computers run out lots of pairs, (y,z)? This is a kind of two-dimensional equivalent to what we did with the function $y = r.x.(1-x)$, and we might think that we will find similar behavior, with a critical *curve* replacing the critical value.

What happens is much more surprising. We can plot our (y,z) values in two dimensions, just as we plotted out speeds and positions for the case of the pendulum. And, just as was the case with the pendulum, we will find that the whole plane is divided up into separate regions, with boundaries between them. The boundaries are the boundary curves of the "Mandelbrot set", as it is called. If, when we start with an (a,b) pair and iterate for (y,z) values, one or both of y and z run off towards infinity, then the point (a,b) is *not* a member of the Mandelbrot set. If the (y,z) pairs settle down to some value, or if they cycle around a series of values without ever diverging off towards infinity, then the point (a,b) is a member of the Mandelbrot set. The tricky case is for points on the boundary, since convergence is slowest there for the (y,z) sequence. However, those boundaries can be mapped. And they are as far as can be imagined from the simple, well-behaved curve that divided the two types of behavior of the pendulum. Instead of being smooth, they are intensely spiky; instead of just one curve, there is an infinite number of them.

The results of plotting the Mandelbrot set can be found in many articles, because they have a strange beauty unlike anything else in mathematics. Rather than drawing them here, I will refer you to James Gleick's book, *Chaos: Making a New Science*, which shows some beautiful color examples of parts of the set. All this, remember, comes from the simple function we defined, iterated over and over to produce pairs of (y,z) values corresponding to a particular choice of a and b. The colors seen in so many art shows, by the way, while not exactly a cheat, are not fundamental to the Mandelbrot set itself. They are assigned depending on how many iterations it takes to bring the (y,z) values to convergence, or to a stable repeating pattern.

The Mandelbrot set also exhibits a feature known as *scaling*, which is very important in many areas of physics. It says, in its simplest terms, that you cannot tell the absolute scale of the phenomenon you are examining from the structure of the phenomenon itself.

That needs some explanation. Suppose that you want to know the size of a given object—say, a snowflake. One absolute measure, although a rather difficult one to put into practice, would be to count the number of atoms in that snowflake. Atoms are fundamental units, and they do not change in their size.

But suppose that instead of the number of atoms, you tried to use a different measure, say, the total *area* of the snowflake. That sounds much easier than looking at the individual atoms. But you would run into a problem, because as you look at the surface of the snowflake more and more closely, it becomes more and more detailed. A little piece of a snowflake has a surface that looks very much like a little piece of a little piece of snowflake; a little piece of a little piece resembles a little piece of a little piece of a little piece, and so on. It stays that way until you are actually seeing the atoms. Then you at last have the basis for an absolute scale.

Mathematical entities, unlike snowflakes, are not made up of atoms. There are many mathematical objects that "scale forever," meaning that each level of more detailed structure resembles the one before it. The observer has no way of assigning any absolute scale to the structure. The sequence-doubling phenomenon that we looked at earlier is rather like that. There is a constant ratio between the distances at which the doublings take place, and that information alone is not enough to tell you how close you are to the critical value in absolute terms.

Similarly, by examining a single piece of the Mandelbrot set it is impossible to tell at what level of detail the set is being examined. The set can be examined more and more closely, forever, and simply continues to exhibit more and more detail. There is never a place where we arrive at the individual "atoms" that make up the set. In this respect, the set differs from anything encountered in nature, where the fundamental particles provide a final absolute scaling. Even so, there are in nature things that exhibit scaling over many orders of magnitude. One of the most famous examples is a coastline. If you ask "How long is the coastline of the United States?" a first thought is that you can go to a map and measure it. Then it's obvious that the map has smoothed the real coastline. You need to go to larger scale maps, and larger scale maps. A coastline "scales," like the surface of a snowflake, all the way down to the individual rocks and grains of sand. You find larger and larger numbers for the length of the coast. Another natural phenomenon that exhibits scaling is—significantly—turbulent flow. Ripples ride on whirls that ride on vortices that sit on swirls that are made up of eddies, on and on.

There are classes of mathematical curves that, like coastlines, do not have a length that one can measure in the usual way. A very famous one, the "Koch curve", is sketched in Figure 4. The area enclosed by the Koch curve is clearly finite; but when we set out to compute the length of its boundary, we find that it is $3 \times 4/3 \times 4/3 \times 4/3 \ldots$ —which diverges to infinity. Curves like

Figure 4: A sick curve

This shape has finite area and infinite perimeter. To make it, add a small triangle at the middle of the side of each larger triangle, and continue doing this forever.

this are known as *pathological curves*. The word "pathological" means diseased, or sick. It is a good name for them.

There is a special term reserved for the boundary dimension of such finite/infinite objects, and it is called the *Hausdorff-Besicovitch* measure. That's a bit of a mouthful. The boundaries of the Mandelbrot set have a fractional Hausdorff-Besicovitch measure, rather than the usual dimension (1) of the boundary of a plane curve, and most people now prefer to use the term coined by Mandelbrot, and speak of *fractal dimension* rather than Hausdorff-Besicovitch dimension. Objects that exhibit such properties, and other such features as scaling, were named as *fractals* by Mandelbrot.

Any discussion of chaos has to include the Mandelbrot set, scaling, and fractals, because it offers by far the most *visually* attractive part of the theory. I am less convinced that it is as important as Feigenbaum's universality. However, it is certainly beautiful to look at, highly suggestive of shapes found in Nature and—most important of all—it tends to show up in the study of systems that physicists *are* happy with and impressed by, since they represent the result of solving systems of differential equations.

VI. STRANGE ATTRACTORS

This is all very interesting, but in our discussion so far there is a big missing piece. We have talked of iterated functions, and seen that even very simple cases can exhibit "chaotic" behavior. And we have also remarked that physical systems also often exhibit chaotic behavior. However, such systems are usually described in science by *differential equations*, not by iterated functions. We need to show that the iterated functions and the differential equations are close relatives, at some fundamental level, before we can be persuaded that the results we have obtained so far in iterated functions can be used to describe events in the real world.

Let us return to one simple system described by a

differential equation, namely, the pendulum, and examine it in a little more detail. First let's recognize that the phase space diagram that we looked at in Figure 2 applies only to an *idealized* pendulum, not a real one. In the real world, every pendulum is gradually slowed by friction, until it sits at the bottom of the swing, unmoving. This is a single point in phase space, corresponding to zero angle and zero speed. That point in phase space is an *attractor* for pendulum motion, and it is a *stable* attractor. All pendulums, unless given a periodic kick by a clockwork or electric motor, will settle down to the zero angle/zero speed point. No matter with what value of angle or speed a pendulum is started swinging, it will finish up at the stable attractor. In mathematical terms, all points of phase space, neighbors or not, will approach each other as time goes on.

A friction-free pendulum, or one that is given a small constant boost each swing, will behave like the idealized one, swinging and swinging, steadily and forever. Points in phase space neither tend to be drawn towards each other, nor repelled from each other.

But suppose that we had a physical system in which points that *began* close together tended to *diverge* from each other. That is the very opposite of the real-world pendulum, and we must first ask if such a system could exist.

It can, as we shall shortly see. It is a case of something that we have already encountered, a strong dependence on initial conditions, since later states of the system differ from each other a great deal, though they began infinitesimally separated. In such a case, the attractor is not a stable attractor, or even a periodic attractor. Instead it is called a *strange attractor*.

This is an inspired piece of naming, comparable with John Archibald Wheeler's introduction of the term "black hole." Even people who have never heard of chaos theory pick up on it. It is also an appropriate name. The paths traced out in phase space in the region of a strange attractor are infinitely complex, bounded in extent, never repeating; chaotic, yet chaotic in some deeply controlled way. If there can be such a thing as controlled chaos, it is seen around strange attractors.

We now address the basic question: Can strange attractors exist mathematically? The simple pendulum cannot possess a strange attractor; so far we have offered no proof that *any* system can exhibit one. However, it can be proved that strange attractors do exist in mathematically specified systems, although a certain minimal complexity is needed in order for a system to possess a strange attractor. We have this situation: simple equations can exhibit complicated solutions, but for the particular type of complexity represented by the existence of strange attractors, the system of equations can't be *too* simple. To be specific, a system of three or more nonlinear differential equations can possess a strange attractor; less than three equations, or more than three linear equations, cannot. (The mathematical statement of this fact is simpler but more abstruse: a system can exhibit a strange attractor if at least one Lyapunov exponent is positive.)

If we invert the logic, it is tempting to make another statement: *Any physical system that shows an ultra-sensitive dependence on initial conditions has a strange attractor buried somewhere in its structure.*

This is a plausible but not a proven result. I am tempted to call it the most important unsolved problem of chaos theory. If it turns out to be true, it will have a profound unifying influence on numerous branches of science. Systems whose controlling equations bear no resemblance to each other will share a *structural* resemblance, and there will be the possibility of developing universal techniques that apply to the solution of complicated problems in a host of different areas. One thing in common with every problem that we have been discussing is *nonlinearity*. Nonlinear systems are notoriously difficult to solve, and seem to defy intuition. Few general techniques exist today for tackling nonlinear problems, and some new insight is desperately needed.

If chaos theory can provide that insight, it will have

moved from being a baffling grab-bag of half results, interesting conjectures, and faintly seen relationships, to become a real "new science." We are not there yet. But if we can go that far, then our old commonsense gut instinct, that told us simple equations must have simple solutions, will have proved no more reliable than our ancestors' commonsense instinctive knowledge that told them the Earth was flat. And the long-term implications of that new thought pattern may be just as revolutionary to science.

VII. REFERENCES

I like articles to be self-contained, because that's fairer to the reader who lacks access to libraries and good book stores. However, in this case there is no way that I can include color pictures of the endlessly-fascinating Mandelbrot set, so I have to offer at least that reference. And I can't resist offering just a couple more.

1) James Gleick: *Chaos: Making a New Science* (Viking, 1987). You will read this book, love it, be swept up and carried along by it, and thoroughly enjoy the exciting ride. And when you are done, I defy you to tell me, on the basis of what you have read there, what chaos theory is, and what its underlying ideas are as an integrating influence in science.

2) Ilya Prigogine and Isabelle Stengers: *Order Out of Chaos* (Bantam, 1984). I am a fan of Prigogine. This book is not primarily a discussion of chaos theory, but in three chapters (5, 6 and 9) it provides more meat on that subject than Gleick's whole book. Prigogine's *From Being to Becoming* (Freeman, 1980) covers some of the same ground, but at a high technical level. Both Prigogine's books are much harder reading than Gleick, and they expect a lot more of the reader.

3) Douglas Hofstadter: *Scientific American*, November, 1981, reprinted as Chapter 16 of *Metamagical Themas* (Basic Books, 1985). Hofsadter, as always, looks for elegance. He finds it in the results of chaos theory, and describes what he finds as clearly as one could ask.

I am a fan of Hofstadter, too. Did you buy his *Godel, Escher, Bach*? So did I. Did you *read* it, from beginning to end? Neither did I. Every bit is fascinating, but it is as rich and dense as chocolate pudding. I still read bits now and again, when I crave intellectual stimulation.

Introduction

I must say that when the idea for an article on the ultimate PC circa 2000 was first broached I thought it oddly self limiting on two counts. First, ten years is such a short span, and second, PCs, personal computers, are hardly the stuff that dreams are made on. If you want real action, look in on what MIT (or Toshiba?) will be doing with networked super computers, right? Right.

And yet... and yet... maybe it's not ultimate capacity that's the real story. Maybe in this one case the true drama is in something as mundane as the price-performance ratio. Maybe its that I can own one. And you can too. Maybe the real story is about empowerment, for you and for me. Here it comes....

2001: THE PERSONAL COMPUTER

Mark L. Van Name

We science-fiction writers generally have not had much success predicting the future. There have been a few notable exceptions—Clarke with communication satellites and Heinlein with waldoes, to name two of the most obvious—but by and large our futures have proven wrong far more often than they have proven correct.

Consider, for example, the personal computer. Few, if any, SF writers even came close to predicting the widespread use or influence of personal computing on American and world culture. Sure, in the last decade or so, when the rise of personal computers was obvious to anyone willing to look around carefully, computers started appearing in many SF stories as integral parts of the lives of their characters. Prior to that time, however, the computers in SF stories were generally the exclusive province of scientists and military men, arcane (and often, quite incorrectly, huge) machines reserved for the rich and the powerful. Today, every eight-year-old in a middle-class American elementary school has played with a computer, and you can't walk fifty feet in a Hong Kong market without bumping into a smiling man selling black market software or hardware with a deal just for you.

Many SF writers have also become hip to what's going on. Today's SF stories are full of predictions about computers, but they're generally predictions of where we will end up *someday*. If you read much SF, you probably already know the litany of hot trends: direct mind-to-computer links (usually via a jack in the neck or skull), molecular computers built with the finest in Japanese nanotechnology, a universal network that links every computer and, therefore, every person, and on and on. Don't get me wrong, I don't want to disparage that list. I even used some of those very ideas in stories of my own.

All of them, however, are guesses about a someday that's an unknown time from now. Few people seem willing to make concrete predictions about the personal computers of a much nearer future, say a decade or so from now. Say 2001, a good SF year. So, I thought I would give it a try.

The Ground Rules

To make it possible for you to file this copy of *New Destinies* until 2001 and then check out my predictions, we need to agree on a few rules.

First, I will address strictly what I believe will be commercially available by the middle of 2001. The leading high-tech experiments in Bell Labs or M.I.T. are always interesting, but they are typically years in advance of commercial products. I will, however, give myself an unlimited budget, cash enough for the best of everything, because the fastest, newest products are also typically the most expensive ones.

Finally, space forces me to stick largely to hardware, to predicting the raw computing power of the high-end personal computers of 2001.

A Brief Taxonomy

Those computers, like the ones many of us use today, are going to be too complicated to discuss as a single item. The only way to understand any even moderately complex computer is to look at each of its major components, piece by electronic piece.

The part of every computer that usually gets the most press is its central processing unit (CPU), the machine's main brain. The CPU, however, is just the beginning. It needs memory to store running programs and at least some of the data those programs will manipulate. It also needs a place to store the large quantities of data and programs that inevitably accumulate on a computer. That means disks, usually both the portable kind (today's floppies) that let you move your data from machine to machine, and the faster, larger storage of hard disks. Any time you keep valuable data, you also have to worry about backing up that data in case your original storage medium dies, so I'll also talk about backup technologies.

Finally, there must be some way for us to interact with our computers. That means one or more input devices, which today almost always includes at least a keyboard, and often a mouse or trackball. There are also always one or more ways for the computer to respond to us, typically a monitor and a printer.

Let's take these components one by one.

Processors

The most important fact about the processors in the high-end PCs of 2001 is that there will be many of them. The best PCs today are already moving in this direction, with separate processors on their video, disk, and network controller boards, and minicomputers and mainframes have long used multiple processors. By 2001, however, this trend will be *de rigeur* on all high-end PCs. My top-of-the-line PC will have at least two main CPU chips, with expansion slots capable of handling anywhere from two to six additional processors.

These multiple CPUs will provide the power to run

many different tasks simultaneously, all at high speeds. At least some of the operating systems available then (as now) will be able to allocate processing power intelligently to the different applications you might be running at any given time.

The individual CPUs running those applications will, of course, be a great deal faster than their current counterparts. In its relatively short lifetime, the computer industry has produced several axioms that are to date inviolate. One is that processors always get faster, denser, and smaller. The speed of light almost demands this statement: despite early SF visions of planet-sized computers, making a processor faster almost inevitably means making it smaller. The longer the stretch of wire between two components of a system, the longer the electrons take to travel that wire, and no truly high-speed system can afford to waste too much valuable time sending electrons over long stretches of wire.

Today's best general-purpose microprocessors, such as Intel's 80486 and Motorola's 68040, already demonstrate the reward of packing electronic components tightly together. These chips, which represent about the sixth generation of microprocessors, can execute around fifteen million instructions per second (MIPS), many times the processing power of the first micros. These newer chips are correspondingly many times denser than their electronic ancestors: both contain around a million transistors each.

By 2001, we'll be several more chip generations in the future. At this stage in chip development, a new generation seems to come along about every four years. For example, Intel's next three generations—the 80586, 80686, and 80786—are due in 1992, 1996, and 2000, respectively. So, by the middle of 2001 at least a few vendors should be shipping premium-performance systems based on the 80786 and its competitors.

Intel's few public forecasts about the 80786 paint it as a single chip that contains four general-purpose processors capable of delivering about 175 MIPS each. That's an increase of over an order of magnitude in raw computing speed per internal processor, with a collective processing power of about 700 MIPS—quite a jump from even the fastest of today's PCs. With this much power, you could, for example, run full wind-flow simulations on an aircraft design instead of having to apply for time on the nearest Cray supercomputer.

Despite its much greater power, the 80786 will probably be pretty much the same size as the 80486: about an inch on a side. Inside the chip, however, will be an entirely different story. The 80786 will hold about 100 million transistors, an increase of almost two orders of magnitude in transistor density over today's best chips. The 80786 will also probably contain two other specialized processors designed to speed graphics and image processing, as well as some high-speed memory. (Today's high-end Intel product, the 80486, has a similar basic design: the 80486 chip contains both a main processor and a floating-point processor, as well as a small supply, 8K bytes, of its own high-speed memory.)

Memory

That 8KB of memory inside the 80486 is a special kind of memory, high-speed static random-access memory (SRAM). Most computer memory today comes in the form of dynamic RAM (DRAM) chips. DRAM chips require periodic refreshing from the CPU, or they lose their contents, effectively forgetting what they held. SRAM chips, by contrast, don't forget, at least as long as you keep power to the system. SRAM chips are also faster—and more expensive—than DRAMs. Fast SRAMs provide the best known answer to a problem that is getting worse all the time: processor-memory mismatch.

The dilemma is actually a fairly simple one: processors are getting faster much more quickly than memory chips. Also, the faster the chip, the more it costs. You might be able to afford a single fast processor, but most folks won't shell out the money for all the fast memory chips that a PC requires. A fairly typical PC today, for example, might have two megabytes (MB) of memory in eighteen one-megabit DRAM chips. Even if DRAMs fast enough to keep up with the 80486 were readily available (and they're not), you'd have to buy eighteen of them for this relatively modest configuration. The result is that nearly all PCs use memory that's not quite fast enough to keep up with their CPUs. The resulting speed mismatch means that every time the CPU has to get something from memory, which is every time it does almost anything, it has to wait. While it's waiting, the CPU can't do anything. The fastest CPU eventually ends up running no faster than the memory it uses.

That's where the small amount of SRAM comes into play. The 80486 uses its 8KB of SRAM as a *cache*. In computer parlance, a cache is a section of memory that holds the portions of the larger main memory that the processor most recently used. Analysis of computer program behavior has shown that programs tend to exhibit a behavior known as *locality of reference*, which basically means that once a program starts working on one section of memory, it tends to keep on working on that section for a while. By keeping the most recently used pieces of memory in a small cache of SRAM that is fast enough to keep up with the CPU, the CPU can get what it needs—most of the time—from that cache without waiting. A special chip, the *cache controller*, keeps the cache and the larger main memory in sync, so that nothing the CPU does gets lost. Even though a PC's main memory is typically 640KB, a small 8KB cache will let the CPU run without waiting over 80% of the time.

The 80786 of 2001, and its competitors, will also have caches, but they'll be both bigger and, necessarily, faster than today's caches. Instead of the 80486's 8KB cache, Intel will probably put two megabytes or more of cache into the 80786 chip.

That won't be the end of the cache story, either. Today's hottest 80486-based PCs usually have a second cache outside the CPU, effectively giving the CPU a much larger total cache. The same will be true of the systems in 2001, except that the caches will be—you guessed it—bigger and faster. I expect secondary caches of at least an additional 2MB, with caches up to 8MB not uncommon.

There will also be a lot more main system memory. The vast majority of the PCs in the world today probably have only a megabyte or less of DRAM in them. The hottest of today's PCs typically come standard with only two to four megabytes of memory. All of that memory is typically either 256K-bit or 1M-bit chips. With 1M-bit chips, you need at least eight chips per megabyte, so putting more than a few megabytes in a system usually means coming up with a fair amount of space for those chips on a circuit board, where space is precious. (Eight chips gives you a megabyte, but many systems also use a ninth chip per megabyte for a form of error checking on the other eight known as *parity checking*.)

By 2001, we won't need anywhere near that many chips to produce the same amount of memory, because we should be just getting seriously into the second generation of DRAMs past today's common 1M-bit chips. IBM and a few other firms already make 4M-bit chips, the next generation, and a few Japanese firms have shown 16M-bit prototypes. The high-end PC of 2001 will use 16M-bit chips, so it'll be pretty easy to make a PC with 10MB of memory: just plug in eight or nine such chips. Many users will have 64MB or more of memory.

A Quick Glance Aside

At this point, anybody not familiar with computers might well wonder just why anyone would ever need or want such fast processors or so much memory. Millions of people work everyday with PCs that have only 640K of memory and CPUs that run at speeds below 1 MIP. Why should future workers need anything else?

The answer lies in another curious axiom of the computer era: there can never be enough processing power or memory. Happy with your standard PC? Load a graphical user interface program like that of the Macintosh onto it, and watch the PC slow to a crawl. Using a faster PC that can handle such programs? Get several applications running at the same time, and once again you'll slow to a crawl. If that's not enough, start displaying real-time animations, while running a complex financial simulation, while downloading the stock quotes from an on-line information service, while printing the entry from your on-line encyclopedia on your laser printer, and you'll soon be doing enough jobs that no current PC can keep up satisfactorily. There are also many jobs, such as weather forecasting, that no computer, personal or otherwise, currently has the power to do really well.

Finally, computer software developers also contribute to the need for more processing power and memory. Give them more of both, and they'll find interesting and useful features to consume those resources. Like gas molecules in a vacuum jar, software tends to expand to fill all the available memory and processing power.

Back to the Fray

On-line data works much the same way: it tends to expand to fill all available disk space. Another computer industry truism is that you can never have enough disk storage.

It should, therefore, come as no surprise that the amount of disk space available on PCs has grown rapidly during the short life of these small systems. The first IBM PC, for example, came with one or two floppy disk drives, each of which could hold a disk with up to 160KB of information. Today's high-end PCs typically use floppy disks that can hold either 1.2MB (the 5.25-inch variety) or 1.44MB (the 3.5-inch variety) diskettes.

More importantly, most of today's PCs also come with hard disks. Hard disks are faster, typically non-removable disks with many times the capacity of floppy disks. A high-end PC today will have anywhere from two to eight disk drive bays, each of which can contain hard disk drives capable of holding 300MB or more. These hard disks are generally no physically larger than the 10MB hard disk in the first IBM PC product, the XT, that came with a hard disk. (In computerese, a drive's size is usually the number of megabytes it can hold; thus, a 300MB drive is "larger" than a 150MB drive, even if both devices are the same physical size.)

These newer hard disks are much faster than the hard disks on the earliest PCs. The most common standard measure of a disk's speed is the average time it takes to find and read a random chunk (block) of bytes on the disk, the drive's *average access time*. The XT's 10MB hard disk had an average access time of around 65 milliseconds (ms). The 300MB disks commonly available today have average access times in the range of 16-18 ms, with some pushing the 10-ms barrier.

Both the capacity and the speed of today's hard disks make them clearly a great deal better than their PC ancestors of eight years ago. It's important to notice, however, that disk-drive technology is generally not advancing quite as fast as semiconductor technology. You could buy a 300MB disk drive in 1982, although it was a huge thing about the size of a dishwasher that cost thousands of dollars and was used almost exclusively with minicomputer and microcomputer systems. You could not, however, find a microprocessor in 1982 that ran at anywhere near the speed of the 80486.

Don't get me wrong: today's disks are definitely larger, faster, and cheaper than ever before. Still, their advances have not quite kept up with the improvements in chip technology, and I expect that differential to continue for the next decade. That statement should not, however, detract one whit from the accomplishment of disk engineers. Those folks have to deal with something that chip makers never encounter: moving parts. It's hard to make anything with moving parts both fast and reliable.

To see the kinds of problems disk engineers face, consider the case of disk heads. Hard disks are stacks of platters, each of which is much like a record. The disks read and write those platters electromagnetically with heads that hover just above each side of every platter. Those heads are much like the toner arms of turntables. All the platters spin at very high speeds. To read or write a specific disk block, the disk drive must move the right head to the right position just as the right block spins underneath the head. The coordination problems alone are enormous. So, too, are the problems of timing and interference: the head must finish with the block before the disk spins that block away, and without messing with any other blocks. Some of today's disk prototypes have heads that are so close to the platters that visible light cannot fit in the gap between head and platter. At the same time, if the head and platter ever physically touch, the platter becomes just so much trash.

Because of the somewhat slower pace of the advance of disk technology, I expect the high-end PC disk drives of 2001 to be only about three times the size of the best such drives available today. With today's largest drives running close to 1GB (yes, that's one gigabyte), that puts the best PC-sized drives of 2001 at around 3GB. Of course, the largest and most expandable PCs of that year will be able to hold from five to eight of those drives, for a comfortable maximum hard disk storage of 15GB to 24GB.

All this disk space won't go to waste, either. In addition to the data and programs you already see on today's PCs, these disks will also have to cope with mass quantities of stored audio and full-motion video images. We're already heading in that direction rapidly, with every vendor from IBM to Apple jumping on the bandwagon for *multimedia*, computer systems that combine traditional programs and data with movie-quality images and stereo sound into total packages that, ideally, anyone can use. Multimedia systems eat disk storage in vast quantities.

Today's partial answer to this problem is usually the CD-ROM (compact-disc, read-only memory) disk. A CD-ROM looks like an audio CD, and like today's audio CDs, it is read-only; you can't change its contents. A typical CD-ROM can hold around 600MB, which sounds like a great deal of storage. Even with the best available compression methods, however, 600MB is nowhere near enough space to hold the complete digital audio and video tracks of a feature film. CD-ROMs are also currently slow. Typical CD-ROM drives today have average access times of around 300 ms, a long way from the 18-ms or better times of the large hard disks.

Bigger hard disks will make room for the upcoming multimedia products. CD-ROMs will also continue to play a big role in those products, and these optical disks will also, as you would expect, get faster and larger. In fact, the high-end PC of 2001 will have both traditional disk drives and one or more optical drives.

I also expect these PCs to contain extremely large blocks of DRAM chips that act as disk caches, to speed the CPU's interaction with the disks. Several vendors today already offer disk controller boards that have caches that range from 1MB to 8MB, and most microcomputer operating systems can now use chunks of system memory as a disk cache. There's a minor war raging between those who believe a cache on the disk controller is better and those who put their money on large system memory caches, but both sides—and all the experimental data—agree that caches greatly improve disk performance. I'm not sure which kind of cache the high-end PC of 2001 will use, but either way I expect the cache to be at least 8MB, and more likely 16MB to 32MB.

There's also a new darkhorse in the disk race: pseudo-disks made entirely of chips. The best entries in this category seem to be the flash EE-PROM (electrically erasable programmable read-only memory) chips. Flash EE-PROMs are based on E-PROM and EE-PROM chips, both of which are meant to be read many times and changed only rarely, and so are, in computer terms, slow and difficult to change. Flash EE-PROMs occupy an interesting middle ground between these two types of chips and DRAMs: they're easier to change than the former, but much slower than the latter. While the typical access time of a DRAM—the time it takes to read the chip's contents—is 80 nanoseconds (ns) or better, a flash EE-PROM's access time is more like 200 ns. That's slow in chip times, but amazingly fast in disk times.

By 2001, flash EE-PROM chips as big as 256MB could be available for around $1 per megabyte. If these chips really reach such capacities, look for them in the PCs of that year. These semiconductor disks will serve two roles. Their primary job will be to hold programs and data that don't fit into the system's main memory, with any remaining space going to general data storage.

Archiving

The disks of 2001 should be at least as reliable as those we use today, but they will still fail occasionally. If the information on those disks does not exist anywhere else, then such failures can be catastrophic. The solution to this problem in 2001 will be the same as our solution to it today: *backups*.

A backup is a copy of the information on a disk or other device. The media that people tend to use for backups is typically removable, so you can store the backups in a location apart from the one where the original data resides. Backup media is also often slower than the original storage form, because you don't need to work with the backup copies the vast majority of the time.

Today's most common PC backup devices are diskettes and computer tape drives. Write-Once, Read-Many (WORM) optical disks are also gaining popularity, as they have high capacities (600MB or more) and are very easy to use.

Some of the most powerful of today's PCs also use another backup method, *disk mirroring*. Disk mirroring is a technique in which a computer system keeps a constantly up-to-date second copy of its hard disk. When the original disk fails, the system switches immediately to the backup disk and alerts you that the original disk has gone bad. The switch to the backup disk is at a sufficiently low level in the system that it is effectively invisible to you; you can keep operating without any interruption, as if the original disk were still working. Disk mirroring will be a standard option on the high-end PCs of 2001.

The other major backup media of that day will still be diskettes and tapes. The diskettes will, however, be optical ones. With a system with several gigabytes or more of hard disk, it's impractical to copy the disk to today's diskettes—you'd need literally hundreds of diskettes. Optical disks, by contrast, already can hold 600MB or more, and we can expect that capacity to double (at least) by 2001.

On the tape front, the standard of 2001 will probably be a medium that is already rapidly growing in popularity: digital audio tapes, or DATs. A single DAT will handle a gigabyte or more.

Input

Making a backup is something that most computer users do all too infrequently, but everybody who uses a computer works with its input devices all the time. You might expect, therefore, that the input devices of 2001, like its processors, memory, and disk drives, will be radically better than the ones we use today, but I don't think so.

In fact, I expect the standard input device to be the good old keyboard. It won't be any funky Dvorak keyboard, either; just the standard QWERTY keyboard of today's typewriters and computers.

There will, of course, be lots of other input devices. Most PCs in that year will also have a pointing device. That device will probably be a mouse on most systems, but many folks will also use the mouse alternatives already around today: trackballs, touch screens, and tablets.

Tablets will be particularly popular with artists and other people who work with graphics. The tablets will also be smarter than those we use today, with the ability to learn to recognize your cursive handwriting as one nice added feature.

Scanners will also be common, and far less expensive than their counterparts today. The scanners will be able to handle both graphics and text, so that any printed matter will become potential input to your system.

267

These basic technologies already exist and are in widespread use today, and they will only get better.

My list so far omits one of the most common of all human input mechanisms, speech. Hundreds of SF books, stories, movies, and television shows have scenes in which a human and a computer carry on a conversation, and everybody seems to assume that this advance will just naturally happen. You can even buy speech-recognition systems today, although those systems are very limited.

I, too, believe that someday we'll be able to talk to our computers, but it won't be in 2001. The problem is more profound than whether the computer hardware of that year will have the power to understand speech; it's simply that we don't yet know how to write the necessary software. Barring a quantum leap forward in this area, we'll still be typing at our computers in 2001 far more often than we'll be talking to them.

Output

They will, however, be talking to us. As multimedia applications grow in popularity, our computers will bombard us with sounds of all kinds, from spoken words to music. It will all come out in high-quality, digital, stereo format, too, so that you will, if you wish, be able to run it through your standard household stereo system.

Those applications will also deliver movie-quality images to us, all of which we'll see on screens as large and vibrantly colorful as the best of today's TVs—and better. Not every PC will have such screens, because they'll always cost more than simple monochrome displays—there are still black-and-white TVs around—but the monitors on the best PCs will be stunning.

They already are. If you're willing to shell out several thousand dollars, you can today buy a twenty-one-inch-diagonal Macintosh monitor with a graphics board that can display millions of colors at once. By 2001, that level of output quality will be the norm. It will also run easily at real-time speeds, even with multiple images on your screen at once. You should be able to watch the latest

James Bond movie in one window, while a soothing fractal display runs in another, and you edit text in a third, all at natural speeds and with wonderful clarity. (Today's best displays offer around a million elements, or pixels; that image resolution should at least double by 2001.)

These screens will also be a great deal thinner and lighter than today's large monitors. Monitors with diagonal sizes from 21 to 35 inches will be common, and none will be more than a few inches thick. The key will be a change in basic display technology. Instead of picture tubes, these color monitors will use a thin film of transistors and layers of color filters. Black and white thin-film transistor screens are already common in portable computers, and NEC is even shipping a color portable computer that uses this technology. The resolution and colors on that color portable are poor compared to today's desktop color monitors, but by 2001 they should be comparable.

The other major form of output, printing, will still be popular in 2001, and the major technology will still be the same one we use today, laser printers. Those printers, however, will be able to print colors on normal paper, and their output will have typeset quality, around 1200 dots per inch (dpi). These high-end, color, 1200-dpi printers will still be very expensive, maybe even as costly as the entire rest of the system, but they will be available to anyone who can afford them.

Who Needs All That Power, Anyway?

Earlier I discussed some applications that require the processing power of the kinds of systems I've just described, but I haven't really explained why anyone will need so much personal computing power. There are two basic reasons.

The first one has to do with the market for computers. So far, using a PC is an arcane and even intimidating process to most people. That hasn't stopped PCs from being phenomenally successful in the last decade, but they still are not the kind of simple appliance that anybody can use. They are not, for example, TVs.

Anyone can watch TV without any training. For computers to continue their infiltration into the muscle and tendons of everyday life, as I believe they will, PCs must become as easy to use—at least for everyday tasks—as TV is to watch. The first step in that direction is to make the PCs as attractive as the best of today's TVs. That, by the way, is where the multimedia applications come into play, because at heart they represent little more than the fusion of computing and television.

The other step, of course, is to tie PCs more closely to the huge flood of information that already comes into our homes. The vast majority of us, whether we like it or not, live under a never-ending torrent of information rain. It assaults us from all sides, oozing into our homes like water through coral: TVs, phones, stereo systems, books, cassettes, radios—it's hard to escape the information onslaught. Information is quite literally in the air around us. Information is the future.

To maintain the pace of their advance into our lives, computers must become the sink for that information onslaught, the place where the information pools collect. The same fiber-optic cable that supplies your cable TV programs will also link your computer to the outside world. You ultimately will be able to watch TV on the same system that you use to pay your bills, look up a phone number, run a spreadsheet, learn to speak Russian, and help your child do his or her homework. The PC will become an information appliance. Why bother flipping through a morning paper, when your computer can get the same information, sort it according to the priorities it has learned by observing your past use, and then highlight important items for you?

We won't have reached this goal by 2001, but we'll be getting closer. To handle those jobs, we'll need not only all the PC power I've predicted, but much more.

Even if you don't, your children will: they'll just shove you away from the keyboard and screen, put on a *Star Trek* rerun for you to watch in a window in the screen's lower corner, and then continue building their future without you.

Introduction

It seems like only yesterday—it was only yesterday!—that we were all on tenterhooks over the prospects of cheap, easy, and maybe even portable ("Mr Fusion!") fusion power. The returns still aren't all in, but it's beginning to look like a fast-talking Mormon chemist and his British sidekick (religious affiliation unknown) were having us on. Oh, doubtless they were as sure of their facts as a typical public relations spokesman, but no more than that; apparently the lure of unimaginable wealth led them down the garden path—and so they led us down the garden path.

But wait! There's hope. All the benefits S.M. Stirling sees arising from safe, cheap, clean power are already here. One hardly dares to use the word, but if you take the "u" in "fusion" and change it to an "i," and add an "s" next to the "s" that's already there you'll know what I'm talking about. Global Warming? We don't need no stinking Global Warming. Just replace all our genuinely stinking coal- and oil-fired plants with Mr F*s*ion and our problems are solved.

FUSION ENERGY AND CIVILIZATION

S. M. Stirling

Humans have always depended on fusion power; the terrestrial biosphere is powered by that great big unshielded reactor in the sky, spitting out radiation at us . . . why, it's the primary cause of skin cancer . . .

More seriously, the natural condition of any closed system in our universe is towards maximum entropy, a situation where all energy is evenly diffused and no motion can take place. Evolution—the increasing complexity, order and specialization of life—can occur only because Earth is *not* a closed system. Sunlight rains down on it continuously, and radiates away, maintaining the energy gradient on which all life depends.

In human terms: the *upper* limit on the standard of living, the leisure, and the public morality of any society is set by the amount and degree of concentration of the energy available.[1] Our remote hunter-gatherer ancestors had a rather lavish amount of energy available, because they were so few in relation to the Earth's surface and so skilled at making use of the biological

[1]. There is no lower limit.

energy-collectors known as plants and animals. Recent studies have shown that before they were pushed into marginal areas by herders and farmers, hunter-gatherers could make a good living with as little as three or four hours of work a day, leaving the rest free for fighting, singing, making ornaments, performing ceremonies or just lazing around the fire and meditating. A lifestyle many contemporary urbanites might envy, at least in a warm climate! The hunter-gatherers were also healthier than their peasant descendants, being less crowded and more prone to washing.

This leaves the vexed question of why humans invented agriculture at all. One current theory holds that it was done to enable the cultivation of barley for beer . . . The answer, I feel, is again one of power. For the bulk of humanity, agriculture represented a step *down* the food chain. It meant that humans ate, essentially, grass and tubers—a diet which represented a more diffuse source of energy than meat. The wheat, rice and potatoes which provided the bulk of the peasant's diet mostly served as fuel for the production of more grains. Grinding, day-in, day-out toil became the lot of the overwhelming majority of humans, along with crowding, squalor and disease. Our primary religion remembers it as the expulsion from Eden: "In the sweat of your brow shall you earn your bread."

But for the *elite* of peasant-based societies, agriculture represented a wonderful concentration of solar fusion power . . . at the expense of the peasantry. Farms and their attendant peasants served to collect the diffuse energy, which was further concentrated—often on the backs of the peasants—in cities and manors. From this surplus the aristocrats were fed, and their hangers-on; soldiers, priests, scholars and bureaucrats, specialized artisans. Despite entropy, you *can* get more out of a system than you put in, as long as somebody else gets *less*. The colloquial version of the Three Laws of Thermodynamics states: "You can't win, you can't break even, and you can't get out of the game." You can, however, cheat.

The State was a product of this agricultural revolution, and once launched it had an irresistible tendency to spread for the simple reason that no hunting people could rival its concentrated military power and dense population. In terms of horsepower per acre, it was vastly more efficient than hunting and gathering—although vastly *less* efficient in terms of energy available per person-hour of labor.

From this springs the stony cruelty of early agricultural civilizations, their utter indifference to human life and pain; the inscriptions of the Assyrian kings, boasting of whole cities flayed alive, the sadomasochistic *grand guginol* of the Roman arena, the slave children driven to die in the silver mines of Laurion to sustain the glory of Periclean Athens. This slaughterhouse century of ours has seen mass wickedness enough, but this has represented a (hopefully) temporary falling-away from grace. The cruelty of the preindustrial era was *necessary*, for without an utterly oppressed and exploited peasantry there was simply no surplus for cities, books, a leisure class. From the viewpoint of the overwhelming majority the structure of civilization was a mechanism for grinding bread out of their bones. As a Dorian aristocrat of Crete said:

> I have great riches, spear and sword
>   And rawhide shield at my breast
> My land is ploughed, my harvest stored
>   The sweet wine from the vintage pressed
> The peasant trash has learned its Lord
>   By spear and sword.
>
> And all who dare not walk with spear
>   And sword and rawhide fluttering
> Must needs kiss my feet and cling
>   And cowering in their fear hail me
> "Lord" and "Great King."

This parasitism was in turn self-reinforcing; the upper classes were uninterested in production since their specialty was extracting the maximum surplus from their subjects, while the producers were quite rightly convinced that any improvements they made would simply be appropriated by their social superiors. For six thousand years after the basic neolithic breakthrough, innovation in the basic technologies of production was glacially slow. What progress there was tended to be in the fields of administration and military technique, rather than agriculture, or in extensions of scale. Kings and emperors built glorious cities, with peasant-forced labor; fought wars of increasing size and sophistication, over the backs of their peasants; their scribes learned better and better methods of record-keeping, so that the surplus might be more efficiently gathered; dams and irrigation schemes were dug so that more tax- and rent-paying serfs could live lives of animalistic squalor and brutality. In fact, as erosion, population growth and salination reduced the carrying capacity of the core areas of agriculture, standards of living had a long-term tendency to *fall*.

The parasitic nature of early civilizations also made them unstable. They represented a tiny peak on a huge mass of illiterate poverty. When their overlords reached the point of no longer being able to trust any substantial portion of their subjects with arms, tribal peoples from beyond the frontier of city-and-peasant culture could overcome them; for the bulk of the population, a "Dark Age" could represent a temporary relief. As in a crystalline substance that has two phase-states, peasant economies could support either a bureaucratic empire or a decentralized, slightly less oppressive but barbarian alternative. In the long term, the pressure of war and its economies of scale always began the process of empire anew. Once an area had reached the maximum that could be achieved with the classic means—iron tools, walled cities, paper and a literate scribal class—it tended to fluctuate in place, the long "middle passage" of human history. Kingdoms and empires and religions came and went, but the basic structure remained unchanged. And the limiting factor was energy.

But humanity was lucky. Out on the western extremity of the Eurasian supercontinent, an exception arose: Western civilization. As early as the ninth century A.D. the peoples of Western Europe were making more use of inanimate sources of energy, principally water and wind power. Earlier civilizations had known of them, but made only sporadic use; by the High Middle Ages tens of thousands of water and wind mills were scattered all over Europe. Grinding grain, eliminating the killing labor that Homer's heroes blithely assigned to their slave-women; fulling cloth, sawing wood and stone; every groan of wooden wheel represented one less whip-mark laid on a human back. Improvements in agriculture occurred at the same time—better ploughs, the substitution of horses for oxen, more productive rotations. And significantly, this was the first era to make widespread use of the highly-concentrated fossil fuels, solar energy gathered over millions of years. The intellectual innovations of the West, individualism, rationalism, the prescient scientific optimism of men like Roger Bacon, built on this foundation.

By the Renaissance, Europe had the first cities in world history which traded mass-consumption goods for their food rather than extracting it at swordspoint. The standard of living had improved to the point where humble folk could add bacon to their porridge once a week, and there was a broad stratum of not-so-humble bourgeois. Not aristocrats, nor luxury artisans and traders catering to landlord demand, but a literate and self-confident middle class, perhaps the first such large class in human history. The same period saw the abolition of serfdom west of the Elbe, because for the first time there was a society productive enough not to need forced labor. Not that there was much luxury or leisure among the wage-laborers and tenant-farmers of early modern Europe, but a threshold had been passed; a threshold of available *per capita* energy. Life need no longer be a zero-sum game, if humans chose otherwise.

The series of historical accidents which lead to the Industrial Revolution preserved this fragile beginning, saved it from petering out into a Chinese-style high-level equilibrium trap. Most of the technologies which made the Revolution were imported from the Orient, but in China they were introduced gradually, without disruption. The pressure of population and the massive conservatism of the Mandarin-landowner scholar-bureaucrats made sure that the population growth swallowed up all the increased productivity. This is a much-needed reminder that human beings do not embrace change and growth naturally; change always menaces strong vested interests, whether those are material or ideological/religious. It is almost always easier to maintain the status quo. Western Europe's structure of quarreling nation-states probably had much to do with maintaining the momentum of change, since a state which fell behind would be devoured by its neighbors; its elite had a direct personal interest in increased efficiency.

Even more important was the competitive commercial system; the economic war of all against all generated a razor-keen appreciation of comparative costs. The unique circumstances of eighteenth-century Britain then produced a series of crucial innovations in the use of stored solar-fusion energy (coal, and then oil) that allowed, for the first time in history, the widespread use of energy sources more concentrated than sunlight; sources that it seemed could be expanded infinitely and applied to every form of human economic and military use. The sheer *power* these innovations produced was irresistible, and forced every neighboring state to follow suit, however much violence was done to hallowed social orders and ways of life. Even the closely similar societies of Western Europe had a generations-long struggle to adapt, for the innovations were not free; they required a wholesale adoption of the world view and social structure that had produced them. Even in our own time, many peoples—Iran would be a good example—are convulsed by the contradictory forces of modernization and outraged tradition.

With fossil-fuel based industry, humanity was liberated from the Neolithic paradox of progress built on slavery. Growth became exponential. By the twentieth century the standard of living of the masses in the advanced countries had risen back to the level of their hunter-gatherer ancestors, and then surpassed it— *without* sacrificing any of the advantages of civilization. A high culture had become a good deal for the bulk of humanity, something without precedent, and the realization that poverty was not inevitable began to sink into the collective consciousness of the human race.

The concept of "progress" is an outgrowth of this realization. Yet this century has also shown how fragile this achievement is; science fiction has been ringing changes on the post-holocaust barbarian world for fifty years. More ominous than the risk of self-annihilation is the simple fact that we are living on the planet's capital. Fossil fuels are limited: at present rates, we have only a few centuries worth of oil and this does not allow for growth. Worse still, the energy densities available are not enough for us to control the environmental consequences of our industrialization. With sufficiently cheap energy, pollution would become a thing of the past; at *current* levels of energy usage, this is impractical. Most of our species is still locked in the subsistence-agriculture trap, and simply extending the First World system of coal and petroleum fueled industrialism to them would probably destroy the planet.

This knowledge is the spectre at the feast of progress, now that Western civilization is overcoming the self-inflicted wound of 1914 and its consequences. The so-called "soft" path is nothing more than a return to the animalistic misery of preindustrial times; sunlight is simply too *diffuse* to maintain even the present level of world consumption. Hard, concentrated energy is the essential prerequisite for an economy like ours; conservation and increased efficiency merely delay the problem without solving it. Restricting growth in output means a boot in the face of the world's have-nots; it means freezing the current distribution of wealth, a tiny island of comfort on a swelling mound of resentful pain; eventually, it means impoverishing everyone.

Nobody will consent to be poor, and nobody will give up anything, whatever the fantasies of the spoiled, rich, white city people who make up the constituency of the "limits to growth" and "Earth First" movemements. The neo-Luddites imagine a future of organic vegetables and hand-woven rugs; the reality of their policies would be a mad-dog scramble between nations, classes and races over scraps of water and fuel and food, a global Beirut. Followed by restabilization right back in the post-Neolithic norm of human history, a society of starving peasants ruled by bandits, perhaps with a few high-tech trinkets for the elite. The ability to tap near-infinite supplies of concentrated non-organic energy gave us a glimpse of a world where life was not a zero-sum game, and it was possible to have affluence and culture without being a predator on other human beings. To maintain that vision and extend it to all we need something more: we need more than that one fusion reactor up in the sky. The knowledge is there. What we need is the will.

Science fiction can show us the possibilities of . . . *fusion!*

Introduction

Anyone who reads New Destinies *knows that we follow a fairly strict privatist line. But here Marc Stiegler has gone us one or two better. And while his conclusions may seem a bit drastic, he was a professional in the defense consultation biz for many years; perhaps his proposal deserves consideration. Certainly it would be fun, which would make it unique in this venue.*

THE B-2 LOTTERY

Marc Stiegler

In recent years there have been a number of scandals about the quality of the Test and Evaluation programs for military weapon systems. The impressive price tag on the Stealth bomber makes test and evaluation particularly important. The recent flying of this aircraft gives us a critical opportunity to reduce the cost of the project while at the same time ensuring the quality of the testing program. The answer is simple: conduct a B-2 Lottery.

The lottery follows a simple 2-part procedure:

1) Every night for a year, the Air Force must fly the B-2 at least half way across the United States. They must fly over a different part of the U.S. every time. The B-2 pilots are urged to use every evasion technique they have available to avoid detection.

2) Lottery ticket holders attempt to shoot the Stealth out of the sky. The first lottery ticket holder to knock down the Stealth receives an award equal to the cost of a production model Stealth bomber, i.e., the lottery

pays off a single cash prize of $500 million. When the Stealth is downed, the bomber program is canceled; even a $500 million prize is a bargain basement price for this reduction in government spending.

Lottery tickets cost $100 apiece. Since every man, woman, and child in the U.S. has already paid $100 for the development of this aircraft, all U.S. citizens automatically qualify as lottery ticket holders.

In the spirit of *glasnost*, Soviet fighter pilots are encouraged to join—but they must buy their tickets with hard currency.

STYLE POINTS

Elegance should qualify for a bonus. Cessna pilots can double their money by flying up next to the Stealth, tucking their wing under the Stealth's wing, and flipping it over into the ground. Since the Stealth will normally fly low and slow, this should work very nicely.

Farmers can also get style points by using vintage firearms from World War II or before. Once again, if the Stealth chooses to fly low, this should be a clean kill. A triple bonus is available for anyone shooting down the B-2 with a black powder musket.

Style points are deducted for using modern assault rifles. Assault rifles used strictly for sport (i.e., rifles which have never been fired at human beings) are exempt from this penalty.

Team play is encouraged. For example, suppose a suburban housewife hears a Stealthy sound flying overhead. She fires a roman candle that bursts and spews spray-can metallic-glitter paint in all directions. As the Stealth passes through the cloud of fine droplets, it receives a glittery new paint job. The nearest F-16 homes in on the now brilliantly illuminated target and blows it to ashes (yes, no restrictions on the Air Force playing the game: after all, who is better qualified to test it? Goodness, I hope they have a better chance of shooting it down than the housewife). The housewife and the F-16 pilot each receive half the total prize money. In this scenario, gun cameras on the F-16 will be critical. We expect many photo finishes, as dozens of roaming F-16s zoom in from hundreds of miles at Mach 2 to claim the first shot.

BIGGER PRIZES, BIGGER PLAYS

The best way to destroy the Stealth bomber, of course, is to drop a bomb on it while it sits on the ground, from another craft that is just as stealthy as the Stealth. Such a demonstration would show the military an alternative vehicle to act as a Stealth bomber, possibly at a significant savings. The first person to sneak past Air Force defenses with a package the size and weight of a 25 kiloton warhead (noticeably larger than the bomb dropped at Hiroshima, which is adequate for most purposes) receives, not merely the cost-based value of the B-2 airplane, but rather the cost-based value of the entire B-2 Research and Development program, minus the cost of the craft used to deliver the bomb. The Navy might be very interested in this prize—a carefully placed cruise missile could handle the job on the first night. And though the basic $500 million is a pittance, a complete B-2 R&D project represents real money.

Senior citizens with World War I biplanes also have excellent chances at the R&D award, since cloth and fabric aircraft have low radar cross sections. The Goodyear Blimp, with a suitable coat of paint, is another fine candidate. They'll have to hurry, though, to beat the fleets of plastic ultralights that would swarm over the landscape seeking prize money. Even after deducting the cost of his ultralight from the award, the proud adolescent pilot's remaining $23 billion should be enough to buy most of Massachusetts after the tax hikes there depress real estate prices. Once again, this is a cheap price to pay, since every man, woman, and child in the United States may have to pay another $200 to complete the program if we don't find an alternative.

RESTRICTIONS

Because nuclear devices are so small these days, certain delivery techniques must be barred to encourage reasonable play. Delivery of nuke by briefcase, for example, is disallowed. Similarly, if you deliver your bomb by Federal Express to a Stealth runway, the prize goes to Fed Ex, not the shipper. Estes hobbyist rockets, however, make legitimate vehicles.

Finally, business executives cannot use their Lear fan aircraft in the competition. Lear fanjets already must carry transponders, because their plastic fuselages reflect so little radar that air traffic controllers cannot track them reliably. So the Lear fanjet would make a fine alternative for the Stealth, except in one regard: the Lear fanjet flies far too fast to be like a B-2. It is also far too maneuverable. You could never flip a Lear into the ground with a Cessna.

Could the lottery become self-supporting? Certainly, the B-2 swatting game is fun for the whole family. Perhaps we should demand that future projects like the B-2 be funded by the lotteries themselves rather than by taxpayers. With a family of four, would you have bought $400 worth of B-2 lottery tickets if you had been given a choice? Especially since you can't even win the prize?

Anyone care to buy a ticket?